Patricia Marcantonio was b won awards for her journalis

Patricia's short story collecti
Cuentos has earned an Ann
and was a Commended Title for an Américas Award for
Children's and Young Adult Literature, and one of the Wilde
Awards Best Collections to Share; with recommendations from
Bulletin of the Center for Children's Books.

Her website is http://patriciamarcantonio.com/

BB   bookbub.com/authors/patricia-marcantonio
f   facebook.com/MarcantonioStories
O   instagram.com/santos_stories

MISBEHAVING AT CACTUS LANES

PATRICIA SANTOS MARCANTONIO

One More Chapter
a division of HarperCollins*Publishers* Ltd
1 London Bridge Street
London SE1 9GF
www.harpercollins.co.uk
HarperCollins*Publishers*
Macken House, 39/40 Mayor Street Upper,
Dublin 1, D01 C9W8, Ireland

This paperback edition 2024

1

First published in Great Britain in ebook format
by HarperCollins*Publishers* 2024
Copyright © Patricia Santos Marcantonio 2024

Patricia Santos Marcantonio asserts the moral right to be identified
as the author of this work

A catalogue record of this book is available from the British Library
ISBN: 978-0-00-862639-6

Printed and bound in the UK using 100% Renewable Electricity
by CPI Group (UK) Ltd

For those who get a second chance in life and love.

Chapter One

Thunk, thunk, thunk.

I prayed good taste would win out in the end. That my soon-to-be buried husband of almost forty years would go to his maker with dignity and without one goddamn reference to golf.

Thunk, thunk, thunk.

I was dead wrong.

Three men in black suits stepped out from the crowd at the graveside. They held golf clubs like soldiers carrying rifles in a military parade, except these guys were old and overweight in expensive clothes. But in seamless synchronization, the men teed up a ball and slammed it into an empty field next to the cemetery for a twenty-one golf-ball salute to my late husband, Robert Thomas Adams.

Thunk, thunk, thunk.

As each ball hit the ground like a fat, round bullet, the mourners behind me emitted a surge of tears and sniffles. The pastor standing beside me discretely rolled his eyes at the

1

send-off. Those rolling eyes seem to say, "By God, no dignity or good taste at this funeral." Then again, when was death in good taste? But he had a point.

I couldn't have stopped the golf-ball salute anyway. Bob had written the details for his funeral into his will years ago after watching a similar tribute on the *Golf Channel*. Dead man's wish or not, the embarrassment of it all made me want to crawl into the hole too.

Thunk, thunk, thunk.

Within the shiny copper coffin, my husband's body wore his best polo shirt, shorts, and golf shoes. The outfit was also written into his will, and I guessed I should have been grateful he wasn't a WWF fan. Beside him was his cherished club, a Calloway driver, with which he had won the country club championship senior division for seven years straight. His will had also requested his body be arranged so his deceased fingers held the grip as he had in life, but the mortician couldn't make the arrangement work unless they buried him standing up. I made an executive decision to nix that.

Thunk, thunk, thunk.

The crowd at the grave was sizable. Most of the people were Bob's business and golf acquaintances because he had belonged to three leagues and served as sergeant-at-arms of the Clearview Country Club Men's Association. That group sent a spectacular flower arrangement with the figure of a golfer done up in roses. Bob's favorite golfing sweater was eerily mimicked in red and white petals.

I glanced over at my children. All through the church service and at the grave, Mike and Kyla were distraught and distressed. Weepy and waily. Red eyes and ruddy noses from crying. The pictures of grief.

That's how I should have looked. In other words, widow-like. Throughout the morning, I sniffed and dotted my eyes with a tissue because I didn't know what to do with my hands in an attempt to project the grief I should have felt. I'm not boasting to say it was a performance worthy of a Golden Globe nomination. I had cried when Bob died ten days ago. Tears for a human being lost to this world and never to return. Tears for the pain his death had caused our children. And yes, for the man I had lived with for almost forty years. Even though we'd gotten used to each other like memorizing the PIN for our bank card. And we'd become roommates keeping each other company rather than sharing laughs and love. One of those couples I hated to see at restaurants. Married, sitting at the same table eating dinner, and not speaking the language of each other. But I'd bet most couples married that long were probably no different. No matter, it was still tragic for both of us.

Now, with my Manolo Blahnik heels digging into the cemetery sod, a dreadful realization smacked into my head. Not all my tears had been for Bob.

Bob.

Soon to be buried under a turf where he could no longer chip and putt. I wanted to shout to those assembled, "Hey, I'm the one left behind, still breathing."

"Oh, hell," I whispered. "Oh, hell."

Thunk, thunk, thunk.

My black dress suddenly felt three sizes too small. I worried my kids would finally notice the total absence of real

3

sorrow on my face. I wished I wore a hat with a long black veil like the one Gladys George wore in *The Maltese Falcon*. But my veil would have to be thick as a shag carpet so no one could see my tearless cheeks.

Staring at the casket, I racked up my reasons for not crying at the funeral. Emotional shock. Yeah, that was it. The sudden end to a man's life at the age of seventy-eight. A new vacancy in my life, not unlike checking into the corner room at the Bates Motel. If nothing else, I excelled at justification and excuses so much I could have earned a Noble Prize. But another emotion overpowered those. A jolt of mighty guilt for *not* crying crashed down on me. I was a good person and good people cry at funerals.

I couldn't catch a damn break.

Thunk, thunk, thunk.

When the last golf balls fell, the service ended.

"Daddy would've been thrilled with such a salute." Kyla choked out the words.

I touched my daughter's shoulder. "He'd be hitting balls alongside them if he could." That spurred another crying jag in her.

Hell.

"I thought it was a bit cornball." Mike adjusted his sunglasses.

I loved my son even more for saying what I was thinking.

"Mike!" Kyla hissed in anger at her brother but cut it short when people walked over to us to extend more hugs and sympathy.

The funeral was held early to beat the Las Vegas heat, but the temperature caught up with us and we started sweating like monkeys in a marathon. This signaled it was time to hit the air conditioning, which was the natural state of things if you lived in Southern Nevada.

The pastor took one of my hands in his, spoke rote words of comfort, and headed off – probably to preside at the next funeral without a twenty-one golf-ball salute. As the mourners departed, I turned paranoid. How many saw my emotionally challenged appearance during the service? Did they spot eyes drier than the desert one step out of Vegas? Hopefully, they'd just think I was courageous.

"Margaret, you're so brave in this sad time," a few people did tell me.

"Margaret, you're holding up so well," others declared. I nodded with thanks, giving an artificial sniff. Another great acting job to rival Meryl Streep.

I was going directly to hell.

After everyone walked to their cars, I couldn't move away from the shiny casket, as if leaving meant going someplace even more frightening. My refuge throughout my marriage had been *Lifetime* movies. When life didn't jibe with what I hoped it would be, I imagined myself in one that did. My way of avoiding a stronger dose of antianxiety pills or a fifth of whiskey at bedtime. I imaged one movie now. About a woman, a thinner version of me, who just lost her longtime husband. She wondered what in blazes lay ahead for her as the music swelled up in time for a commercial touting laundry detergent with dazzling whiteners. Stay tuned for a preview of next week's show.

"Time to go, Mom." Mike took my elbow and led me toward the limo.

Kyla's husband, Jerome Anderson, gently held my other elbow as if I were two hundred years old. I smiled at my son-in-law. A CPA, Jerome was thirty-five going on seventy when it came to his near maddening reserve. The man cared exclusively about his wife, young son, and getting numbers to balance by April 15th. But all evidence indicated he was a good husband and father. An asset in anyone's books.

"You all right, Mom?" Mike said.

"I think so."

"We're all here for you, Mom." Kyla sneaked her brother a look of concern, which I saw.

Kyla sucked at sneaking looks.

I glanced back at the graveside, which was even sadder now with no one around. Rows of empty chairs under a tent, a phony Astroturf padding surrounding the hole. Flowers already wilting from the heat. I touched the golf tee in my pocket. It had been among Bob's belongings when he collapsed on the ninth hole at the country club. I'd intended to save it as a keepsake of the man I'd lived with for so long, the father of our children. I pressed my forefinger to the sharp end of the tee.

"Hold on."

Returning to the casket, I placed it on the extravagant flower arrangement on top. The tee was where it belonged.

In the limo, Kyla and Mike flanked me, and each held one of my hands. Jerome sat on a side seat. The inside of the long car reeked of lavender, the aromatherapy answer to calm the grieving, or so I'd read. The smell just succeeded in giving me a headache.

I squeezed the hands of my children. Bob lived on in Kyla's

bright red hair and blue eyes, and their belief that they were the centers of the known universe. Since this was the day for remorse, I felt guilty I couldn't keep Bob from spoiling her, nor prevent him from placing the yoke of perfection around her delicate neck. All of which had placed me in the perennial role of bad cop mom.

Three years older than Kyla, Mike had Bob's squarish jaw and slightly receding hairline. He had refused any yoke placed on him by his father. My son also preferred skittering around the edge so he could take in the bigger picture rather than see himself as the epicenter of all things. He had my sense of humor and thick skin, which he called an absolute requirement for his job as a news magazine writer.

"How's Jonathan?" I asked. Everyone decided it best to leave my nine-year-old grandson with a babysitter.

"Good. We talked to him about how his grandpa went to heaven," Kyla said.

"And?"

"It's confusing to him but he'll be fine." She sniffed back genuine tears.

"It *is* confusing."

"A touching ceremony. A respectful turnout." Jerome squirmed as if questioning whether those were the proper remarks.

We all nodded and traveled in silence. Mike loosened his tie, Kyla checked herself out in a compact, and Jerome nicked lint off his pants. I shifted in the seat and thought, *none of us know how to behave.* The comportment of mourning was a precarious thing.

A police escort had accompanied the limo to the cemetery

in East Vegas. Without the escort, the limo now stopped and started with the traffic on its way to my house in the southern part of town. The ride was the longest I'd ever taken. Even longer than the one to visit Bob's mother, who hated me, or when I drove the kids to Disneyland by myself because Bob was too busy working. Outside of the air-conditioned limo, another hot and dazzling white day rushed by. The tinted windows turned everything gray and off-kilter.

As the limo waited at a red light, I noticed a striking neon cactus plant over the doors of a bowling alley on a corner. This wasn't the simplistic neon of a beer sign, but more an expressionistic art piece. For a better look, I leaned past Mike and opened the tinted window. The neon piece was even prettier with colors echoing the greens of a new summer. The words, CACTUS LANES, lit up over the plant. Each letter blinked on, the sign darkened, and then the letters illuminated all over again in a friendly invite.

C-A-C-T-U-S L-A-N-E-S

The neon hinted of a distant memory. Something about those blinking lights comforted me more than all the hugs and handshakes to which I'd been subjected at the funeral service. I wish I knew why.

The light changed, and the limo drove on. Twisting back in my seat, I watched the sign and its winking call until we turned a corner.

C-A-C-T-U-S L-A-N-E-S

For the first time since Bob died, I smiled. My son and daughter looked at me as if I was running naked alongside the car. Kyla rolled up the window.

My daughter made good on her threat to plan a splendid and flawless funeral reception. A week before, she had appropriated the arrangements from me. She commanded I rest and leave the planning and execution in her efficient mitts. I yielded without an argument because I had no strength to challenge her dazzling organizational skills so I stayed up in my bedroom, read, slept, watched old movies, and signed checks to pay for her vision. She had told me, "Mom, I'm going to make sure everything is perfect."

The result: A reception that deserved a layout in *Funeral Vogue*, if there was such a thing. But then, perfection *was* my daughter's vocation and vice simultaneously. It drove Kyla onward and everyone else around her silently insane. She'd been like that since she was a child. She used to arrange Barbie's tiny shoes by style and her outfits according to occasion. Formal, sport, and career. Her own closet was the same. Shirts, skirts, and shoes in order or color coordinated. I'd once read how serial killers were very orderly, which prompted me to watch Kyla closely for weeks to make sure she wasn't killing neighborhood dogs and burying them in the backyard at midnight. But I understood I was being silly, and Kyla would grow out of the need for precision. Unfortunately, I was still waiting. Thankfully, my daughter wasn't dispatching dogs. At least, none I knew of.

"Everything looks beautiful, Kyla." This was true. I neglected to add that perfection carried a price – aloofness when there should have been warmth, especially on the occasion of a death. The whole setting left me colder than sleeping without socks.

"Thank you, Mom." With more tears, her grief turned her utterly vulnerable. "I miss him a lot."

"I know, baby."

"What will I do without him?"

"You'll live."

Her spine straightened as if this wasn't the answer she wanted. Drying tears, she walked into the other room, probably to check on whether the perfection continued elsewhere. She'd seen to all the reception details, even the unseen ones. From the thoughtfully arranged flowers around the house to the monogrammed guest book to an enlarged photo of her late father on an easel in the foyer. She even selected the photo. The one of Bob holding the club now buried with him. He wore his usual half smile as if he was saving the other half for a good game on the links.

Kyla had hired a bartender to serve drinks and two parking attendants to guide the many cars soon to pull up to my large house. She picked a caterer specializing in memorial services. In other words, someone who wouldn't serve flashy food.

In preparation for the arriving guests, the hired staff rushed around, mostly following my daughter's directives. I stood in the middle of the foyer feeling like a lump in a black dress. I wanted to help somehow or somewhere, so I stepped into the kitchen because doing the dishes or cleaning countertops meant I wouldn't have to think.

The kitchen was a designer's dream. Marble tops and stainless steel. Amber lighting. Oak cabinets. Two ovens. Appliances shiny as they were pricey. Bob had hired a contractor and decorator to create the kitchen. Though I lobbied for homey and small, he objected. Such décor clashed with the home's aesthetic of affluence. So I ended up with the ballroom of kitchens. I had joked to him how I should wear a gown just to have a cup of coffee in there, but my late husband had been born without a sense of humor.

This is a real condition.

The last time I'd seen Bob alive was in the kitchen.

He was heading out for a quick eighteen before dinner. Usually, he waved to no one in particular, though I was the only one in the room. I was bent over the newspaper drinking coffee and didn't look up at him.

"Have a good game, Bob." That was my usual response because years ago I'd stopped giving a shit whether he did or not.

Now the upscale kitchen was busy with the funeral caterers. At a counter, Consuela Rivera placed smoked salmon canapés on a silver tray.

I smiled when I spotted her.

"Con, I'm so happy you're here."

Reaching my chin, Consuela planted her sturdy arms around me and squeezed. Her curly black hair smelled of strawberry shampoo. Then she let go.

"How are you really, *mujer*?" Her voice was raspy as dried chilies.

"I don't know."

"That doesn't sound right." Her eyes tensed with worry.

I wanted to change the subject because if anyone could tell I hadn't cried, it would be Consuela. "Thanks for being here, Con. It means a lot to me."

"I'll always be here for you."

Her smile reminded me of a headlight beam, a sincere light to guide the way home. For the past eleven years, she cleaned the house every Tuesday and Thursday. Whenever Bob wasn't around, which was most times, I helped her clean and afterwards we'd go out to lunch or talk in the backyard over cheese, crackers, and bottles of beer. I counted Consuela a friend more than an employee and padded her paycheck. In her fifties, she was built firmly for work and love of family, either her own or the people she regarded as extended relatives. I was exalted to be in the extended category.

"Wait a minute. Why are you wearing an apron, Con?"

"Kyla hired me and my cousins to help with the reception." She waved at two cute young Hispanic women who waved back.

"I wanted you to be a guest today. Please take off the apron."

She placed a hand on my arm. Her hands were rough from work. "I could use the extra pay for my grandson. He's going to college and needs all the money I can afford to give him." Her smile shone. "I love my daughter, but she don't earn crapola at her job and her husband, the S-O-B, is worthless as a dead battery."

Within three months of employing Consuela, I had learned everything about her family. Their good and bad points, although sometimes I felt a little uncomfortable knowing so much. Still, I was flattered she liked me enough to share part of her life. I had plenty of female acquaintances in book club and garden club, but not any good friends because I would have had to share. Con saw my life so I didn't have to.

"Well, if you're going to work, then I'll help. I need something to do other than play the widow." I was instantly ashamed about that remark.

"We're fine, but thanks for the offer, Mrs. Adams," said one of the young cousins. "And so sorry for your loss."

I nodded. "At least I can put dishes into the dishwasher." I donned an apron hanging over a chair. "And I'm good at filling up trays and making coffee. I worked as a waitress once and made damn good tips."

"Cool," replied the young woman.

As soon as I started helping Consuela with the salmon appetizers, Kyla walked in, her head leading her body. I knew that walk. The determined walk. The get-things-done walk. The walk-over-people walk.

"Mom, what are you doing in here? The guests will be arriving any minute. Take off the apron."

"I'd like to help, honey."

"You don't have to. We hired these people." Kyla pointed to the younger women and the caterers. "Space those crackers out like I told you. I want them uniform." She then threw her attention at Consuela. "Is the coffee ready?"

Kyla's condescending tone made me feel like I'd shoved a wet finger into a socket.

"I'm taking out the coffee urn right now." Consuela's smile disappeared.

While Consuela thought of me as a friend, she designated Kyla as an employer with a capital B. I wasn't offended because my daughter always barked orders at Consuela as if she was an indentured servant.

"Consuela and her cousins are working hard and doing a nice job, Kyla. Let's leave them alone." I took off the apron.

"But, Mom…"

Gently, I turned her towards the door of the kitchen. "Con always does excellent work on every job."

"I'll be watching just in case," Kyla told them.

"I'm sure you will." On the way out, I delivered yet another apologetic expression to my friend who smiled with understanding. God love her.

We stood outside of the kitchen. "Kyla, I've mentioned this a thousand times before. I hate the way you talk to Consuela. It's disrespectful."

"She's a paid employee. They're used to accepting directions." Kyla straightened her dress.

My jaw constricted with frustration. "She's my friend. You owe her an apology."

"Maybe, later."

I wasn't convinced about the maybe part. "Be sure you do."

Kyla glanced toward the dining room where the bartender had set up. "I hope we have enough wine."

"Well, if we run out of the stuff, everybody can all just go home."

"I don't want that to happen." Kyla hurried off, presumably to continue her precision campaign, leaving me standing alone in defeat.

Bob had indeed left his imprint on her, as if our daughter was a piece of wet cement.

"No, it has to be this way, not that way. It must be perfect," Bob advised Kyla on anything from homework to golf.

"Perfect, perfect, perfect. I don't want to see less." He spoke to her as if she was an underling at his engineering firm.

Kyla's eyes would round to the size of blue Titleist golf balls and glaze over with tears. "Yes, Daddy. You're right. I will be perfect. I promise."

When I intervened, which was a lot, he told me striving for perfection was the way of the world.

"Not this world." But he ignored my point.

In her room, I tried to comfort Kyla by letting her know her father was so wrong. "You don't have to be perfect, Kyla. No one is perfect. Just be good and kind and do the best you can."

She gripped her small hands together. "Oh yes, I do have to be perfect. Daddy is right."

Kyla had adored him. Even when he didn't make time to watch TV with her, hang out on vacations, or even attend her parent-teacher conferences with me. I'm no Dr. Phil, but I think she took up golf just to be with her dad. It did work. On the greens, they were pals. Of course off the links, she was left behind like Mike and me. Her desperation to be noticed by him mushed my heart into Malt-O-Meal.

Damn Bob. Damn dead Bob.

Chapter Two

The house was noisy, which was a bit ironic considering it was a funeral reception. I hadn't heard the place that loud since Bob cranked up the TV while watching the U.S. Open, Masters, or one of the hundreds of other golf tournaments that seemed to go on year-round.

"Golf is such a quiet game. Why do you have the TV blaring?" I used to ask him.

"Adds to the excitement," he answered with a wink.

"Maybe you need to get your hearing checked."

Without taking his eyes off Phil Mickelson sinking another putt, Bob put his hand to his ear and shouted back, "What'd you say?" At first, I thought he might be joking, but then I remembered the humor lobe of his brain had been scooped out at birth.

The crowd of funeral guests spread all over the first floor and trickled out to the sprawling patio. They chatted, held drinks from the bar, and carried around small plates of the tidbits carefully selected by Kyla from the caterer's menu. For the first hour, people continued their condolences. Later, they seemed to forget about me, for which I was grateful. I thought about going upstairs to watch *Casablanca*, which I'd recorded off TCM. But I had an obligation to Bob's death and the kids, so I bowed to duty as always.

I was the Samwise Gamgee of Vegas.

Earlier I had visited with Bob's remaining family members who consisted of cousins so old their handshakes felt like soggy rolls of toilet paper. When Bob was alive, I had sparsely chatted with them at birthdays and other funerals. That was a good thing because we had nothing in common except Bob, and now not even him. His family was "Comfortably Wealthy," a term earning quote marks. Not rich enough to buy an island, but they all inhabited substantial houses and investment portfolios. No hugs of comfort from them. Instead, they remained distant as a mountain range. I believe that after all those years, they still thought of me as a gold digger, which I found hilarious.

Once in a while, I spotted Mike among the mourners and he threw a thumbs-up. I didn't see Kyla at all and hoped she wasn't bothering Consuela and her cousins with more commands.

Moving among the visitors, I tuned into their conversations. At my parents' funerals, I had learned things about them from listening to the mourners, things I never knew. Like how my dad had wanted to be a professional baseball player but injured his wrist in a bike accident that ended his dreams at age fifteen. Or how my mom played the accordion better than Lawrence Welk and gave it up when she married. Hearing about their unfulfilled dreams should have given me more of an affinity for them, but only made me feel worse.

Stopping around a corner, I eavesdropped on two older men from one of Bob's golf leagues. Maybe the Tuesday group. I couldn't keep them straight. Jack Jonas was the heftier of the two with a polished bare head. Louis Tucker had a dense carpet of white hair and broken vessels in his nose.

"Good ole Bob Adams." Jack moved around his whiskey glass, making the ice cubes clink.

"A heart attack on the ninth hole." Louis took a bite of a spinach-dip-covered baguette. "The man did love the game." He spoke though a full mouth.

"Well, if you're going to go, go after a good round, I always say."

"I heard he was buried wearing his golf shoes."

"In them right now."

"Hope they're comfortable. He'll be wearing them into eternity."

Richard Steven, a man slender as a nine iron, joined them. "Bob was one great golfer." He carried around a gin and tonic.

"I wonder if his handicap will get him into heaven," Jack said.

"If it does, then I'm screwed."

"Well, until he's invited upstairs, I'm sure Bob will be swinging away at the driving range in purgatory."

The men laughed and then Jack focused on the mound of spinach dip on Louis's plate. "That looks good. Think I'll try it."

I continued my eavesdropping but didn't hear anything new about Bob. I wished his friends might whisper about how he had kept a sultry mistress in a luxury condo downtown, or how he'd been a compulsive gambler, or perhaps, a closeted gay man. If nothing else to give Bob some personality and chip away at the guilt I hadn't shaken for not weeping at the funeral. But they just commented on his business acumen and golf skills. They didn't call him funny, generous, or even the salt of the earth. Not even Bob their best friend. He was just Bob the businessman, or Bob their golfing buddy. I sighed with sadness for my dead husband. Was his life so emotionally barren that only business and golf helped? Apparently not his kids, or roommate wife who didn't weep for him.

My guilt level spiked.

The wives of Bob's other golfing buddies waited in line for the bathroom. Gert Thompson filled out her clothes with an immense bosom that appeared to expand like the universe. Reedy as a cornstock, Sarah Crenshaw served on the library board and only read biographies. I sneaked around the other side of the hall so they couldn't see me, but I could hear them, which was easy. Gert's voice carried farther than an announcer at a prize fight.

"Poor Margaret. All alone in this big house."

"She should be used to being by herself. Bob was never home. Always golfing or away on business. Least that's what my Joseph says. How she put up with it for so long is a miracle."

"I never saw a woman take so much shit."

"Still, what's a woman without a man?"

"Happier?"

The women giggled and quickly stifled it before anyone could hear them.

I tapped my forehead on the wall at their right-on description. Then someone took my hand.

Mitchell Cross.

I hated to shake hands with him. He worked in my husband's office as a marketing executive. In his early sixties, Mitchell was twice divorced from younger blonde women with tiny waists and obvious boob jobs. Though I didn't fit the pattern, he outrageously flirted with me and right in front of Bob. I couldn't figure out his interest unless he was going to suggest I join him in a scheme to knock off my husband à la *Double Indemnity*. Whenever Mitchell flirted, I had the icky sensation he gazed right down to my XL panties. I truly believed he had bought a pair of X-ray contacts on Amazon.

Mitchell drew me to him, and I leaned back. My eyes watered from his high-priced cologne, which I had dubbed "Man in Heat."

"So sorry for your loss, Margaret." He pulled me closer.

"How kind of you." I took a step away.

"The days ahead will be trying and lonely." Mitchell opened the palm of my hand and slid his manicured fingers up and down. "Bob was a good provider."

I tugged my hand out of his as politely as I could without having to punch him in the head.

"And a good companion."

I gave a faint noncommittal smile.

His fingers tiptoed up my arm. "All by yourself, Margaret. What a shame. I've always admired your…"—he stared right at my chest—"your bravery. But there's no need for you to be alone."

Rescuing my arm, I desperately wanted a jug of hand

sanitizer. "Excuse me, Mitchell, but I've got to check on the refreshments."

"If you ever need someone to comfort you, I'm your man."

"Try the cheeseball."

"Cheeseball, hmmm." Mitchell licked his lips. He stepped forward, but Carol Cunningham came right in between us. She grabbed me with a tight hug. Fortunately, Mitchell spotted another woman and headed in her direction, sending me a last lascivious wink. The man had one set of golf balls for trying to drum up a date at a wake.

"I am so sad for you, Margaret." A slab of a woman, her white curls resembled shavings off a block of ice. "Still can't get over losing my Henry." She started to cry. "I understand what you're going through."

I patted the woman's wide back and thought up a gentle way to escape.

Carol began beating the walls with her fist so hard a painting trembled. "I miss him so much I don't know how to go on." The woman clutched me with so much power I could hardly breathe.

"Time heals everything." I wrestled my way to freedom.

"Well, they goddamn lied." Carol snuffled back tears but they didn't stay snuffled back very long. "I can't believe it's been twelve years." She sobbed so loud that more than a few people turned their heads to look.

I vamoosed in the opposite direction.

By three in the afternoon, people began to file out through the ornate glass and iron front doors. From all the hugs and handshakes, I felt bruised as a week-old avocado.

Consuela, her cousins, and the caterers cleaned up. I tried to pick up a glass or plate to help, but Kyla shooed me back to the living room to sit down. Mike headed upstairs to watch a World Cup preliminary match on the television in my bedroom. Though he loved sports, he wasn't cursed with the fanaticism of his father, for which I thanked heaven, paradise, and Valhalla daily.

Kyla supervised the workers and had nothing bad to say when they finished, which meant they did a better job than she expected so she couldn't find fault with them.

Nearing five, Consuela and the cousins left the kitchen immaculate. I insisted they accept the leftover catering food.

"But Mom, you can freeze it for later," Kyla said.

"No way will I be eating a boatload of shrimp cocktail, cheese, spinach dip, and cookies. They have bigger families who'll enjoy it."

Kyla shrugged and left.

"Call me when you're ready and we'll go out for a drink," Consuela told me.

"You bet. Best to Joey and the kids."

I hated to see her go.

At the front door, Kyla bear hugged me. "Mom, I still think you should come and stay with Jerome and me for as long as you like. Right, Jerome?"

Jerome didn't answer right away. She encouraged him with a slight jab to his third rib.

"We'd love to have you." His voice raised an octave.

"Thanks for the offer, but no."

Jerome and I got along well. Unfortunately, he was as fastidious as Kyla was obsessive. As I was nowhere near their neatness and exactness, living with them would drive me nuts enough to take a dive off Hoover Dam. I'd just save everybody the trouble and stay home.

Kyla mildly kicked Jerome in his calf.

"Yes, come for as long as you like." He squeaked it out.

"Quit torturing your poor husband. I'll be all right. Now go home. It's been a long day for all of us. And Kyla, the reception arrangements were beautiful."

Her eyes lit up.

Mike came from behind and nudged Kyla out the door. "Get going, sis. Let her rest."

"Don't be so pushy. Call if you need anything, Mom. No matter what time of night, I can be here in twenty minutes."

I looked at my watch. "If you can make it in that time, I'll have to call you Kyla Diesel."

"Kyla Diesel? I don't get it."

"She means you'd have to be driving like someone in the *Fast & Furious* movies." Mike helped his sister.

"Fast and what?"

"Go home, please, Kyla." I put my head down and sighed. Like my late husband, Kyla never got my humor or attempts at it.

Jerome took Kyla's hand and led her toward their car. She cried all the way.

Mike held my hand.

"You're probably worried about me too, son, but I'll be fine."

"I know you will, or else I'll tell Kyla."

"God, no. Mike, it's a long drive back to San Bernardino. Stay the night."

"I could use the alone time, Mom."

"I totally get it."

"I know you do. That's why I love you."

We understood each other, but not enough to admit to my son I hadn't cried at all that day for his dead father.

"I'll buy a huge cup of coffee to keep my eyes open. Text you when I get home." Mike walked to his car. He stopped and glanced back at the house with a whisper of regret shading his handsome face.

Shutting the double doors, I locked them behind me to keep out any more mourners. My heels *clicked, clicked, clicked* on the marble floor of the foyer. The Morse code echoed through the empty house.

N-O-W W-H-A-T

N-O-W W-H-A-T

Buck up and be a man, Margaret. I aligned my spine to support the pep talk. *You must learn to be alone.* The kids were kids no longer and hadn't been for a long time. They had their own lives and were gone.

"You're alone now, girl."

Then I bent over and laughed hard because I'd been alone ever since the kids moved out.

Removing my shoes, I rubbed my feet. A quarter-sized blister had formed at the back of my left heel. From the downstairs closet, I retrieved a pair of blue fluffy slippers and moaned from the memory foam comfort. In the living room, I clicked on *The Who's Greatest Hits* CD. I proudly admit to being an ultra-rock 'n' roll fan. Had been ever since I heard the Rolling Stones song, *Satisfaction*. Bob had preferred classical and more than once told me I should have moved on from rock music.

"Never," I replied and turned up the Stones, Beatles, Kinks or whatever band I was listening to at the time. For all the prosperity I gained through marriage, my most beloved possession was the Time Life Anthology of Rock 'n' Roll hits that I'd bought for three payments of $29.95 when I was still a waitress. If I ended up in a nursing home someday, I wished for a place where my music would be shaking the hallways. With my walker, I'd be strolling to bingo to the tune of Led Zeppelin's *The Immigrant Song*. Somehow that image consoled me about old age.

I cranked up the tunes as I did when Bob was gone playing golf or working. Sometimes, I danced around like I was at Woodstock. But even with my beloved rock music booming, the house seemed to have doubled in mass and emptiness. When Kyla got married eleven years ago, I wanted to downsize. Bob resisted as always. He liked its proximity to the country club and the spaciousness. Five-thousand feet of largeness over five bedrooms and four bathrooms.

"You could chip in the dining room," I had kidded Bob.

"You can't chip on marble," he replied in all seriousness.

His total lack of absurdity had been a constant nail in my tire of life.

In the dining room, I passed my hand along the fine wooden table. Bob and I ate in there twice a week because the rest of the time he ate at the office or the golf club. When we did sit down together, he talked about the pro golfers as if he personally knew them. Come to think of it, he might have met them as he hung around golf courses so much. He infused golf terms into our conversations like pints of blood dripping into a sick man's arm. He'd provide a play-by-play of his latest games. Of his bogies, birdies, and eagles, which sounded like the name of a law firm. I could even hear the receptionist answer the phone. "Bogies, Birdies, and Eagles. How may I help you?"

When I attempted to direct our talk to politics, books, films, or the environment, Bob steered it back to golf or in terms of how it affected the game. "Hey, I heard the President has a sixty handicap" or "I read the latest book on the golf techniques of champions" or "Global warming isn't real. It's always hot out on the fairway."

He only turned animated with chat of backspins, fades, and mulligans. Bunkers, chips, and drops. The latter three could have been a different law firm, this one focusing on criminal defense. "Bunkers, Chips, and Drops. What crime did you commit?"

Though I didn't know what the heck most of the terms meant or who the hell the players were, some golfese rubbed off as if I'd taken a Rosetta Stone course on sport linguistics. At the beginning of our married life, I had learned to golf so Bob and I could be closer and have something to share besides children and living in the same home. But his long disapproving breaths at my ludicrous swings made me play worse than someone with a broken rotator cuff. I quit after two years with a handicap lurking somewhere in the hundreds. So with habitual politeness, I'd listen to Bob's dinner golf talk with a smile that could have been painted on with acrylics.

Afterward, he watched the news and sports, while I watched old movies and read books. Such was our life after the kids, except for the occasional dinner or dance at the country club where Bob seemed to be most at home.

I left the dining room and shuffled around the imposing house with too many rooms. After all those years, I was still a trespasser because I'd started out with so much less.

My mom, dad, two brothers, and I had packed into a three-bedroom house in Henderson. As the sole girl, I scored my own bedroom and never let my brothers forget it. My childhood had been solid and level as skating over cement. Not as bouncy as the Cunninghams on *Happy Days*, or as miserable as the Joan Crawford household.

Dad worked in construction, usually building casinos because most people's livelihoods in Vegas were connected to gambling in one form or another. Brusque as a bulldozer with gigantic hands, my father considered rich people the plague of the earth only because he wasn't one of them. If he had lived, he'd have lots to say about the size of my fancy-shmancy house with its copper faucets, four-car garage, decorative wrought-iron railings along the stairs, premium hardwood floors, high ceilings and multiple fireplaces in a town rarely cold enough to need them. Where palm trees surround the pool with its own cabana and tasteful décor drenches every room.

Dad would have wanted to know what everything had cost and then shake his head when I told him. But he would've been secretly impressed, probably, because he lived with enough money to survive and not a whole lot more.

Mom had worked in the cafeteria at my elementary

school. She was content there was sufficient income for us to live in a respectable house, buy us new clothes every school year, and take an annual family vacation to a national park. Having enough should be good for anybody, according to her motto. Come to think of it, she said that quite a lot. Having enough is enough. No expectations for more. That should have doomed me right then, but I didn't let it happen, at least at that point.

Thanks to student loans, work study, and saving up from jobs all through high school, I attended the University of Nevada, Las Vegas full-time to become an elementary school teacher. Sharing a small apartment with one of my friends, I did what I wanted. Stayed out all night when I wanted. Studied all night when I wanted. The air was easier to breathe, and it wasn't because I was forty pounds thinner then. As I started my third year of college, I loved my life. I loved my purpose and accomplishment. Then, as often happens when you're happy, fate kicks your ass. One night my father woke the house with painful moans while he urinated in the bathroom. Within another three months, he was dead from an advanced case of prostate cancer. Following his funeral, I moved back home, reduced my class schedule, and worked part-time at a restaurant to help mom, who fell apart like a thousand-piece puzzle dropped on the floor. Both my brothers had already moved to California, so that left me to help put her back together.

Then one day, Bob came into the restaurant ... and kept coming in, leaving me huge tips. He began to pursue me with flowers and took me to classy restaurants and concerts. I got to dress up as he picked me up in his expensive car. He'd see me and smile. *Maybe for once I felt I had exceeded expectations*, I thought.

Then he opened his mouth. "Not too bad."

I should have bolted then but I didn't.

Though twenty-six and old enough to know better, I became dazzled—or more accurately, dazed—by a guy who wore a shirt and tie to work. He loved golf though he had no athlete's body. A regular guy of regular looks and height. His cheeks had a touch of the cherub to them, and his hair had begun to ebb like a tide. But he had a gentleman's air as if he'd been raised by a PBS affiliate, well-mannered and soft-spoken. Such a contrast to the men I'd dated previously. Men in work shirts and jeans right out of the wash. Stubborn dirt lining their fingernails. Men with muscles and baseball caps. Stalwart as a semi and as sensitive, they took me to the movies, bars, or dancing, and I necked with them in their trucks.

I once asked Bob why he liked me.

"You're grounded and won't let me get away with anything. And you're funny."

I thought that strange since he never seemed to get my jokes.

After seven months, he proposed and I convinced myself I loved him. He was a nice, kind man who'd probably treat me well, but I'd really fallen in love with the possibility of more.

Damn those expectations.

Bob said he loved me when he asked me to marry him and on our wedding day. After that, he didn't say it much, as if those other times had been plenty.

Mom had disliked her younger sister's husband because he was way older and not well off. But she had no objection to

Bob, who was sixteen years older than me. I hated to think his wealth played a factor, but I suspect that was the case. Many times, my mom had pronounced her own family, as well as my father's side, was not worth the ground from which they were formed. She had lobbied hard for Bob, saying I'd never get another man like him and how I'd be secure as the Federal Reserve. On his end, Bob promised to financially help her.

How could I pass up such an offer?

I had yielded like traffic.

Shame on me.

Our wedding reception was an extravagant affair at the country club where Bob's relatives gave me looks that could burn money. On the other hand, my brothers beamed at me as if I'd married a Kennedy. Whenever they visited Vegas, which wasn't often, they continued to congratulate me on hitching myself to such a bankroll, as if that amounted to the single achievement in my life. And who knew, maybe it was. Taking one look around our house, they'd pat my back and say, "Good going, sister." I wanted to tell them I hadn't earned any of this other than by saying "I Do."

On our honeymoon in Hawaii, I lost my virginity—this time officially. The initial occurrence took place with my first boyfriend, Chuck Rutherford, a truck driver who kept going down the road.

So I became Margaret Adams. Like my childhood, my married life wasn't Cunningham happy or Joan Crawford miserable.

It just was.

Within five years, the expectations for more in my marriage evaporated like water on a sidewalk. But by that time, we had children and I stayed to raise them. Bob wasn't a bad dad, just an absent one and that made me work harder to be a better mom. He wasn't a bad husband, but not all there. I tried to be a better wife, but got tired after a few years and fell back on being polite. I dreamed of leaving him and taking the kids but then go where? I had no completed education and worried that with all his money he'd get better lawyers and keep the kids. So I stayed.

After Mike and Kyla went out on their own, I had no excuse not to pack a bag. But all of a sudden I was in my fifties and even more scared. Then I was sixty and wondering what the hell had happened. What happened to that feisty college girl who wanted more out of life?

She apparently got buried.

Ding ding ding.

Ladies and gentlemen, I give you … the still reigning queen of excuses. Maybe all those years leading to now was the real reason I didn't cry at Bob's funeral. He wasn't to blame really, and *that* made me want to cry.

Here was a second chance to do something right.

In my fluffy slippers, I walked into the foyer, which was an airy and pretentious thing. Even when Bob was alive, the house created a vacuum, sucking the air out of my lungs. With Bob permanently disappeared, something else invaded my body. I picked up the large photo of the late Robert Thomas Adams, gave it a close look, and smashed it to hell on the floor. Careful not to step on the broken glass, I hauled myself upstairs, both excited and damn terrified at what I was going to do now that I was finally free.

Chapter Three

W hen people die, you sign a lot of papers. That was all I'd been doing since Bob passed on. I'd just finished signing more and slid them across the shiny desk of our accountant.

"You're in very good hands, financially speaking." Ralph Felding's words were neat as if extraneous syllables cost him money.

Felding eyed the papers to make sure I put my signature on all of them. I hated stereotypes, but this guy was full-on typecast by his profession. A CPA. Pricey but somber suit, not too flashy otherwise his clients might think he was playing blackjack with their money. Old-fashioned glasses bordering on geeky. His tie, conservative as a church prayer meeting. He was a Ken Doll of accountancy.

Before this, I had visited his office to sign the annual tax forms with Bob. We always owed because of the amount of money made by my late husband. All the way home, he groused about paying taxes to the government, *ya da, ya da, ya da*. When I reminded him those taxes paid for roads, law enforcement, and other services from which everyone benefited, he turned up the classical music to drown out what he referred to as my "liberal leanings." More than once, I was tempted to jump out of the car.

Felding's office was well-organized and professional. Behind his long wooden desk were shelves filled with books about tax laws, auditing, and other accounting jargon I could only guess at. A huge but plain coffee mug sat on a coaster in the corner. The flashiest thing in the room happened to be his accounting licenses framed by ridiculous gold ornateness more at home in a brothel.

"Bob provided for you with an insurance policy, stocks, and other good investments. Plus we've found a buyer for the engineering firm. This will add up to a tidy profit. Exceedingly tidy. The house is paid off and you have a generous monthly living allowance."

Felding owned a slight lisp. Polithy. Houth. Generouth.

In his will, Bob provided a goodly amount for Kyla and Mike, but the rest was all mine and the amount was nothing to shake a calculator at. He had inherited a successful engineering business from his father. Bob was a hard worker, he expanded the company and made it even more profitable. He was supposed to retire at seventy but kept going because he couldn't relax anywhere except out on the golf course. I had wanted to travel and we did once a year. But usually ended up at places with famous golf courses: Augusta, Georgia. Pebble Beach, Florida, and St. Andrews Links in Scotland. While he golfed, I took day trips to the sights by myself or read in the hotel room. I might as well have stayed home. The kids and I had taken real vacations to Disneyland, the beach, and the mountains. Nowhere near a golf course so Bob didn't come with us.

"Yes, you're in very good shape, Margaret. Other women would be fortunate to be in your position." The accountant's cheeks flushed. "I-I mean..." he stammered. "Not about losing their husbands."

"It's strange, Ralph. I never knew how much Bob was worth. I never asked him."

The accountant's smile flashed very white teeth. He apparently spent lots of money on brightening. "That is so common with wives who don't work. If they have a job outside the home, then they know every penny."

While it could have been an insult, it wasn't. The accountant stated facts as he saw them. Anyway, I'd been a fool for not asking Bob about our finances. If nothing else, we could have had something to discuss at dinner. He'd been talky talky on our dates, but maybe he had said all he needed and left it up to me to fill in the blanks when he settled into marriage. So during our first years together, I exhausted myself trying to get Bob to open up on subjects other than kids and golf. Later, I realized I needed a nuclear bomb to make any real headway.

"Margaret, you have nothing to worry about money-wise." The accountant checked his watch. "Questions?"

"Ralph, I'd like to work – you know, be useful."

"But why work if you don't have to?"

"I just answered that, Ralph."

"Go on a cruise, Margaret, travel to Europe. Buy yourself something nice."

"I can still contribute to…"

"To what?"

"To the community, to society."

"Forget useful. Forget work. If I didn't have to work, I wouldn't. Work ages you. If I were you, Margaret, I'd relax. Bob would have wanted it this way."

I sat back in the chair with defiance. I wasn't going to let Bob have his way from beyond the grave. "Thanks for the advice, Ralph."

"It's free." He laughed at his CPA joke.

With the Nevada heat thumping down on my head, my feet dragged. I was also hauling the mental and emotional weight of all that money. So unsettling having so much after growing up with just enough. More guilt slammed me between the shoulder blades. I should have thanked Bob for all his work. But at the time, I saw it as taking him away from the kids rather than giving.

Not only did I feel guilty, I felt captive. I stumbled as I walked to my car. I was newly imprisoned in an air-tight tower constructed of hundred-dollar bills, stocks, and investments. My chest grew taut and my heart started to palpitate. Gene Kelly tap danced on my aorta. I couldn't breathe after realizing this new sentence ran consecutively with the thirty-six-year stretch I already served with Bob. Gene quickened his steps in my chest.

This was no heart attack. No, it was something else. A panic attack. Not sort of but full blown.

I breathed in and willed my heart and Gene to settle down. *Be grateful for what you have, Margaret. No one likes a whiny wealthy widow. You could always donate a chunk of what you inherited to Greenpeace, the ACLU, and Habitat for Humanity.* Of course, no one except Mother Teresa would do that, but I did plan to up my annual donations to them.

Still, when I drove home, I swear I could hear the prison door slam behind me.

Chapter Four

Birds twittered overhead and dashed through the fountain spouting in the middle of the man-made lake. Gemstone-green grass surrounded the forever blue water. Palm trees stood with purpose, as if protecting treasure. A crisp freshness rode the air.

How beautiful.

Damn, I hated this place.

I waited on the terrace at the Clearview Country Club. Simone Sanderson had invited me to lunch, otherwise I'd never have gone back.

The country club was named runner-up as one of the most beautiful golf courses in the West by a national golf magazine. The managers acted as if the private course had won first place. They blew up copies of the article, had those framed, and placed over the entrances and in the bathrooms to remind members how lucky they were.

Under the terrace came the regular snap of the sticks against balls where golfers teed off at the nearby tenth hole.

Cleats ticked on the floor as other players headed in for lunch or cocktails in the clubhouse. No doubt the golfers were worth as much green as they played on, considering the amount of money required to buy a membership, not to mention the annual fees. For the amount, however, they got to recreate at the runner-up most beautiful course in the West and avoid the riff-raff of public ones. They rode the links in quiet electric golf carts and a drink cart came to them with scotch and gin and tonics. At country club dances, they boogied regularly to live bands after enjoying steak and lobster Newport dinners in a très classy atmosphere. Like their less affluent counterparts at city courses, the club members drank too much, but here they threw up in pricey suits and called taxis, Ubers, or private drivers to whisk them home.

At the beginning, I believed the country club a rival for my husband's time and attention. Ultimately the course won and I let it go. I'd never been a sore loser. Besides, how could I compete with a place offering year-round entertainment, good food, and companionship in a twosome or foursome?

I checked my watch. Simone was running late, which wasn't unusual for her.

Her deceased husband, Stan, had been the CFO of Bob's engineering firm. One year younger than me, Simone still had her abs because she worked out regularly with a personal trainer. She also dressed ten years younger, but on her the style worked—most times. There were occasions, however, when she showed up in brazenly too-young outfits that made me think of how Eleanor Roosevelt would look in pink leggings. Although we were acquaintances rather than friends, I didn't want to hurt Simone by telling her so. A friend I could be honest with.

Speaking of lack of style, I wore a simple blouse and capris. In the chair, I shifted around the thirty-plus pounds I'd gained over the last eight years. I attributed everything to menopause and growing older, but the explanation was getting thin, and I wasn't. I hadn't halted my slide into full-figuredness and hit rock bottom when I started wearing pearls and tall bouncy hair to the country club dinners Bob and I used to attend. After that, I'd browse websites showing celebrity women in their sixties who still were rated, if not hot, well, smoldering. Alas, I was no Goldie Hawn, Kim Basinger, or Susan Sarandon. The fact that few women my age did look like them was no consolation.

I nodded resolutely. I'd have the chef salad instead of the club sandwich and fries for lunch.

Simone finally entered with a curl of her hand and a cloud of exclusive perfume. She swept over and bestowed a light hug.

"Margaret, you look good, considering."

Simone talked in a rushed manner, like she had so much to say she had to fit it into one breath.

"No, *you* look good."

Simone nodded with acceptance as if entitled to the compliment. She turned her head to provide a view of her profile and patted under her chin. "Botox and a face peel."

"Sounds like a cocktail. I'll have a Botox on the rocks with a twist of face peel, please."

Simone didn't get it.

I cleared my throat.

"I'm fighting off the years as hard as I can, no matter how much it costs." She tapped at her cheeks. "I'm going to have more work done next month. Just a little off the jowls and reduce the wrinkles around my eyes."

"Good for you." I smiled with support.

I'd never go under the knife because I was secretly petrified of plastic surgery. Although I could probably afford a whole new face, I worried I might end up on one of those what-went-wrong-with-plastic-surgery pages popping up online. As a teenager, my nightmares had consisted of running naked around the school right as the lunch bell buzzed and the halls were packed with kids. These days I had bad dreams about coming out of plastic surgery with lips reaching ear to ear, skin shinier than aluminum foil, and a mug resembling the cat in a Whiskas commercial.

Simone winked. "I know a fabulous surgeon. Think about it, Margaret, we could look better than our mothers when they were our age."

"Yeah, who'd want to look older than Mom?" She still didn't laugh. "Anyway, Simone, I think of my wrinkles as a badge of courage."

I could talk such bullshit.

Simone wasn't listening, anyway. Standing at our table was a server who could stunt double for Brad Pitt. I'm talking about the ripped Brad Pitt from *Thelma & Louise*, not the *Twelve Monkeys* disheveled Brad Pitt. He wore the country club wait staff uniform of black pants, white shirt, and a heap of attractiveness.

Simone's voice lowered and her glossed lips lifted in a smile. I shook my head a little. She appeared to be the type of woman who felt good about herself only when a man paid attention. If I'd gone by that criterion, I'd never feel any damn good.

"You must be new," Simone told the young Brad Pitt.

"Yes, ma'am." He had a patronizing voice suitable for recruiting generous tips from customers.

"Call me Simone. Go on. Say it."

"Simone." He smiled.

What a smile.

"See that wasn't hard. What's your name?"

"Travis."

"Anyone ever say you look like Brad Pitt?"

"The *Thelma and Louise* one. Not the *Twelve Monkeys* one," I added to help out Simone.

"Never saw those movies. You ladies want to see the senior menu?"

I laughed. Simone did not. The poor kid had lost one huge tip from her.

"Give me a Margarita, no salt on the rim." She spoke tersely at being reminded of her age.

He turned to me. "Anything for you?"

"Botox on the rocks with a twist of face peel."

"Huh?"

"Just an iced tea."

The server left, but Simone still checked out his butt, which was indeed magnificent. Suddenly, she sat up as if she'd remembered she left on the gas at her four-thousand-square-foot home. She touched her Botoxed forehead that looked stiff as an ironing board.

"I'm so stupid for asking you to meet me at the club. This place is probably full of memories of Bob."

I sipped water and glanced at a group of young players teeing off. They had the air of stockbroker about them. "Bob was more at home here than he was at home. I'd like to think he's just playing the back nine … forever."

"My poor Margaret. How long has it been?"

"Seven months. That long?" I added with a little surprise at the span of days. What the hell *had* I been doing?

"See, you've lost track of time because of your grief."

I laughed, which summoned a look of concern on Simone's face. "I'm not going insane, promise I'm not."

"Then it's time to move on with your life."

"What'd you do after Stan died?"

"Went on a cruise to the Bahamas, had a tummy tuck, and took samba lessons."

"That's one interesting list."

"I know what you're thinking."

I was thinking it all sounded trite and shallow.

"You're thinking it's superficial."

Man, Simone was so close.

"But all those things helped me enter the next phase of my life. I was no longer Mrs. Stan Sanderson, and I had been her for such a long time. Now I was just Simone, and I had to find out who she was." She sat back in her chair.

For the first time in the twelve years I had known her, I kind of liked her.

"So good things are ahead of you, Margaret."

"You mean drooping boobs and vaginal dryness?"

Simone's lips twitched like she couldn't decide whether or not to laugh.

I cleared my throat again.

"I can guess what you're thinking."

"What?" I asked.

"That you'll never want another man after Bob."

I lowered my head because I wasn't thinking anything of the sort.

"But I'll tell you what will add years to your life." She leaned closer.

"A time machine?"

"Men."

"Oh, God."

"Sex." She took a drink of water and winked.

I clutched my napkin. I'd slept alone for the last fourteen years. The single occupancy began when I'd asked Bob to sleep in the other room because I had a cold and needed rest. He snored worse than five men who ate turkey for dinner with a pecan pie chaser, his rumblings piercing the expensive ear plugs I wore. So he packed off to a guest room during my illness and never returned except for the occasional sex. Then, he stopped coming around at all. Because he was older, I figured he'd burned out faster—sex-wise. Or he might indeed have had a mistress packed away somewhere who met his carnal needs. Either way, he moved into another bedroom and the master bedroom became my domain in the house. In there, I'd watch old movies, read, or scout around the vastness of the Internet. Even before he stopped visiting me at night, our sex life had become more routine than passionate. Perfunctory as an oil change at Jiffy Lube. I did miss the intimacy, fleeting as it was. Bob did give nice hugs, though his kissing was sloppy at best.

Although he didn't sleep with me, every night he'd still knock at the bedroom door, enter, kiss my forehead, and say "good night, old girl." His tender action moved me until I remembered that that was the most we'd talked all day.

"Margaret?"

"Huh?"

"I was talking about men."

"Oh yes, them."

"When you stop thinking about sex, then you are done for, my dear. And I'm certainly not."

"You're seeing someone?"

Simone's smile declared a "hell, yes."

"A retired judge. We have so much fun going to dinner and concerts. We met through *Seniordates.com*. He's very distinguished, divorced, and loves to samba. And he is so good in bed I've had to triple my intake of vitamin E to keep up."

"Oh, God."

She leaned in and whispered. "Exactly what he says. 'Oh, God. Oh, God.'" Then she leaned back in her chair. "You're not through with men, are you?"

"No, of course not, Simone. I've told my children that when I die, I want my ashes spread over Chris Hemsworth or Idris Elba. Whoever they can catch first."

"What? Who?"

"Nothing."

I took a drink of water to stop talking and was thankful the Brad Pitt waiter brought our drinks just then. I picked up my iced tea and saluted the woman across the table. "Anyway, here's to Simone. I'm so glad you found her."

She smiled. "And here's to Margaret."

"Whoever she is. Maybe I'll go on a cruise to Disney World, get a boob job, and sign up for line dance lessons."

This time Simone laughed. "You're just lost. Your loving husband is gone."

I nipped at my lip, a habit I'd formed whenever anybody brought up Bob and how much I must miss him. Truth be told I hadn't. As my mom used to say, don't speak poorly of the dead or else they might haunt you. In my case, I was compelled to keep quiet on the subject or else be cursed with sightings of Bob of the Dead on the Ninth Hole.

"Margaret, you have so much to look forward to. You can join golf or bridge leagues. And I know the library foundation and symphony guild would love to have you on their boards."

"Let me think about it."

"You're so brave."

"Don't know about that. Never been tested."

"I have no idea what you mean." Simone fluttered her false eyelashes. They were too long, thick, and curly to be real.

"Never mind me, I'm just rattling on. But I have to say your eyelashes are fabulous." Now that I'd noticed them, I was having a hard time not staring.

"They're lifted." She fluttered them to demonstrate. "To get back to my point, you're not a soldier having to be brave. You're a woman." She grinned with senior seduction as the server returned for our food order.

He nodded at Simone but looked right at me. "Ma'am, I asked the bartender about a Botox on the rocks with a face peel twist, but he hadn't heard of it either," he said with sincere regret.

"Thanks for trying." He was going to get a nice tip from me.

"Isn't he the cutest thing?" Simone said.

I thanked God for many things in my life. My children. My health, which was relatively good.

I also thanked God for fat pants.

Kyla hated when I called them that, but they were comfortable and familiar. My go-to outfit was black sweatpants and a Beatles T-shirt I scored at the Salvation Army. Bob had disliked when I shopped at secondhand stores.

"It's other's people's junk. You can buy new," he groused.

"I like other people's junk. There's a story behind it."

"What story? I needed money for drugs?"

In my fat pants and oversized T-shirt, I grimaced. The sweats were one size larger than my normal size because I disliked anything tight, especially around my stomach. Perhaps I was getting *too* comfortable. I probably resembled one of those "before" shots in women's magazines. Gray peeked through my dark brown hair, which was ragged at the ends. The last time I went to the hairdresser was before the funeral and hadn't gone back since. I thought it bad taste to look too good right after my husband had been buried.

Once Kyla had dragged me into a Victoria's Secret to buy a new supply of underwear. I glanced at all the lace and silk and pushup wires and couldn't see the point.

"It's not like I'm going to get a job as a part-time hooker on the Strip."

At the word "hooker" Kyla immediately covered the ears of my grandson, Jonathan.

"They'll make you feel more feminine, Mom."

"Femininity is a state of mind." Besides, even if I'd bought all those skimpy bras and lacey panties and jaunted around the house just wearing them and a dimple, Bob would've been oblivious.

In my favorite outfit, I headed downstairs with a glass and a full bottle of Chardonnay. I'd already hauled down a plastic chair from the garage. Bob had wanted to turn the large basement into a family recreation area and in-house movie theater. Terrific, I thought with abundant sarcasm. Then I'd never have to leave the house.

In one section, he had a pool table and a small bar installed for his many get-togethers with golf buddies, but he never got around to the movie theater renovation. So the other half of the basement became a storage annex.

I poured myself a tall glass of wine. Sitting down there, I experienced security as if hiding out from the enemy in a concrete bunker with thick carpeting.

Damn, I hated that feeling and took a drink of wine.

On shelves, plastic bins held my memorabilia, family photos and mementos, and the evidence of my existence. Sipping more wine, I started going through them and marveled at how everything fit in them so neatly.

The heaps of photos of the kids I planned to scan and place onto USBs. Class photos of them from elementary to high school. Prom photos. Photos of vacations to Disneyland.

Opening their many presents at Christmas, patting full tummies at Thanksgiving, or clowning in the pool on July Fourth. So much purpose raising the children.

In many of the photos, it was just me and the kids. As usual, Bob was out golfing or on business. Of course, he did hire a photographer to take an official Christmas photo that went out to his business connections.

What I couldn't scan were the swatches of hair from their first haircuts saved in plastic sandwich bags. Kyla's first ballet shoes. Mike's first catcher's mitt. As I inspected the contents, my children grew up again. How blessed I was having them in my life.

Another bin held photos of my family. These I hadn't seen in years. My mother and father at barbecues in the backyard. Me mugging for the camera at Christmas with my brothers. Cherishing a Barbie wannabe doll I loved so much until one of my brothers bit off its head. Easter in our best clothes. Dressed up for Halloween clutching full bags of candy.

Funny how that life was chronicled and measured by holidays.

I never remembered my parents as young as they were in those photos. In dated hairdos and clothing, yes, but with years ahead of them wearing possibility like a suntan. I examined a photo of my dad. He sat on the porch, smoking one of the many cigarettes he went through in a day. In the photo, he was older and no promise endured. Turning it over, I noted the date, which was just a month before he died, and then placed the photo back in the bin. The glossy paper could have been made out of steel sheeting.

In another bin sat photos of me as a young girl and

teenager. I smiled with abandon in all of them, illustrating the younger me must have known something the older me didn't. Though my body was sixty-two, the inside of me, in my soul or spirit or essence or whatever the hell you called it, the years were fluid. Most days I couldn't believe I'd been stomping on the earth for so long, except when the arthritis kicked my right knee into pain and submission. But then sixty was the new fifty, according to Simone, who seemed to justify more than me. Given such logic, she probably equated death to a day at the spa for all eternity.

Whenever I glanced into a mirror, the ageless me stared out through eyes encroached upon by wrinkles and time. I was an innocent prisoner of age, no doubt about it. The Alfred Dreyfus of decades.

Alfred Dreyfus?

Probably drinking too much wine. Or, not enough. I knew I shouldn't but popped an antianxiety pill with the alcohol. I'd been on them for years to remind me to chill when I wanted to scream. Although I took the lowest dose possible, I was ashamed to need them. That is until I overheard women at the country club dances confess to inhaling pharmacies full of antidepressants. Apparently, I wasn't alone in my misery.

I finished one glass and poured another because all the abstract thinking made me thirsty.

From one more bin, I took out my high school yearbooks. The front of each emblazoned with the mascot Lonny the Lizard wearing a football helmet. The books all smelled musty and I laughed. Like dragging out the Dead Sea Scrolls from ancient Rubbermaid.

In each book, I searched for my class photo and marveled at

the copious amounts of hair on my noggin. And son of a gun if I wasn't sorta pretty. Not one of those cheerleader beauties but cute dammit.

My teeth gnashed.

Bob never called me beautiful or even pretty or cute. Mostly, he told me, "You don't look bad at all." After I came home from our dates, I'd sit on my bed and throw down my shoes. I wanted to be better than not bad at all. I wanted to be prized like the women in those romance movies on television. I wanted to be gorgeous in my lover's eyes. Of course, the notion was all movie bull, but I ached for a brush of it over my life.

On our wedding day I met him at the altar wearing an expensive, lovely wedding dress and looking good, if I do say so. He smiled, winked, and whispered, "Yes indeed, not bad at all." I should have bolted right out of there like Elaine in *The Graduate*.

How I wished I had another bottle of Chardonnay with me in the basement.

Flipping to the back of my junior yearbook, I checked out a list of my extracurricular activities, some of which I'd forgotten along with my locker combination.

"I belonged to the National Honor Society. Was I smart?" I asked the basement.

The inclusion made me proud, although my girlfriends had called the Honor Society membership a badge of social death. Boys never wanted to date a girl smarter than they were, they said. These days, smart women enjoy more acceptance and their own place. I raised my glass of wine to them. Too bad men were still in charge of almost every damn thing.

I'd also belonged to the dramatics club, though my auditions for parts went nowhere. So I ended up painting the scenes for productions or taking care of wardrobe. In pep club, I cheered for the home team and hiked up my skirt to scandalous shortness.

My fingers went cold on the next listing.

I was the goddamn captain of the high school bowling team. How did I forget that? In the yearbook photo, I'm standing in the middle of nine other girls. A state tournament trophy stood in front of us. From my expression, it might as well have been the Stanley Cup or an Academy Award.

The memories slipped into my head like olive oil in water. As part of gym class, I spent two weeks learning how to bowl. I'd shown an aptitude for the sport and the gym teacher encouraged me to join the bowling team. We practiced at the Big Strike Bowling Alley, a few blocks from the school, and it was fun. I carried my bowling average like the Congressional Medal of Honor. The other girls on the team were loud and energetic and all made jokes. Most of the other students who bothered to form an opinion in the first place considered bowlers outsiders and weirdos. My non-bowling friends gave me consistent shit about hanging around the Big Strike. They claimed the bowling alley carpets were filthy and the bathroom walls etched with obscenities. Granted, the place stunk like a truck full of smoked cigarettes, even in the bathrooms. But it still smelled of heaven. I had a great time there.

As soon as the bowling season ended, I succumbed to the taunts of friends and never returned to the Big Strike alley.

It was now the site of a Walmart.

I pointed a finger at my younger self. Age seventeen and

packed with potential and a capacity for happiness. Not to mention a decent bowling average.

"Where the hell did you go?"

Finishing my wine, I pondered the question dogging me since the funeral.

What now?

Standing up, I knocked over the wine bottle. My butt ached, but I smiled at what might be an answer.

Chapter Five

The neon sparked to life, one letter at a time with the slightest *buzzt* sound.

C-A-C-T-U-S L-A-N-E-S

Smiling, I accepted the winking invitation and got out of the car.

The day already burned hot when I woke. And in Vegas, that's the very definition of hot. Heat waves shimmered up from the ground like invisible demons hoping to invade heaven where it was bound to be much cooler. So much brightness I had to shut my eyes. Something about the day seemed to be more blazing than usual. As if the sun emitted a few more rays. Drinking my iced coffee, I speculated whether the additional brilliance was a good omen or more global warming. I went with the good omen.

By the time I walked through the parking lot, it was damn hot. With such temperatures, how could I be cool and collected about what I acknowledged was a somewhat impetuous action? Going bowling after forty-five years.

An adobe-colored plaster covered the front of the building. Along the walls ran three-foot-tall rock planters which I hadn't noticed when we drove past on the way home from the funeral. An assortment of cactus plants filled the planters, and they were all in spectacular bloom. Waves of ornamental fleshy plants packed my flower garden at home. Yet, I was touched by the simplicity and beauty of the cactus flowers. They belonged in the desert of Las Vegas. Not the delphiniums, hollyhocks, and peonies splurging in my flowerbeds.

The short, round barrel cactus displayed orange and pink flowers. Red blooms topped the tall Fairy Tale variety of cactus. Amethyst-colored petals thrived on the Christmas cactus. Small reddish-purple flowers swirled about the round pincushion cactus plants. Cactus roses sprouted from the flat spiny plants. Orange blooms dressed up the prickly pears. The cactus plants in two large terracotta planters near the front doors were also abundantly in bloom.

I teared up from their subtle loveliness and my silly impetuousness.

What the hell was I doing there?

The tower walls closed in. Heart palpitations thrummed up to my throat like Keith Moon in a drum solo. Perspiration slid down the middle of my back. Vegas suddenly ran out of air and I couldn't hold on to a breath. My feet shifted back toward my car.

"So beautiful," I managed to say.

My farewell prayer to Cactus Lanes and its flowers. I cried at their loveliness and my inability to go inside.

"Yes, they are beautiful."

Wiping a tear, I turned. A man holding onto a backpack

also admired the plants. An older version of Ricardo Montalbán with a kick of Edward James Olmos. His face told a rich story—he had obviously thoroughly lived life.

"You okay?"

"Yes," I squeaked out.

"The damn heat."

I nodded.

He smiled and touched one of the cactus blossoms. "Funny how something so full of stickers and thorns can produce these lovely and delicate flowers. But then cactus plants are survivors, so they have to celebrate their endurance."

Like Montalbán, his voice was Corinthian leather. More than that. An audiobook narrator speaking in tones richer than a Cadbury Egg.

The palpitations relaxed a bit. His voice could have been a shot of valium. "That's a very nice outlook."

"Heard it on the *Discovery Channel*."

I laughed. "But I thought the cactus plants only bloomed in the spring."

"Me too. Yet here they are." He scratched his head, which was covered with deliciously thick hair more white than black.

"Miracles in the desert." I took in a breath of air, which had abruptly reappeared.

"Yes, they are. You know, when a cactus blooms, it means love is coming."

"Now you're just making stuff up."

"No, I swear I'm not. I read it on a webpage about Mexican myths."

"Then it must be the truth."

"Not to mention *napales* are also good eating with eggs." He nodded. "Nature never lies."

"No, it doesn't."

He tilted his head. "Have we met before?"

"I would have remembered." God, what a dope I was.

His smile deepened. He had dimples. Of course, he had dimples.

"Well, something about you is very familiar."

"As long as it wasn't on an *America's Most Wanted*."

He laughed now. "See you inside." He went into the bowling alley.

I bent over to take a closer look at the cactus flowers. I could almost believe the blooms symbolized love because their prettiness was almost too good for this world. "If you do signify love, you've definitely got the wrong girl," I whispered to them.

My heart drumming subsided and I straightened my spine. Keith Moon left the stage. I was going in.

Pushing past the glass doors, it took a few seconds for my eyes to adjust coming into relative dimness. When I could see, the first thing I noticed was that this place was a lot cleaner than the Big Strike Bowling Alley of my youth. The carpets appeared new and were decorated with bowling balls and pins on a dark blue background. The designs exploded like stars in a sports constellation. A line of video games, four pool tables, and an air hockey table sat in one section of the alley, and a bar and pro shop were located at the other end. No ashtray smell at Cactus Lanes either. Nevada had banned smoking indoors, an unusually liberal move for such a creaky conservative state.

"Can I help you?"

I jumped.

"Sorry to scare you. I did brush my hair today." A woman smiled behind the curved counter of the snack bar. Tall and durable, she had short, tight curls of red. Lucille Ball red. She fluffed up her do. A spray of freckles painted her billowy cheeks and almost matched the dots of ketchup on the white apron she wore. Her expression was so friendly she could have been Mother Earth's younger sister, Betty Earth.

"You can smile. It was a joke."

I sighed. At last, people with a sense of humor. Except for my son, Mike, they were sorely missing in my life.

The woman removed her apron. Over jeans, she wore a turquoise T-shirt with a Cactus Lanes logo. "Bet you're here for our world-famous Cactus Lanes chili fries."

"The what?"

"Give me one second." The woman swiveled toward a fryer bubbling with oil and calories.

Like all bowling alleys, this one was lit in perpetual sunset so players couldn't tell if it was night or day outside. The place was quiet with just a few bowlers. On the middle lanes, the older man who knew a lot about cactus plants was teaching a group of kids how to bowl. His young students laughed and clapped for each other.

What first drew me to Cactus Lanes was the extraordinary neon sign out front. But inside, lovely neon sculptures dotted the walls. A saguaro cactus and yucca in luminescent greens. A howling coyote in vibrant brown. A southwestern-type lizard the hue of a calm dusk. Indian flutists dancing in bright tints. Elsewhere, the neon light took the shape of bowling pins and bowling balls. Above the snack bar, a neon sculpture of a burger, fries, and malt.

An art gallery of bent light.

"Have a seat." The woman had returned and motioned to a stool at the counter. I obliged, not wanting to be impolite. I ranked rudeness right up there with ignorance, greed, and bigotry. Also high on the list were people who didn't signal when they turned and parents who let their kids scream in restaurants.

Kyla giving Consuela a hard time.

The woman placed in front of me a plate heaped with French fries smothered with green chili and topped by melting yellow cheese. The dish smelled spicy and decadent.

"I'm sorry, I didn't order those." I smiled.

"They're on the house."

"They do look great, but if I eat those, I'll have to move up a size in fat pants."

"Live a little. These fries are guaranteed to raise your cholesterol as we speak. But every year they steal off your life is totally worth it." The woman pushed the plate closer. "Don't be shy. We don't stand for shyness around here."

Not wanting to offend the woman, I took a bite. "Whoa. These are remarkable. They're beyond that. They are dangerously remarkable." I ate a little more and almost felt the fat make its way to my thighs.

The woman's grin at the compliment glowed as much as the neon sculptures. "What'd I tell you? And pay no mind to the rumors we cook our fries in the same oil we use out on the lanes."

My eyes widened as a man sent an oil-spreading machine

down the unused lanes. Without thinking, I checked out the fry in my hand.

"Another joke, honey."

"I get it." After wiping my hands on a napkin, I thrust one out. "Margaret Adams."

The woman took it in a potent grip. "Jo Maple."

Jo filled a glass of water and a Diet Coke and placed them both in front of me. "You'll need this to wash down all our good food."

"I can see how these can become addictive."

"I give samples to hook people into coming back to satisfy their chili fry habit." Jo winked. "The green chili recipe came from the owner's mom and I can make it pretty good. Well, almost as good as hers."

"The food is impressive. But these neon pieces are fantastic."

"You bet." Jo pointed toward the lanes where the man was teaching the children. "Frank Martínez made 'em. He owns the place, and he's an artist and a helluva bowler. He even used to roll on the pro bowling tour. A regular Renaissance man. So you want to bowl some lines?"

"I haven't bowled in years, many years. But I'd like to start up and I need a refresher course."

"Frank's an amazing teacher. Enjoy your fries a little more and then we'll go talk to him after he finishes up with the kids."

The seven student bowlers appeared to be five- to six-year-olds. Parents on seats in back of the lanes alternately cheered on their kids, offered encouragement, or took photos or video with cell phones. The teacher looked right at home with the children, or any place for that matter.

"Jo, why are they bowling in socks?"

"No bowling shoes in their size."

At their turn, each youngster picked up one of the colorful balls from the return. Standing at the foul line, they swung the ball between their legs and let it go. The ball traveled slow and crooked. Frank Martínez watched, clapping along with the parents in the gallery when pins fell down, if they did at all. Most of the balls headed right into the gutters.

"Pete, aim at the second arrow on the lanes," Frank advised a kid with spiked blond hair.

The boy picked up a ball and promptly dropped it on the floor. *Thud.*

"It's okay, Pete. Pick it up and try once more."

Frank could have been a patient grandpa instructing one of his own grandkids.

Pete threw as his teacher asked. The ball rolled over the second arrow on the lane and took down seven pins. The kid jumped up and down. A woman—no doubt his mom—let out a shout in the gallery. Pete's next ball traveled right into the gutter.

"Nice round, young man," Frank said.

A little girl was next. Her ball completely missed the second arrow and departed via the right-side ditch.

The girl put her head in her hands. "Dammit."

"What did you say, young lady?" Frank's hands went on his hips.

"My dad says that all the time when he messes up."

"Maybe I should talk to your dad too."

The girl giggled.

"You have one more chance."

On her second try, she knocked down two pins and danced as if she'd graduated from kindergarten cum laude.

After a few more rolls, the class ended.

"Good job, guys. Now I want you to practice with your parents for open bowling," Frank said. "I'll be around to give you more help if you need it. And when you finish, please put your balls back on the shelves."

The parents donned bowling shoes and joined their children out on the lanes. As I watched, I regretted not taking my kids bowling. An athlete, Mike would have been great and what a good time we would have had together. But I was also certain Kyla would have taken one look at those used, chipped balls and gone running.

Jo came out from behind the counter, took my arm and pulled me close, obviously not a believer in personal space.

"Come on, let's go see him." She led me to the teacher. "Frank, this is Margaret Adams. She wants lessons."

"We know each other."

"Oh yeah?" Jo moved her eyebrows up and down and grinned playfully.

"Margaret appreciates the cactus flowers out front."

Shaking his hand, I wished I'd put on a fresh coat of lipstick or lip gloss. Up close he was even better looking than Montalbán in *The Wrath of Khan* movie.

Okay, he had a paunch under his polo shirt, and his hair needed a cut, and a bald spot claimed a place at the back of his head.

But damn.

In response to his proximity, I became so conscious of my extra weight I sucked in as much of my stomach as I could without passing out. Then I exhaled. Why was I even thinking about how I looked? *You're sixty-some, not sixteen.*

But those eyes.

The darkest brown I'd ever seen. The color of primordial trees. I glanced down and held my purse so tight my knuckles turned into chunky pearls. *Margaret, you're acting as if you'd never met a man before.* I looked up and decided to become all business.

"Do you think you'll have time for me, Mr. Martínez?"

"Call me Frank."

Screw the all business.

"I'll leave you two alone. I got a shipment of mozzarella sticks coming in. My life's just too exciting." Jo returned to the snack bar.

"So Margaret, what's your wood?"

"My what?"

"Your wood? Your handicap?"

"I forget. Do I have to apply for one?"

Frank gave me a sympathetic smile as if I was bowling challenged, which I was.

"Not just yet. How you fixed for equipment?"

"I thought I just needed a ball." I smiled at my joke, my very small joke.

"I'll take that as meaning you need one."

I was coming off like a freaking idiot. "Yes. Yes. A ball. I need a ball. I don't own one, so I'll have to use one of those for now." I pointed to the rows of balls on shelves behind the lanes. "House balls, right?" *Shut up, shut up, shut up.*

"We can talk later about what kind of arsenal you'll need. You can use a house for now. I'll check out your address and swing on the approach. I have to warn you, the back ends are arid as the Sahara, but no worry. In time, you'll be throwing rocks and going all the way."

I had absolutely no idea what he was talking about. But I loved listening to his audiobook voice.

Frank smiled now. "Ever bowled before?"

"About a hundred years ago. I had a 135 average and was captain of the high school bowling team. Fred Flintstone was also a member. We all admired his twinkle toes."

He laughed and my heart swan dived into a warm pool. He thought my bad joke was funny. I wanted to weep.

"A mixed league, huh?"

God, he made a joke back. Cactus Lanes was Shangri-La. Nirvana. Elysium. The all-you-can-eat-salad bar at Sizzler.

"Luckily, the game hasn't changed much. How about starting lessons tomorrow?"

I had things to do but couldn't remember what. I couldn't think of one damn thing I had to do, not with those eyes looking at me, eyes making *me* want to take samba lessons and jump into a large vat of Botox and face peel. Discretely as I could, I checked out his left hand. No wedding ring but there was a silver band on his right. I guessed him to be a widower.

"Tomorrow?"

"Why waste time?"

"You're right, Mr. Martínez."

"Frank."

"I'm not getting any younger."

"Who'd want to? About eleven?"

"Fine. You're going to have to be patient with me."

"I know patience. I once taught a one-armed man to bowl."

"Impressive."

"Well, he had a broken left hand and had to learn to bowl with his other one for the city tourney."

"Still remarkable."

We shook hands again. Definite warmth there. Probably from the green chili fries I'd eaten.

With a wave to Frank and Jo, I stepped outside from the dark alley into the bright light. Taking a deep breath, I said out loud, "What the hell am I doing?"

On my way to the car, I stopped to check out the cactus flowers. What had Frank said about them? Survivors celebrating their endurance.

I could live with that.

Chapter Six

"Arggh."

What an accurate description. I was doing inventory on the clothes in my walk-in closet to find what I could wear to my bowling lesson. My favorite shirt, a stretchy lilac button-down, had a stain right on the front. My second favorite, a white one, had another stain at the bottom. Another knit showed a small hole.

"Arggh."

On my way to the Meadows Mall, I tried to remember the last time I'd shopped for clothing other than buying a new suit and shoes for Bob's funeral. It had been a while. This time, I hunted the shops for something to wear to Cactus Lanes. I needed bottoms and tops allowing me to bend. At the same time, I wanted to avoid clothing that made me look like the modern-day equivalent of a school marm.

In the dressing room of one store, I set aside a pile of shirts, pants, and capris. I planned to swing a pretend bowling ball to ensure the butt seam of my selections would remain strong and not rip. Taking off my clothes, I glanced at myself in those tall, unforgiving dressing room mirrors.

"Holy shit," I hissed.

"Watch your language. There's a young girl in here," came a voice from the adjoining dressing room.

"Sorry."

I silently mouthed a few more swear words at the reflection. My gut hung in a mound under my belly button. I wasn't so much carrying a pooch as transporting a toy terrier. I had a semblance of a waist but my middle was thick as an iceberg. My bosom, meanwhile, rivaled the landmass of Iceland. Large bosoms ran in my family but this was ridiculous. Extra skin under my arms waved back at me when I rotated them. I was grateful for a neck. Some women my age had nothing but sagging flesh between their chin and throat, as if they were storing carbs for the winter. Overall, the site in the mirrors was disheartening. I lay back on the bench in the dressing room.

When I turned forty, I had started walking two miles a day and swimming laps in our pool. In addition, I exercised a half hour each day to one of those DVDs starring women who looked like they never had to exercise. The walking or workout routine apparently was not good enough or long enough. Not nearly enough as evidenced by the bumps and bulges glaring back at me in the mirror.

When had I become so damn old when I wasn't even that damn old?

I slumped with the jarring fact: I'd crash-landed into matronhood.

Matron.

I loathed the word. It sounded like Prison Matron. Matron the wrestler. Big Mama Matron. Old Maid Matron. Matron the Destroyer.

My body had betrayed me. No. I'd done this all myself.

I'd never bought into the image of thin so prevalent in the movies, on TV, and in advertising. Not that I'm messy, or wear the same dress five days in a row, or have elbows crusty as old bread. The decline showed in hips a little too wide and breasts tumbling down my chest. In hair showing gray.

Over the years at the country club dances, I'd seen many of the lawyers, doctors, and businessmen exchange their old wives for younger models. Sometimes, I wondered – and secretly hoped – why Bob hadn't traded me in for a newer mockup. A trophy wife with stellar legs who Zumba-ed and had heaps of blonde hair out of a bottle. A gal with a Barbie waist, the pouty lips of a pug, and a seventeen handicap out on the links. But maybe Bob was just too busy or too tired to make the change. Maybe he balked at sharing half of his fortune with a divorced wife or a newer, thinner model even though he'd probably demand she sign a prenup, which I didn't.

God forbid, maybe he loved me all those years. Truly, it was hard to tell any emotion with Bob.

Whatever the reason, the woman in the store mirrors appeared to have stopped caring somewhere along the line. Getting dressed, I finished my purchases and immediately called my hairstylist Hillary to drive away the image I'd seen in the mirror. Fortunately, she had an open spot.

"Take a seat, Margaret."

Hillary was mildly perky but not annoying. Her own hair was impeccable, like a synthetic wig. The salon walls displayed large photos of models showing off different styles of hairdos. They mocked me. But I needed to distance myself from the word "matron."

"Hillary, can you give me a new look? I mean one of those where I won't recognize myself?"

"Know how long I've been waiting for you to ask?"

"Forever?"

"Yes."

"So you're giving me carte blanche?"

"I don't want to look like the old Margaret."

"I don't blame you."

"What?"

"I mean it in a good way."

As the stylist placed my hair into aluminum foil wraps, a question needed answering. Why the hell was I doing this? The new clothes. The new hair. The name "Frank" bounced around my head like a wayward ball in a pinball game. I pushed it out, although it crept back in throughout the afternoon. He was probably married with ten grandkids who adored him. *But he wore no wedding ring*, a voice chimed in. *Hey, your husband has been dead for less than a year*, another voice argued. *Why are you getting dolled up? Because it's about damn time*, one more voice added. *Bullshit*, answered the other voice. All the arguments and voices were giving me a headache.

Overthinking was what I did best.

Under the salon apron, I wrung my hands. I disliked women who improved themselves only to please men. Women like Simone. And here I was doing the same thing. I loosened up my hands.

No, I was doing this for myself at long last. Frank Martínez was just a mitigating factor. And dammit, at least it was good to *have* a mitigating factor. I saw myself through his eyes, though I'd just met him.

"All done." The stylist tapped my shoulder.

"I'm afraid to look, Hillary." My eyes remained closed.

"How long have I been doing your hair?"

"More than ten years."

"You trust me?"

"I think so."

"Come on, girl. Look."

I opened one eye at a time.

The cut was layered, tousled, and chic. Long bangs and two-toned highlights worthy of a California girl. "Not bad," I found myself saying, echoing the usual compliments of my late husband.

She crossed her arms. "Forget that not bad crap. You look fabulous."

"Hillary, don't bullshit me, please."

"I'm not."

"For a good tip you might." Good thing we'd known each other for years.

"You *always* give me a good tip. And you still look very good."

"If I'm going to get rid of the old Margaret, then let's go for a pedicure and manicure."

"Hallelujah, Goddamn."

———

When I walked into the kitchen from the garage, the phone was ringing. Checking the time, I knew who was calling. "Hi, Kyla."

"Mom, how'd you know it was me?"

"Because you call at the same time every evening to make sure I haven't been kidnapped and I'm not lying dead somewhere."

"I worry about you."

"Please, don't."

"Still coming to dinner Thursday night? I want to try this grand new recipe for lamb. And Jonathan wants to see you."

"And I want to see my grandson."

"What are you doing with your time?"

I tightened my lips. I wasn't about to tell Kyla about the bowling lessons. She'd have nothing good to say about any activity not associated with a country club and where I didn't pay a hefty fee to participate. I predicted my daughter would also call bowling "common".

"Mom?"

"Not much of anything. Hey, you and I should do lunch and a movie together. It's been a long time since we've done that."

During one summer after Kyla's freshman year in college, she'd been fun to hang out with. We laughed and went to the movies, got our nails done, went shopping and out to lunch. But come fall my daughter had slipped back into a stiff attitude as if rigor mortis had set in early.

"Lunch is fine, Mom, but most of the movies now are trash."

I tapped my toe against the counter. "You sound like your father now."

"How is that a bad thing?"

I made a date for Thursday dinner and hung up.

Upstairs, I tried on the new outfits. I felt like the times when my mom had bought me new school clothes and I put on each article as if it was new skin, a new me. For tomorrow's bowling lesson, I settled on jean legging capris and a top stylishly hiding what I was trying to hide. Fluffing my new highlighted hair, I fell back on my bed, spread out my arms, and grinned with a single thought.

What'd you know? I was more than not bad.

Chapter Seven

My bowling lesson started at eleven, but I was there by ten thirty. Sitting in my car, I spent the time second-guessing my decision to go through with this. If I chickened out, at least I'd racked up a new wardrobe and haircut. Fifteen minutes later, Frank drove up in his truck. Slouching down, I spied on him as he got out and walked spritely to the building. First, he stopped to admire the cactus flowers appearing even more beautiful that morning. He smiled and whistled as he opened the front doors.

I shot up in my seat and quit second-guessing. Passing the cactus blooms, I winked at them.

Jo was wiping down the tables located near the snack bar counter. "Hey, Maggie."

"Margaret."

"You look more like a Maggie."

"How do they look?"

"Like you."

"Maggie." The name felt good on my tongue. "I've always

hated the name Margaret. It sounds like one of those characters on the soap operas my mom used to watch. The ones who drank scotch for brunch and were cheated on by their husbands."

"What'd you want it to be?"

I fluttered my eyes teasingly. "A Felicia or Starlight." I laughed. "You always want to be a Jo?"

"I wanted to be Marianne after Marianne Faithful." Jo smiled large.

"Then, please call me Maggie. Just like Rod Stewart's 'Maggie May'."

She laughed. I laughed. A shot of humor whiskey had been pumped right into my jugular, hot and jolting.

Jo leaned closer to me. "Get a new hairdo?"

"Yes?" My eyes looked up as if to make sure my hair was still there.

"Well, I love it." Jo winked and glanced over at Frank who sat in a glass-enclosed office at one end of the lanes. She bumped her hip against mine. "Frank and I had a bet you wouldn't show up today."

I didn't take offense. Someone else actually cared about my whereabouts, aside from my children. "How much was the bet?"

"Five bucks. I lost and I'm glad."

Frank had bet on me.

Get out of here right now, a voice proclaimed in my head. A palpitation threatened.

I ignored them both.

"Need shoes, Maggie?"

"Bowling ones?"

Jo nodded with great tolerance for a bowling novice.

"Yes, I do need shoes." The reply a bit too enthusiastic.

"Let's get you a pair. Frank'll be ready for you on lane seven." Jo headed to the main counter and asked my size. She brought out a pair of shoes, which were red on one side and cream on the other.

"Jo, why are bowling alley shoes two colors? I've always wondered that."

"No freakin' idea. Probably so no one steals them because who'd want to wear them outside of Cactus Lanes? They're all sorts of ugly."

"My late husband Bob was a golfer. He had six pairs of golf shoes in various colors. Black, cream, and even argyle."

"How late?"

"Seven months."

Jo placed large hands on each of my shoulders and drew me close. She smelled of French fries and hamburgers. Fantastic.

"Sorry, Maggie."

I'd known Jo less than two hours in total but was moved by her sincerity. So easily given. Nothing attached.

"You two just met and now you're best friends," Frank said as he watched us.

"We're special women," Jo said. "Now, I got to prepare for the lunch crowd. Good luck, Maggie."

Frank shoved his hands in his pockets. "Thought your name is Margaret."

"I guess I'm going to be Margaret out there." I pointed to the doors of the bowling alley. "And Maggie in here." That made me never want to leave Cactus Lanes.

Smiling, his eyes narrowed. "You changed your hair."

"Yeah. I needed an update." Not even my husband had noticed when I had cut or styled my hair.

"I approve."

I glanced down at his left hand. Yup, no wedding ring. Coming soon, a new *Lifetime* movie about a woman – thinner than me – attracted to a man less than a year after her husband dies. She goes straight to hell.

"Then let's get started, Maggie." He emphasized my new first name. "How about we start with the right ball. I'll get everything set up and you find yourself one."

Surveying the selection on the racks at the back of the lanes, I carefully placed my fingers in the holes of different ones. House balls weren't new or shiny. They were scarred and marked like veterans of bowling wars, and there were rows of veterans at Cactus Lanes. I could barely get my fingers inside some of them. With others, I could fit more than one finger in each hole. Despite my body shape, my hands were slender and delicate. As a result, I took good care of them, such as using pricey lotions and doing my nails every other day as I watched television. If nothing else, I could find work as a hand model for Depends.

I set my sights on a bright purple ball. My slim fingers slid into the holes, but when I picked up the ball I almost dropped it on my foot. The number eighteen was etched above the holes. Obviously, the weight was more than I could handle. I replaced it.

A ball next to it was more manageable. Thirteen pounds. Black with pink swirls. This was the ball to bring me the strikes. I saw myself bowling with the pros. The music of ESPN's theme accompanying my throws.

Da da da. Da da da.

With such aspiration I shoved my hand deeper inside the holes.

I couldn't get my fingers out.

"Oh, hell." I placed the ball between my legs and pulled. The thing held onto me.

"Ready?"

With cheeks burning like Mount Vesuvius on a summer day, I showed Frank my predicament. "I *thought* I had the right ball."

He tried not to laugh. "Snack bar. Come on."

I followed with the stuck ball. A loser on my first day.

Frank went into the kitchen area in the back and returned with a cup of frying oil. Jo looked on.

She laughed. "Oh my, God, you didn't?"

"Yes, I did. You guys probably think I'm a moron."

"Nah," they said.

"I'm so embarrassed I want to rush out the door but I'd have to take the ball with me. Please tell me this has happened before."

"To lots of people but not on someone's first bowling lesson. Must be kind of a record," Frank said. "We may have to put up a plaque in your honor, Maggie."

Jo placed a supportive hand on my back. "Don't worry. Frank'll help you find the right one."

Jo greased up my fingers with the frying oil, while Frank tugged on my arm. The ball released me with a slight pop. I held onto Frank's forearm to stop from falling backwards. I was sure my cheeks were pink as the swirls in the bowling ball that finally released me. All three of us looked at each other and began to laugh.

"I'll keep the oil handy, Maggie," Jo said.

"Thanks for your confidence."

While I had spent a good ten minutes searching for a ball, Frank found the right one in two. The weight and size were ideal. And my fingers moved in and out of the holes with ease.

"Let's get to work."

On the lane, he demonstrated the approach and release with his own ball. He moved gracefully as a dancer. He was the Fred Astaire of bowling. I could watch him all day.

"Now your turn."

"Oh boy."

Holding out the ball, I hoped my high school prowess would come hurling back to me. Like how genius children suddenly begin playing Mozart on the piano or how people painted masterpieces after one Bob Ross lesson. Taking three steps and swinging back, the ball dropped off my hand and crashed to the floor. The few other bowlers on other lanes all froze and looked my way. I chased after the ball, which rolled off the approach, onto the waiting area, and bumped into Frank's foot.

"Maybe you need a different ball."

"It's not the ball."

"I've had tougher challenges."

"You kidding me?"

"Yes."

I smiled.

"Please roll."

"Do I have to?"

"You're paying good money for your lessons."

"I'll pay you twice as much if you bowl for me."

"Get going." He pointed to the lane.

I threw balls that skidded more than rolled. They either landed in the gutter or followed a course crooked as a lightning bolt. My first game was fifteen. I wanted to place my head in the ball return.

For the first frame in the next game, I stood on the approach, started my walk, and let the ball fly. It headed straight and at the very last second, the ball swerved and missed everything.

I shook my head. "That roll was 'Tales From the Crypt' strange."

"I'm not going to give you an argument there. But you have one more ball left, so blast them all down, Maggie."

"You're going to be proud of me, teacher."

I threw. My ball came to a dead stop right before the pins.

"What the...?" Even Frank was mystified about that one.

Each time I rolled, he offered tips on how to improve. But I couldn't tell whether I was nervous because he was watching me butcher the game or because he was just watching me. To avoid more nervousness, I attempted not to look into his eyes. The eyes of Omar Sharif in *Dr. Zhivago*. Eyes better than a whole box of Girl Scout mint cookies. I pressed my lips together. I was hopeless as a teenager dealing with a first crush. He probably had a girlfriend, a dancer in one of the casino shows most likely. A good man like him. He couldn't be alone. God wouldn't allow such a thing.

"Maggie?"

I avoided making eye contact.

"Huh?"

"You've got to concentrate," Frank advised gently.

"Somehow I've lost control of my limbs."

"You're just nervous. You'll get better."

"I don't have that long to live."

He grinned. "Quiet. Now, get up and throw boulders."

Regrettably, I wasn't any better for the rest of the hour-long lesson. When we finished, I placed the ball back in the rack. Depression turned my insides into knotted old ropes after a score of twenty-eight on the second game and thirty on the third one.

"Don't be discouraged. You haven't bowled for a long time, and this was the first lesson." Frank sat beside me as I slipped into my street shoes.

"I beat up the lanes today."

"Kind of, but they can take it."

"How'd it go?" Jo took a seat next to us.

"Bad enough to make you cry." I was honest.

"She'll improve," Frank added.

"You both need a drink." Jo motioned us to the snack counter and poured Frank and me an iced tea. She winked and went off to help other customers.

"How long have you owned Cactus Lanes, Frank?"

"About twenty years. Whew. A long time. I bought it with my pro earnings."

"Amazing. How many years were you a professional bowler?"

"Twelve years and that was long enough. I wanted to stay home. I needed to stay home." His eyes darkened.

"I didn't mean to get so personal." But damn I wanted to know more.

Two six-year-olds and their parents rushed through the doors.

"Sorry, Maggie, but it's time for my next lesson." Frank got up.

He placed his hand on my shoulder and I felt it down to my heels. "And don't be so hard on yourself. You've no place to go but up." He greeted the young students with a wave and smile.

A man wearing a Cactus Lanes logo T-shirt and jeans walked up to the counter and nodded a hello. I'd seen him spreading oil on the lanes on my first visit. Taller than Frank, he had an ample chest, along with a wickedly thick mustache and black hair. Pockmarked cheeks gave him a tough appearance, but his eyes were soft.

Jo handed him an iced tea. "A cool drink for a hard-working man."

I stuck out my hand. "Maggie Adams." I amazed myself I was so forward. Usually at country club parties, I was the woman who sat at the back and counted the minutes until I could go home and watch classic movies on TV. Maybe my new hairdo had given me bravery.

He wiped one hand on his pants. "Ernie Sánchez. I do whatever needs to be done at Cactus Lanes and boy, it's a long list." His voice was grumbly.

"I imagine it does take a lot of work to keep a bowling alley going. Taking care of the machines and the lanes and all."

"See?" he told Jo. "At last someone who appreciates my duties."

"We do because you remind us all the time." Jo wiped the counter.

Laughing, he added three spoonfuls of sugar to the iced tea.

"We are lucky Ernie's working for us, when he's not complaining, that is."

"I don't complain. I observe."

"Same difference. Ern used to work at one of the monster casinos in the maintenance department. But he decided to leave it all behind and join us here. Mostly, he came to us because Frank is his best friend. They've been bowling together since high school."

"Hey, you're lucky to have me, remember?" Ernie announced with a straight face and then grinned. "And I'm humble."

He downed the rest of his tea. "Well, because of all those many responsibilities, I've got to go back to work. Nice to meet you, Maggie."

"And you, Ernie."

Jo pointed her chin at him. "Ern may come off as grouchy, but he fixes cars for his friends and doesn't charge anything, including to me. He also repairs appliances for family and lends money, which drives his wife, Linda, *loca*."

"That is a good man."

"He is, but he still can be grouchy."

I picked up my purse but stayed put. "Jo?"

"Hmm?"

"Frank got so sad when he talked about the pro tour. Was the experience bad?"

Jo's whole body solidified, except her eyes, which blinked with seriousness. "His wife, Anna, got sick while he was out on the PBA tour. She died about two years after he quit. I never knew her, but Ernie says she was a wonderful, wonderful woman, if a terrible bowler." Jo glanced down the lanes. "When she died, Ernie was scared Frank would never come out of his grief. They're both very good men. I'm fortunate to call them friends."

She leaned over the counter to watch Frank teach the little kids. "We all seem to lose what we love, don't we, Maggie? Like you and your husband, or when I couldn't roll for six weeks when I broke my arm. But thank the Lord, there's bowling to make life just right."

"Yes, thank the Lord."

On my way outside, I sneaked a look at Frank. He waved and smiled. I ran into the glass door and shook my head with embarrassment.

Back at home, I rested my right elbow in ice water. From the aches in my arm, I could have been throwing javelins across the Rocky Mountains.

Before getting into bed, I took the highest dose of Tylenol allowable without going into a coma. My arm throbbed, but I tallied up the hours like they were golden pins until next Wednesday and my lesson with Frank.

Frank.

Just mentioning the PBA tour made him think about his late wife and his sorrow was palatable, a shroud in the air. My own emotions about my late husband were thin as a one-ply tissue.

I wanted nothing more than to comfort him.

Chapter Eight

I was on a roll and I didn't mean just at the bowling alley.

The next morning, I drove to the office of the Nevada Department of Employment, Training & Rehabilitation on East St. Louis Avenue. According to its website, the department helped people with job training and placement. The night before, I worked up a résumé, which I conceded was pitiful with heaps of white space on the page. High school. Two full years of college, although I quit in my third year. To save myself embarrassment, I omitted my work experience at the restaurant where I'd met Bob. I had typing skills, though probably not fast enough to earn a paycheck. I knew how to use the Internet. But who was I kidding? Everyone knew how to use the Internet. Even my nine-year-old grandson showed me how to view cute kitten videos on YouTube.

"I'd make a great greeter at Walmart or churn out Whoppers like the devil," I said as I pulled into the parking lot.

Yet, I gained a bit of hope by taking this initiative. I had to prove to myself I wasn't just a hot, gaseous mound of talk. I needed to take action. More than bowling lessons. A *Lifetime* movie could tell my story. A woman—much thinner than me—gets a second chance at life when her husband dies. She starts a successful business, allowing her to break free from her old unsatisfying existence, though I couldn't imagine what type of business I'd start. And, in the *Lifetime* movie tradition, the woman finds a new love along the way.

Well, probably, not the last one.

Inside the office building, a proficient-looking woman in a nice business suit called me into a cubicle, shook my hand, and examined my sad résumé. From her restrained reaction, it was as tragic as I'd assumed. So much for my *Lifetime* dreams.

"I left college, got married, and had kids. Now, I could kick myself for not going back to school. Bet you've heard my story before."

"Gazillions of times."

"I'm a fast learner and hard worker." I sat up to highlight the point.

"That's a start."

"Am I qualified for anything?"

The woman put down the paper. I could tell she was going to give me bad news. Her eyes went dark as her business suit.

"Frankly no, Mrs. Adams. Unless you want to work as a store greeter, in fast food, or other minimum wage jobs in a mall."

"Not surprising given my résumé."

"You can always return to college and complete a degree or even take business office courses to bring you up to speed."

The idea of going back to school left me exhilarated and horrified. "I'm not too old for college?"

"Heck no." The woman smiled. "But I'll be honest here, even if you went to all the trouble, a lot of employers don't usually hire people your age unless it's for those low-paying gigs."

"Age discrimination is illegal, right?"

"Heck, yes, it is, but ageism still goes on, according to some of my other senior clients."

"You'd think employers would want people with life and work experience."

"Most of the time, they just want young and cheap. Hold on." The woman swiveled around in her chair and took a pamphlet from a credenza behind her desk. She gained more faith in her eyes. "You might try volunteering. There's a variety of things you can do. Like being a companion to other seniors or working with children. Volunteering at libraries. Helping out at food banks or delivering meals to shut-ins."

"Those are damn exciting." So much so I even cursed in front of a state employee.

"For a widowed woman like yourself, this will be a good way to get back into the world."

"The question is am I ready for the world?"

"You already took the first step by asking what you can do. Now, here's information about a senior volunteer program. I think you'll find volunteering tremendously rewarding. It'll add ten years to your life."

"I'd like to have ten years to live again."

That afternoon I called the senior program to schedule an appointment.

The morning sun coated the sheer curtains in yellow. They moved from the slightest of morning breezes through the open window. Such cool welcomes were rare in the desert town, and I was more than ready to take advantage of it when one showed up. This was my favorite spot in my inherited colossus of a house. On a royal blue leather chaise in front of the large window in my bedroom. The walls were painted cream and on them I had hung prints of flowers not unlike those in my garden. Though now I was thinking about adding paintings of cactus.

The furniture and bed coverings were simple. In the corner was a desk for my computer and a large flat screen was on a wall across from the bed. I liked this room because I had decorated it myself. The designer who worked over the rest of the house initially had the room in a French style, which reminded me of the bedroom of Louis the Sixteenth right before he was beheaded. Little by little I bid adieu to the Frenchness.

Over my right arm lay an ice pack the size of a small pillow. My elbow still ached from bowling practice. Such a good ache. But heaven doesn't always last.

A car pulled up out front and I walked onto the small balcony off my bedroom. Down below Kyla pointed an accusing finger at Carl Méndez as he raked up trimmed limbs from the rose bushes lining the driveway.

"Why'd you kill these plants?" Kyla picked up one of the limbs. She spoke in her polite superior voice.

"The aphids got to the roses. I wanted to clear out the diseased ones." A fine-looking young man, Carl was as resolute as Kyla.

"You giving me attitude, Carl?"

"No. I'm just talking about aphids." He was more amused than angry at her immaturity.

"My dad loved those roses and you've cut them." Her voice cracked.

"I am sorry about your father, but the aphids are bad this year."

"Kyla," I called from the balcony. "Carl's right. The bugs killed the roses."

She turned to Carl. "Just be careful." She moved into the house as if she had won the point, aphids or not.

"On behalf of my daughter, I'm so sorry, Carl."

I apologized a lot for her.

"No *problemo*, Mrs. Adams. She reminds me a lot of your late husband." He smiled and trimmed more limbs.

Too bad I had to agree with him.

"Mom, Mom?" Kyla called from downstairs.

I hid the ice pack under the chaise. "Be right down."

When I entered the kitchen, Kyla poured herself an iced tea. She was dressed in a fashionable workout outfit. Black leggings. Tight purple top. Kyla had a collection of such items. Her closet was a convention of color-coordinated workout nylon. The expensive kind, though I couldn't understand why they cost so much if she was just going to sweat into them.

"You were rude to Carl, young lady. On your way out, please apologize."

"I still say the Mexican guy messed up the roses."

"He knows what he's doing. He's a pro."

"Probably an illegal. They steal jobs from Americans."

"Kyla, you're giving me a gut ache."

I had plenty of them with Bob within the last ten years of his life. He hadn't always been so thin-minded. He didn't talk about politics at the beginning, and then he became mostly kind of tolerant. But the older he got, the worse it became until his mind closed up tighter than a clam in ice water. When I asked him why, he said he hadn't changed at all. I gave up arguing the merits of tolerance because I knew I couldn't change his mind without performing a lobotomy with one of my gardening tools. I believed his attitude was related to his wealth. Namely, the more he amassed the less he had to give—the less of everything.

Worse, the intolerance was another Bob-lesson Kyla had picked up as she watched him deal with anyone who wasn't him.

Once again, I tried to help her by pointing out that she was remarkably wrong.

"Well, Miss Information, Carl was born right here in Vegas. His dad's worked for us for twelve years and I don't know how they've endured our family for all that time. Carl's helping his family part-time. He's going to college to become an engineer."

"I'm done with this conversation." Kyla checked her phone.

I sighed down to my toenails. My daughter had also adopted her father's method of avoiding conflict and shutting out any subject they didn't want to hear. Bob would say, "End of discussion."

Kyla stared at me.

"What?"

"I'm not sure about your new hairdo."

"What's wrong with it?"

"You don't look like you."

I glanced at myself in the chrome shininess of the refrigerator. "That's not a bad thing."

"Hmmm. I had a good workout today."

"I'm happy for you."

Kyla stopped tapping at her phone. "Mom, you've got to answer your cell."

"They're annoying and small."

"I can never find you."

"If I get in real trouble, I'll call you to bail me out."

Kyla poured a glass of tea for me. "Daughters worry about their moms. And you're all alone here. So I brought you something for your personal protection."

She handed me a device resembling a pink electric shaver.

"What the hell is this?"

"A taser."

"Come on, Kyla, I don't need this thing. The house security system is good. I feel very safe."

"But not out there on the streets." She clicked it on, and it hummed.

"This is Vegas, not Tombstone." I placed the thing on the counter.

"Best to be careful."

She gave you this strange device out of love and caring, I reminded myself. "It's very thoughtful. Thank you."

My daughter changed the subject. "So what have you been doing with your time?"

I sat down. Kyla had been asking me the same question every week. This time, I had an answer, but no way I was going to tell her about bowling. I didn't want her spoiling my fun.

"I'm going to volunteer for a senior companion program. I've even started training."

"Sounds awfully depressing. Hanging around with a bunch of old people."

"I'm an old person who can still help."

"You should sign up for a symphony fundraiser. They always need volunteers."

I sighed. "And you'd call that more socially acceptable?"

"I don't know what you're talking about, Mom." Kyla scooted through texts on her phone, not looking at me. "I know the symphony board secretary; I'll call her right now."

"Please don't. The symphony has enough volunteers, but seniors need companionship."

"You need more to do, Mom."

"Well, I also started a new hobby." It just came out.

She smiled at me. "Wonderful. Daddy always wanted you to golf. You know I love to golf."

"Yes, I know. But I'm a terrifically bad golfer."

"Maybe, we can go out and play. I just joined another league."

"That's nice." God, how I hated golf. I took a bag of macaroons out of the cupboard and winced because I could barely open the bag of cookies from my sore arm. Turning my back, I ripped the plastic with my teeth.

"Then, what hobby did you take up, Mom?"

I was now going to lie outright to my daughter. "I'm taking an art class." I sounded convincing.

"What kind of art?"

"Pottery." That just popped into my head.

Her attention went to her cell phone, and I was grateful. "Good. I was afraid you'd be wasting away in this house."

"Nope. No wasting going on here."

Kyla glanced around the house. "I never noticed how big this place is."

"Especially when you're the only one home, honey. I'm thinking about selling."

Kyla's face dissolved with upset as if I'd told her I was going to become a senior citizen drug dealer.

"I was raised here. I love this place."

"It's too big for just me."

The distraught melded into mourning. "I miss Daddy."

"He loved you very much. I was his wife, but you were his girl."

"Ahh." Kyla hugged me and I winced in pain.

"Anything wrong?"

"My arm is just sore from throwing pots."

"I'd love to see one of your projects when you're finished."

"Me too."

"What?"

"Nothing."

"Maybe you should redo the kitchen." Kyla smiled as if picturing a whole different and costlier room.

"Have a cookie."

"I shouldn't. I'm doing Keto."

"Have you told Jerome?" I thought that was funny.

"I don't understand."

"I know. Take a cookie."

"But I'm trying to cut out sugar from my life."

"Every once in a while, you need a little sweetness." I moved the bag closer to my daughter. "Live a little."

Kyla smiled and took a cookie. Maybe there was hope for her.

After she left, I sat in the kitchen. All those lies tired me. Without thinking, I reached for a cookie but accidentally touched the tip of the taser. A zip rocketed through my body.

"Fuck!"

I saved that curse word for special occasions. But the shock served me right for lying.

Chapter Nine

Frank stood near the foul line. "Maggie, I want you to become acquainted with every part of the lane."

"And never cross this." With my toe, I pointed at the white line separating the approach from the lane. "I do remember that from high school."

He laughed.

"Frank, I like making you laugh at something other than my bowling."

"You're funny and not just because of the way you throw the ball."

"That's good to know."

He cleared his throat. "Anyway, if you do cross the foul line, whatever pins you knocked down won't count."

I knew that too, but still nodded to show I paid attention to every word he said. I checked out the white line and smiled. "But it looks so innocent, Frank." I stepped over the line as a joke. *Stop showing off.*

"Careful, Maggie."

My shoe slipped out from underneath me because of the excess oil on the other side of the line. With a thump, I landed on my behind.

"You hurt?"

"Not really. I fell on my large ass." I rubbed my backside. "I was just being flirty. No! I mean I shouldn't have been messing around." *God, shut up.*

He extended a hand. "I was going to say it's very oily and slippery on the other side of foul line."

"I figured that out on my own."

I took his hand and started to stand but my foot slid on the oil again. I tumbled back down taking Frank with me. He fell on top of me. My heart sizzled like Jo's fryer behind the counter. I hadn't expected such a sensation. I looked at him. His Omar Sharif eyes were smiling.

"Frank, you okay? I'm so sorry."

"I'm good. You broke my fall."

"Yeah, there's plenty of me to do that."

"Maggie, please don't say such things."

"Humor is my shield."

"Let's stand, but carefully."

We did so and laughed. He handed me a towel.

"You might want to clean the oil off of the bottom of your shoes."

I sat down and wiped them.

"All ready."

"Then please roll."

"It might be safer for all concerned."

I picked up the house ball I always used for my lessons. A thirteen-pounder the godawful color of old cheese. I exhaled to calm myself and started the approach. I might hit a bunch of pins this time. I was giddy with confidence. Halfway down, however, I tripped on a dangling lace of my bowling shoe and twisted. The gravity of the ball caused it to swoop forward, and it zoomed horizontally down the approaches of the other lanes.

"Watch out," I yelled.

Bowlers on other lanes jumped out of the way of my speeding ball, sending it on with curses or laughs. An older man eight lanes down caught the ball and returned it to me.

Frank's mouth, meanwhile, formed an O.

"In all my years of bowling, I never saw anything like that." The older man chortled as he handed me the ball.

"I'm so sorry. But there's no bowling equivalent for 'fore'."

"No worries. I was a newbie myself a hundred years ago." He left, shaking his head and laughing some more.

"Maggie, this is another first for Cactus Lanes," Frank said.

"Yeah, I'm breaking records for the weirdest moves. I'm just glad no one is hurt."

"My insurance is excellent. As long as you don't bonk anyone on the head with a ball, it's all fine. Go on and this time, shoot this way." He pointed towards the pins.

"Very funny."

"I thought so."

I stooped to double knot the laces on my shoes to avoid another sideways throw. With more deliberation than I thought possible, I sent the second ball right into the gutter. The black hole of bowling from which no light or ball escapes.

"Shit."

"This time, aim the ball over the second arrow. Remember, aim for the pocket."

"Remind me about the pocket."

"The pocket is the sweet spot on the pin placement. Since you're a right-hander, it's the place between the number one and three pins. Hit the pocket and *bam*, the pins should all go down. In theory."

"The pocket," I repeated with reverence. "The pocket."

"Maggie, hit one little pin and more will go down."

"Sounds easier than it is."

"No, it's beautiful. The pins stand within an absolute Tetractys triangle. Four pins on each side."

I felt as if my eyes might pop with such a new fact. "Unfortunately, I suck at math."

"Never mind, show me what you got."

"The pocket. The pocket." I chanted like a battle cry.

I was too cautious. My ball rolled so sluggishly it stopped halfway down the lane.

Frank scratched his head and then walked along the small alleyway between lanes to retrieve it and send it to the back so the pins could reset. "I wish I had a video of that one. It would've gone viral."

I plopped down on the seat.

He sat beside me.

"Oh, Frank." I began to cry. "After four lessons, I still stink. Honest to God, I *could* bowl in high school. I *was* captain of the team. What the hell happened to me?" I was talking about more than bowling.

"You said you haven't played in forty-some years."

"Right."

"You just forgot how to use the muscles you used to bowl back then."

"I've forgotten a lot of things."

"It's not like riding a bike. There's skill involved, and with practice, your body will remember. Then watch out for those strikes."

Another tear slid down my cheek. He handed me his handkerchief. "You've got nothing to lose by believing, especially in yourself."

"You sound like a recruiting commercial for the Marines."

"Doesn't mean it's not true."

"You make me almost believe, Frank."

"Can I tell you something, Maggie?"

"What? Get out and don't come back?" I asked in earnest.

Frank's expression was so genuinely gracious my whole body warmed from it. "I've been bowling since high school and I love the game. But sometimes I take it for granted, even after all these years. But you show such enthusiasm, yes, even when you suck. And it reminds me why I fell in love with bowling in the first place. How had *I* forgotten that?"

"Now you're just being kind so I won't quit."

"I'm saying this because it's true."

I wiped my tears with his handkerchief. "All right, Frank. Time for someone who's completely terrible at this game to remind you why you love it."

He patted my arm. "Let's try something first."

Walking out between the lanes, he stopped at a set of small arrows painted on the wooden boards about fifteen feet from the foul line. The arrows formed a larger arrow pointing toward the head pin. He placed his fingers on one of the marks on the side of the larger arrow.

"Remember to throw your ball over this arrow. This mark will help guide you."

Winding my arm back, I threw the ball, which traveled over the mark. Too bad, it was the mark in the other lane.

"At least it's the right idea. Once more," Frank said.

The next game was better. I knocked down five pins with the first try, three on the second. On the last frame, five pins went down. Half of that damn triangle.

I couldn't help but feel exultation at my record score of sixty-six.

Chapter Ten

"Ah, there you are." I took a left turn and drove into the Desert Palm Assisted Living complex.

While I detested cell phones, I loved the map feature because it provided directions anywhere I wanted or needed to go. I even liked the pleasant voice guiding me while I sought out an address.

"Turn left at the light."

"Turn right at the next exit."

"Proceed for one mile."

The digital voice imitated a very polite woman who never tired of people asking her for directions. Technology served a purpose in this case.

Inside the walled Desert Palm complex were smaller cottages encircled by neat lawns and landscaping. Palm trees lined the roads. No seniors were out because the temperature had landed at ninety-eight degrees. The older people probably huddled inside their cottages waiting out the heat, which in Vegas was a long wait until November. As a result, they transformed into creatures of the morning to avoid the dreadful Nevada temps. They woke early. Had dinner at four and were in bed by eight.

So much to look forward to.

Driving around the complex, I thought more about putting the house on the market and moving into something as comfy and contained. Definitely no apartments with neighbors stomping upstairs or complaining about me dancing to rock and roll. A townhouse was out because I wanted a small garden and lawn, something I could manage before I became too old to raise a spade or plant a seed. Although the little houses in this complex appeared restful and secure, I wasn't ready to move in.

"Not yet."

I had visited real estate websites and checked out homes with two bedrooms and a small yard. Clicking on the photos of the houses for sale, I fantasized myself in one of them. Playing my music loud and displaying all the bowling trophies I dreamed of winning. A place to boogie around in my underwear if I wanted and strut like Mick Jagger. Where I could decorate the place in shabby chic, so it looked lived in instead of resembling a model home in a ritzy development. When I moved into a smaller house the first thing on my list to do was adopt a dog from the animal shelter. One of those whopping labs adoring me. Bob disliked dogs. He called them messy animals who left shit in the yard for someone else to pick up. He even objected to the idea of a cat because he termed them too sneaky to love.

I'd definitely get a dog and maybe a cat, just to spite Bob's spirit.

How very nice to live small. Gripping the steering wheel, I promised myself not to abandon the idea. I'd simply go to Walgreens and buy earplugs to drown out my daughter's protests about selling the house that held way more attachment for her than me.

I glanced at the name given to me by the Senior Volunteer Program, which had offered me lots of different roles, such as delivering meals or working at a hospital. At local senior centers, I could serve lunch, man the front desk, or teach computer skills. But I loved the idea of providing friendship to seniors, well, someone ten years or more senior than me.

Once the program staff had checked out my background and I completed training, I was assigned the person I'd be visiting twice a week. The coordinator said I'd most likely drive the woman to doctor appointments or to go shopping. But I researched more interesting places to take her. The Clark County Museum twenty miles from the Strip had exhibitions of old houses and historic buildings. I hadn't even been there. We might ride out to Hoover Dam, which I'd visited once in high school. The city also boasted several art galleries, including a nice one at the Bellagio casino. The public library offered craft classes, and concerts were always going on around the city. While I loved rock 'n' roll bands, I'd be open to classical and or jazz music if that's what my senior pal wanted.

"This is going to be fun." I slapped the steering wheel with joy.

"You have arrived at your destination," advised the friendly map voice.

Pulling up, I was reminded of one of those fairy houses—

large sized, of course. It was so quaint, I was surprised a unicorn wasn't parked out front.

I knocked. No one came to the door. One more knock and I waited.

Gritting my teeth, I worried my senior had died before we had a chance to have a good time.

Then, the door opened. Barely.

"Mrs. Ruth Granger?"

"So?"

"I'm Maggie Adams with the Senior Volunteer Program."

"Right. Come on in and shut the door quick. Don't let out all the cool air."

The house was neat and not overly filled with photos and ceramic knickknacks like at my grandma's house. Several photos of family hung on one wall, but otherwise, the place was quite Spartan and the furnishings modern. A large recliner sat in front of a flat-screen. On a table beside the recliner was an open book and tissue box. The house smelled of Icy Hot. I immediately recognized the odor because I'd been dipping into the ointment for my aching shoulders after bowling.

Ruth Granger was eighty-two, according to the paperwork, and she made a definite impression. The short, slender woman wore tennis shoes, jeans, a pink blouse, and a black baseball hat with the words *Sons of Anarchy* sewn on the front. Her blue eyes raged with feistiness. Although she was almost a foot shorter than me, she walked as if she'd been formed out of pure steel ingot or the stuff they shot into the Wolverine. Nothing matronly about this woman. She leaned slightly on a wooden cane carved with the letters SOA.

She checked me out also and then smiled. "You look passable."

"Thanks."

"The reason I called the program for help is because my daughter and her husband moved to L.A. and she was the one who took me everywhere. My son drives a truck and is gone a lot."

"Didn't you want to move to Los Angeles to be with your daughter?"

"Hell, no. Las Vegas is my home."

"Mine too."

"So why'd you want to entertain old farts like me?" Her laugh whistled like a deflating tire.

I raised my eyebrows "My husband died."

"And you need to fill your days, huh?'

"More like that I wanted to be of service."

"Fine by me."

"So as one old fart to another, what'd you like to do today?"

The older woman laughed. I liked her instantly.

"I can drive you to the doctor or the grocery store or to pick up your prescriptions at a pharmacy. And I also researched some ways to spend our time together. Concerts, museums, crafts classes, art shows."

Ruth held up a tiny right hand. "Put on the brakes, lady. I know exactly what I want to do. We're going to the horse races."

"Horse races?"

"They're televised in the sports book at Caesars Palace."

"Caesars Palace?"

"You having trouble hearing, sweetie?"

"No."

"Well, hear this. There's more to life than getting sick and dying. More than shopping and going to the pharmacy."

"Is this allowed? I mean this scenario wasn't covered in the training." I had my volunteer program manual out in the car. Perhaps I should call the supervisor to confer.

Ruth pointed her cane at my chest. "I won't tell if you won't."

"I believe I can keep a secret."

"Excellent. I want to bet on a horse with the same name as my late husband."

"How do you know about the horses running today?"

"The racing forms are available online. I do love the World Wide Web."

"Me too." And if Ruth Granger wanted to go to the races, it was more than fine with me. "Then we're off to Caesars Palace."

Ruth grinned. "I think we're going to be good friends."

"I hope so."

Before we left, I suggested we take her wheelchair. The info was in her file. She had trouble with her legs at times.

"I hate that thing."

"It *is* a hike through the casino so it might come in handy. It'd give you more time to gamble."

"Dammit, then. Let's take it."

As soon as we stepped into the heat, we both sucked in our breath and hurried to my car, at least as fast as an eighty-two-year-old woman could hurry.

"From your hat and cane, you're obviously a *Sons of*

Anarchy fan," I said as I drove to the famous line of casinos on the Strip.

Ruth smiled. "Ever watch it?"

"I hate to admit it, but no."

"Oh, sweetie. You're missing the best show ever. Good stories about a family gone wrong. People loving each other as much as they betray and hate each other." Her eyes flashed like lasers. "In other words, a true American family. It's on Netflix."

"Sounds like a soap opera all in black leather."

"'Cept this one has more sex and violence." Ruth placed her head back on the seat. "My late husband used to ride motorcycles when he was young. Maybe it's why I love the show. I fell in love with him and his bike. He wasn't in any gang or nothing. Just liked to ride."

"A fine memory."

Ruth pulled down her hat. "Not to mention the young guy who plays Jax in the show kind of reminds me of him."

"Then I'll definitely watch it."

The volunteer program had loaned me a handicapped placard so I could park close to destinations and aid my senior companion. But as I approached Caesars Palace, I decided to use the valet parking out front to save Mrs. Granger even more steps.

Ruth eyed me when we got out in front of the entrance. "You rich or something?"

"More like well off."

"So you can bet too."

"I know nothing about horse racing, but I want to learn."

"Been doing it for thirty years. I taught math in junior high, and I excel at figuring out the odds."

"Then I bow to your experience."

The valet removed the wheelchair from the trunk.

"Still hate this thing." She eyed it with animosity.

"Look on it as your own Sons of Anarchy cycle."

She smiled with small yellow teeth and sat. "You're smarter than you look."

"The best compliment I've had in years. Besides I'm a good driver."

On our way to the sports bar, Ruth bent forward and breathed hard as she sat in the wheelchair. I stopped and dashed in front of the woman.

"You okay, Mrs. Granger?"

"No fussing over me. Didn't those volunteer people tell you not to fuss over old people? We don't like it."

"Sorry. Let's get moving."

"No worries. And call me Ruth. What shall I call you?"

"Maggie." I was beginning to love that name.

Like the other mega casinos on the Strip, Caesars Palace was enormous, almost a city unto itself with shops, restaurants, hundreds of workers, and even more tourists.

"I really admire the detail they put into these casinos, Ruth. The statues, artwork, the fountains, cornices. Even the restrooms smack of ancient Rome—of course as seen through the eyes of a corporation making huge profit off gambling."

"Yeah, the casinos are very beautiful. But I think they're just trying to make you feel better about losing hundreds of dollars."

"Sounds logical."

We passed a bar with an almost full-sized Egyptian barge as the centerpiece.

"Look, Maggie. Vegas's idea of history."

"It's still cool."

"You're one of those easy-to-please type women, aren't ya?"

I slowed my steps. The slot machines chimed in louder than usual. Had I been insulted by an octogenarian? The older woman picked up on it and held a fist up. A sign to stop used in every war movie I've ever seen on TV.

"Just meaning you're the sort who endures life whatever it is."

Yeow, I *had* been insulted—by the truth. "You've known me for a little while and you nailed my personality, Ruth."

"Stick with me and we'll cure you of that." The old lady motioned for me to continue pushing the wheelchair.

"Promise?"

"You bet." She laughed at her own joke.

As expected, the sports bar was gigantic because there was never anything small in Vegas. A line of oversized television screens stretched across an arched wall, all showing a variety of sports, including one where men rode on little carts pulled by horses. I had no idea what the competition was even called but people bet on it. If gamblers didn't want to sit on the seats facing the large screens, they could also sit at booths and watch the action on way smaller screens.

Ruth wanted to sit up front. "The live races take place at tracks in Florida and California, but we can bet on them at the sports book." She studied the racing forms as if they were the recipe for eternal life.

"I've passed by this part of the casino and never stopped in, Ruth. My son and I gamble, but I usually play the slots."

"You've lived a sheltered life, sweetie."

"Unfortunately, it was all self-imposed."

"You're in serious need of a good time."

"You're right, I am."

After a few minutes, Ruth made her selection and handed me money. "Please bet two dollars on Little Joe to win in the first race at Santa Anita."

I repeated the bet and Ruth nodded.

"It's what I called my late husband, Little Joe. He was a short little bugger."

"I'll put two dollars on him, also."

After placing the bets, I returned to Ruth who sipped a Bloody Mary. Even if drinking wasn't part of the volunteer rules, I figured anyone Ruth's age should have whatever she wanted.

"I love it here because drinks are free when you bet." She held up the glass.

"It does make the losing easier to stomach."

Ruth pointed to one of the large screens in front of them. Young handlers posed with the horses one by one. "Hey, it's Little Joe."

He was a gray beauty.

"Let's hope he's also fast."

A bell rang and a line of men and horses tore out from the gate.

"Hold onto your girdle, Maggie."

The riders wore bright colors and the horses moved with poise and power around the track.

"Come on, Little Joe." Ruth waved her small hand in the air.

"Yeah, move it, Little Joe."

In a few minutes, the race was over. Little Joe came in last.

"So sorry your horse lost, Ruth."

"Serves me right for betting on him. My husband was kind of a loser too. God rest his poor soul. But I loved him mightily. Oh well, who do you like in the next race?" She handed me the racing form.

We stayed through several races at the track and then for the last four at another track in Florida. She went through three Bloody Marys and I was glad the glasses were small.

I stuck with Diet Coke because I had to be the responsible driver.

"Do you like living in Desert Palm?" I asked in between the races.

"Not a bad place. I go to Bingo every Wednesday and there's a movie theater and a library. I exercise three times a week in the rec hall, and a crew cleans my house twice a week. Plus I eat at the dining room. Food's edible most days."

"Sounds like a good life."

"Any life is good at my age. When did your husband pass, Maggie?"

"Nine months ago."

"You really wealthy?"

"Afraid so. How about your husband?"

"He passed twelve years ago." Her blue eyes glistened with tears. "Still miss that man every damn day even though he lost more than he won in life."

I placed my hand on Ruth's, unsure of the woman's reaction. But she smiled with those small teeth.

By late afternoon, I had learned how to read a racing form.

The older woman proved a good teacher. I also promised myself to read up on wagering so I could be a better participant and companion and not such a dumbass on our next visit to Caesars Palace.

Upon returning to the complex, I accompanied Ruth to her door.

"Had a fun time with you, Maggie."

"I had fun too."

"So see you on Thursday, sweetie."

"Bet on it."

After dropping off Ruth, I grabbed a fast-food salad and went home. Gambling was exhausting business.

Eating in my bedroom, I found *Sons of Anarchy* on Netflix. If Ruth's husband looked like the guy in the program no wonder she fell in love. I binged five episodes until I fell asleep. I had a dream that I was bowling down at Cactus Lanes. Frank, Jax Teller, and I were all on the same team and wore matching leather vests with the SAMCRO logo on the back. We racked up strike after strike.

I woke up laughing the next morning.

Chapter Eleven

The score on my last game hit one hundred and one. A personal high. I snapped a photo of it with my phone in case I never reached the mark again in my lifetime.

"How was today's lesson?" Jo asked afterward.

"I broke a hundred."

"Outstanding."

"I still stink but the odor might be clearing. I should go to the bar and order a cocktail to celebrate."

Frank came out of his office grinning and holding several pieces of paper in the air. "Ha! We got it. We got it."

"All right." Jo raised a frozen French fry in the air.

"What's going on?" Ernie Sánchez ambled over to join everybody. Wiping down his hands with a cloth, he sat on a stool next to me.

Jo handed him a lemonade. "Ern, you never listen to us. We're going to host the city tournament."

"How exciting," I said. "What is it?'

"Teams from every house in town compete for the title of city champion."

"Yup, that's exciting."

"Also means lots of work," Ernie said.

"Yeah, but whatever comes up you can fix it, Ern," Frank said. "We're talking about the city tournament. And it all adds up to a whole lot of business." He began to pace. "First thing is we paint the inside, replace two of the basins in the women's bathroom, and buy a new fryer for the kitchen. That's just the start."

"And guess who'll be doing all the work. I'm getting too old for this shit." Ernie chugged his drink.

"You could find a rainy day in heaven." Jo pointed the fry at him.

"It doesn't rain in heaven." His grin was devilish.

"We're all going to pitch in to make Cactus Lanes shine. And I'll hire plumbers for the basin work," Frank said.

"You can't trust them. I'll do it."

Jo's thumb aimed at Ernie. "You just can't please this guy."

Ernie's laugh emulated small canon fire, which made everyone else laugh.

I envied their camaraderie and wished I could help. "Anything I can do?"

They all looked at me.

"We are going to need extra help at the front counter," Jo said.

"Whatever you need me to do is fine. To warn you, I haven't held an outside job in decades, but I'm a fast learner."

"At least we know she's not a crazy person," Jo told Frank and Ernie.

I smiled to reiterate that I wasn't crazy.

"Thanks. We may call on your services," Frank said. "Unless you're going to be competing." He winked at me.

"Do they have a remedial level?"

He smiled and turned to his employees. "Guys, I realize the improvements are going to be a bitch, but the tournament will be fun and good money for Cactus Lanes."

"Whatever you say, *jefe*," Ernie said.

"Bring me your ideas about how else we can spiff up Cactus Lanes."

"And whether we can afford them," Ernie added.

"Jo, please get me a plate of our famous Cactus Lanes chili fries." Frank placed a hand over his stomach.

"I thought you said you couldn't touch them since your doctor put you on cholesterol meds last year."

"What the hell. We're celebrating."

I had to be part of this and the only way was to get better at bowling.

After clearing the area in front of the television in my bedroom, I hit the DVR button and found what I wanted. The pro-bowlers tournament on ESPN.

Da da da. Da da da.

ESPN.

When Bob was alive, just hearing the theme music made me want to spit. I'd grown to dislike the channel for taking up so much of his time, time he didn't spend with his children. It surprised me he hadn't bought shares in the thing. For several years the *Da da da Da da da* held menace, as if it was Darth Vader's theme music. *Da Da Da da da da da*.

Now I looked forward to ESPN, although not the golf coverage.

The pro bowlers competed in Fort Wayne, Indiana. Why there, was a mystery. Slowing down the action with the DVR player, I studied their approach. How they stood. How many steps they took before throwing the ball. Their swing. Their concentration. How I longed to attain their air and intensity. Their bowling scores.

"Check out their hooks," I told myself. "I want to bowl like them. So I just have to keep working on it."

I'd gotten used to talking to myself aloud after all those years alone in the house, even when living with Bob.

The pros threw balls curving like a question mark. Their solution: the Tetractys triangle of pins exploded. I just had to learn how to throw a hook like theirs. So graceful. My ball just rolled straight and boring. However, I had to conquer the straight part first and then think about a hook.

Replaying the recording of the tournament, I mimicked their moves over and over until my arm ached.

I could do this.

After a shower, I parked myself on the bed with a tall glass of wine and my laptop. When I had first started bowling lessons, I searched online and found more than 179 thousand sites about the sport. From its history to game strategies to how to drill a bowling ball. Not including all the videos on YouTube.

This was my habit. If I saw a movie or TV series related to a real event, I googled it. After watching *Lawrence of Arabia* and

My Left Foot I became a Wiki expert on T.E. Lawrence and Christy Brown, though I favored the romanticized versions of their lives.

I had enough of reality.

Years ago I had studied the history of golf to find a way to communicate with Bob. At dinner one evening I was eager to share a conversation. I told him how golf had originated in Scotland around the Middle Ages.

"William Wallace probably swung a mean club when he wasn't shouting 'Freedom!'" I joked with Bob. "Isn't it wild? The game you're playing is hundreds of years old." I prepared for a lively discussion.

"Who cares about its history? The game is here and now. Any more roast beef?" he had replied.

Such were our tête-à-têtes.

I prided myself on the bowling knowledge I was acquiring from the online searches, as if cramming for a final exam. Just ask me. Sixty feet of lane ran between the foul line to the head pin. The lane itself was forty-one and a half inches wide made up of thirty-nine skinny wooden boards.

I glanced up from the laptop with hope. That meant a mere sixty feet of lane to master.

Bowling pins stood fifteen inches tall and each weighed three pounds and six ounces, supposedly based on the notion a single pin should be about twenty-four percent of the weight of the heaviest bowling ball. Why that much? Heaven knows why but it sounded mathematically enchanting.

I had already studied regulations from the United States Bowling Congress, especially bowling terminology. When Frank and Jo tossed around such terms, I stood there like an

English speaker listening to people chatting in Japanese with an Italian accent. So each day I memorized a couple of the terms so I could speak bowlese with the rest of them.

That night, the subject was how bowling had roots in ancient Egypt, according to what an English anthropologist dug up in the 1930s. The game was even trendy under the rule of Henry VIII. I laughed at the thought of fat King Henry on a bowling team with his six wives. No one dared win against Team Tudor or else they got the executioner's axe.

In older versions of the game, the player heaved a ball—without any holes—between his legs towards the pins. To celebrate, he "flopped" on his stomach. I'd already flopped on the lanes but without much reason to party.

Immigrating Europeans brought bowling to the United States, and it was first played on lawns. Hence, the name Bowling Green in New York, the first American bowling site.

Balls used to be wood. Now they're made of a hard rubber. The days of the pin boys ended in the 1950s when automatic pinsetters came into fashion. I got on YouTube and saw how the device worked.

After all this I could be the Stephen Hawking of bowling data.

"This is so cool." I sipped more wine and wiggled my feet under the blanket.

Nobody knew who came up with the ten-pin game, according to Wikipedia, which I believed the best thing to happen to the universe since Cherry Garcia Ice Cream. Awareness of the world at your fingertips. In appreciation, I donated annually to the online encyclopedia even when it didn't ask for one.

I rested my head back on the pillow. In high school, my friends joked that only lower-class people bowled. *They smoke and drink beer all night,* my friends proclaimed with the twisted smirks teenagers could do well. *Why do you think they call them alleys,* they added with snarky glee.

I wished those so-called friends were there right now so I could set them straight. I'm playing the game of kings with a history dating back to the pharaohs. The pyramid-building pharaohs. The pharaohs who came up with a writing system, astronomy, mathematics, beer, and those great costumes Cleopatra wore. I had read that on Answers.com, but same difference as Wikipedia.

My fingertips itched.

In the Google search bar I typed "FRANK MARTÍNEZ, PRO BOWLER". I couldn't help myself.

More than two thousand results came up. I whistled. At one time, he'd been ranked sixth in the nation.

"Sixth. Man, oh, man."

That was my instructor. He held a 240 average. I was not worthy. Mine was a pitiful eighty-one. If I had his average, I would've tattooed it across my chest. But he'd not even mentioned his triumphs, though he had every right to. So humble, which said loads and tons about his character.

Frank had served four years in the Army, specializing in electronics. But he had always tried to find a bowling alley wherever he was stationed, according to one interview. After his discharge, he worked as an electrician and decided one day to go professional at the age of twenty-nine.

"It had been the dream of my life," I read his quote out loud. "And how could anyone turn away from their dream."

Another site showed a photograph of a young Frank in mid-swing. In another he laughed with a group of friends. He was great looking at thirty years old. But the photos didn't do justice to the profoundness of his eyes. Nevertheless, his image produced landslides in my body not unlike the time Russell Crowe removed his chainmail armor in *Robin Hood*.

Frank had pursued his dream.

I chewed on my bottom lip. I knew exactly when I had turned from mine. The moment wasn't so much a sharp swerve as a slow veering. I'd have liked to blame it all on Bob but couldn't.

Sitting up in bed, I straightened my nightgown. I wasn't dead yet although I'd come close a few times.

Closing the laptop, I sat back and finished the wine in celebration. I was falling in love with the game of the pharaohs and a second chance.

Chapter Twelve

"Whoa."

That word was so inadequate to describe the pinsetting machines. They were among the best inventions in the world. Electricity. Telephones. Television. Bagless vacuums.

As part of his mission to teach me about every aspect of bowling, Frank gave me a tour of Cactus Lanes, which included checking out the machines. To get there, we entered one of the doors leading to the back of the alley located at each end of the forty lanes.

At first glance, the place was nothing to get excited about. A long utility-type room extending from one side of the building to another and painted a simple cream with fluorescents overhead. Along the exterior wall were shelves with boxes of supplies and a garage door type entrance.

On the other side of the room stood the pinsetting machines. They resembled larger than life clothes dryers. But instead of towels and underwear, pins swirled about. The machines were effective squat robots in the name of entertainment. From them came the constant sound of crash and whir.

"The pins smack into the cushion assembly at the back of the lane. Via conveyors the pins clatter into a bin, get reset back on the lanes then placed in their perfect triangle shape." Frank smiled and his voice rose with enthusiasm.

As he talked, we stood on a small rise between two machines and looked down into the mechanism.

"After knocking down the pins, the balls are returned to the bowler on metal rails."

Wheels, gears, and pipes rotated and spun as he explained.

He leaned closer to me so I could hear among the clatter. He smelled great.

"There's almost two thousand parts in these machines, Maggie."

"Wow." But I already knew this having watched a video on YouTube the night before about how they worked. The pinsetters were staggering and simple productivity. They made me want to be a mechanical engineer.

He stepped down and held his hand out so I wouldn't fall. Then he patted one machine with admiration. "A mess of knocked over, scattered dead wood are placed back in their eternal position in ten seconds or less. Forget sending space vehicles to Mars. The pinsetter is the miracle of modern man."

"I agree." This was all incredibly sexy.

Frank downright grinned. "The machines do break down, or something gets jammed, but I'm constantly astonished by their efficiency."

"Frank, number six is stuck." Jo's voice came over a speaker.

"Sorry. I've got to fix it. Ernie's better than I am with the pinsetters, but I can't find him half the time. I think he's got another job someplace else."

He first turned off power to the machine. Stepping up on the side, he examined the innards for the problem and sighed. He motioned for me to join him and extended his hand. "One of the pins got caught up in the conveyor." With a quick movement, he removed it and set it right. "Easy peasy."

Turning the power back on the machine, it returned to its competent run.

"The machines *are* a wonder, Frank."

"You betcha. I wish life could be so damn orderly. But it's not."

"Unfortunately, no. Somewhere or another, pins get stuck."

"But maybe it's not always a bad thing. It gets you out of your rut. Doing the same thing, over and over." He gave me another smile.

I don't think he was talking about the pinsetters.

After the lesson, I put on my street shoes.

"Maggie, you know anything about shawls?" Frank asked.

"What?" My fingers fumbled. Was Frank thinking of me as a shawl-wearing grandma? Well, I was a grandma.

"It's my mom's birthday tomorrow. I want to buy her a shawl but I don't know what to buy. Do you have time to help me?"

I tried to hide my relief. "Let's go shopping."

"Sure?"

"It's the least I can do for putting up with my awful bowling."

"You *are* improving. I'll even drive."

"How old is your mom?" I asked as we headed to the parking lot.

"Eighty-seven."

"A good life."

"She worked as a nurse at the St. Rose Dominican Hospital until retirement. Then she volunteered at a community center giving immunizations and health checks to low-income families. At the age of seventy-five she finally had to leave the volunteer job due to terrible arthritis pain in both her knees." His voice lifted as he spoke about her.

"She sounds great, Frank."

"She is. I love her very much, but also greatly admire her strength and courage."

"I've met few people with those qualities." My mouth dried. I wasn't among them.

"And she's a character. She makes me laugh. We're having a little party for her at the alley. You should come."

"Now, you're feeling sorry for the widow who fills her time with bowling lessons."

"I'm inviting you because you're a nice person. Come to the party."

"I'd like that."

"I want to buy a very nice shawl for her. But don't know much about women's fashion or men's either, come to think of it. When I buy clothes for myself, I see something and buy it. No torture. For the Cactus Lanes employees and other relatives, I pick up a bunch of gift cards for the holidays. But shopping for my mom is always tough. I usually buy her books but I wanted something special this time."

"What's her name?"

"Aurelia."

"So beautiful. I'd kill for her name. Margaret sounds like stale oatmeal."

Like most men, at least the ones who don't read *GQ*, Frank stood adrift in the middle of women's accessories at Nordstrom. He was still as a mannequin. Unable to move. Unable to shop.

"Not too many men around here." He fidgeted.

"You don't have our predilection for purses, necklaces, and scarves. But I'll confess this—men are lucky not to be troubled by all these accessories."

"Thank, God. I even hate to pick out a new wallet." His eyes gathered in all the glass and chrome in the store. "You shop here a lot, Maggie?"

I gave my head a shake. "Shopping is torture for me, also." It *was* daunting, like being behind dangerous enemy lines of upscale commerce. Even my hands sweated being there. In addition, I hated to see myself in those mirrors but I didn't mention that part. "Come on, shawls are over here."

Though carrying high-end merchandise, the store wasn't outrageously pricey as some of the casino shops. In other words, it stocked items real people could afford. The shawl selection was good. Fine, silky ones with graceful patterns and cashmere in rich colors. All of them soft as a lover's hair.

Frank browsed the shawls carefully, touching a few so gently, which I found goddamn endearing. Two white-haired and well-dressed older women joined us at the display, but they checked out Frank as much as the shawls. They weren't so much looking at him as staring, gaping, glaring as if he was going to shoplift the item. One woman whispered to the other, who nodded and tapered her eyes with suspicion. Their perfume reeked of overpriced old ladies. I wanted to knock them in the head with my purse.

My gut shifted into high gear. Was this how Kyla was going to turn out? How the hell could I stop that from happening?

"How about this one, Maggie?" Frank held up a red shawl with an embossed design.

"Beautiful choice, Frank. You have good taste, don't you agree, ladies?"

He winked at the two women, who scrunched lips at me.

Where'd I find the bravery to speak up? Could be the source stood right next to me.

We walked back to his truck. "Maggie, I knew those women were giving me the eye, and not in a good way. My mom calls it the *ojo*, the evil eye."

"They got me mad."

"I'm very familiar with that look."

Me too. I'd seen it on my late husband. On my daughter.

"Hell, I've heard insults in front of and behind my back all my life. Lazy. Criminals. Illegals. Drug dealers. Etcetera, etcetera."

"You'd think it'd get better."

"Most days it is, when the number of good people far outnumber the others. For those who don't know any better or care to, what I look like will always be an obstacle. I could tell them I'm a third-generation Mexican-American, but I'm sure they'd just see the differences between them and me."

I took his arm. "Doesn't it make you angry, Frank? They were staring like you were going to go out to the parking lot and steal their car. If it was me, I'd egg their ride."

He laughed. "Come on, Mrs. Spunky."

We walked for a bit. Then he slowed, forcing me to slow also.

"What is it, Frank?"

"You know the first thing I noticed about you, Maggie? There was no difference in your eyes, no difference at all."

Chapter Thirteen

The blooms I saw on my first visit to Cactus Lanes had long dropped off, but I always took a few minutes to look at the desert plants before I went inside. I guess I was expecting the flowers to return in force. I hoped so anyway.

The party for Frank's mother was held in one of the rooms in the back reserved for private events. To prove to myself I wasn't a lonely, dismal woman, I wore a new summer dress. I'd lost ten pounds, which I directly credited to the horrifying vision of my body in the dressing room mirror while buying new clothes for bowling. But I had a long way to go before I could eradicate that image from my mind. Still, ten pounds was better than nothing.

I kept thinking about what Frank had told me. No difference. No difference in my eyes. At his remark, my body experienced the same charge as when I'd accidentally tased myself. I'd been so tempted to write the name "Frank" repeatedly on my computer at home. Like the time I had a crush on Mitch Donaldson in my English class in the seventh grade. At home I wrote "Mitch" on my notebook fifty times as if concocting a voodoo spell to raise his interest in me since he had no idea who the heck I was. The spell didn't work, however. He never spoke to me.

Crush. Was that word even used anymore?

Other than Mitch Donaldson I hadn't developed many infatuations during my lifetime. The only other significant one was Gregory Peck when I was thirteen and saw him in *Moby Dick* on TV. His handsome scar drove me wild. On the rare times when Bob and I made love, I'd fantasize about Gregory Peck's Captain Ahab—without the whalebone leg. But wishing was not the same as getting and having a crush was no guarantee the interest was going to be reciprocated. Such was my discovery with Mitch Donaldson and Gregory Peck.

What really propelled me forward toward the party room was my affection for the people at Cactus Lanes. They were fun, open, and generous. I wanted to be around them. I could be myself with them, which was cornball, but unconditionally true. And yes, I was also anxious to see whether Frank brought a date. After four months of lessons, I still hadn't worked up the courage to ask him or Jo if he was involved with a woman. He never mentioned anyone, and no woman ever met him at the bowling alley. If there was a woman – or maybe a man? – I'd settle for friendship. I could deal with rejection, and hopefully not in an Anna Karenina type of way.

New *Lifetime* movie. A woman had a crush on a man, who loved another woman or man. The woman threw herself in front of a pinsetting machine.

"Here goes nothing," I whispered to myself before entering the party.

I received an honest-to-God sincere welcome wave from Frank and Ernie and some of the other part-time alley employees I'd come to know during my lessons. No woman stood at Frank's side, causing my smile to grow larger than I thought possible. But his squeeze might also have been working at a job or unable to attend.

Jo met me at the door and gave me a hug. "Looking good, Maggie. Nice dress."

"Oh, this old thing. I found it in a store yesterday."

Jo laughed. "Some of Frank's relatives are here but not a lot of them. Aurelia didn't want a big gathering."

Aurelia Martínez was tiny, even shorter than Ruth Granger. But she held herself as if twenty years younger and six-feet tall. Such determination in such loveliness. She wore black capri pants and a white blouse. From her ears dangled long silver earrings and a fine chain hung around her slender neck. This woman was the picture of class.

I envied her. I never quite reached the classy stage, not even with my husband's money. Then again, I didn't try hard to do so.

"Join the party, girl." Jo pulled my arm.

Jo loved to tug people this way and that.

On top of one table were pizzas, a huge bowl of salad, drinks, and a tall birthday cake decorated with marigolds in icing. On another table were the gifts. I added mine. I had bought Aurelia an Afghan blanket. Before joining Frank and his mother, I took a breath.

"Maggie, so happy you could come," he said.

"Thanks for letting me crash."

The older woman held out her hand. "Aurelia Martínez."

"Maggie Adams." Her hand was smooth with a bit of a grip. She gently drew me in a little closer. This small woman was sizing me up. I smiled, not knowing what else to do.

After she had her look, Aurelia released my hand. "Have a good time."

In the room, I couldn't hide out like I usually did during Bob's parties at our house. At those I was the quiet wife of Bob Adams who was the golf party animal. He loved to entertain his buddies, and they mostly talked about golf and business. Their wives chatted about exotic vacation sites, clothes, TV shows I'd never heard of and books I didn't want to read so I coated on a smile, nodded like a bobblehead version of myself, and talked about my children.

But unless I was going to hide under the pizza table, I had to interact. Time for the changes to be more than hair color and dress. First taking in copious amounts of air, I talked to as many people as I could, and it turned out to be way less painful than I thought. We talked bowling, yes, but also politics, most of theirs in line with mine, thank the stars, as well as what was happening in Vegas and the wider world. I asked about their lives and work and they were generous with their answers. I expected my head to explode with so much good conversation. Other than with my son Mike, and Consuela, I hadn't talked this much in a long time, and it struck me how isolated I'd become. Now I couldn't shut up.

I liked talking with Frank's cousin, Roberta, a massage therapist. She was an attractive, sturdy woman with large hands.

Roberta let out the longest of breaths. "You know, after my divorce, there I was, thirty-five and no love in the foreseeable future. I was down. I thought I'd end up a dried old woman like my Aunt Juanita."

"What's she like?"

"Aunt Juanita's been a widow for almost as long as I've been alive. She's bitter as dandelions dipped in sauerkraut when it comes to love. She says, 'Once love's gone, it's gone. It ain't never coming back.'"

Roberta turned her voice shrew-like, which made me happy I never met her Aunt Juanita.

"The strange thing is, my family says she'd always complained about her husband when he was alive." She gave a blow of a laugh, and I couldn't help but laugh with her. She exuded so much life the room felt small, but not in a bad way.

"So your Aunt Juanita scared you away from love, Roberta?"

"No, siree. One day, I said to myself 'To hell with it. I'm going to open my arms to love.'"

"I like that."

"The moral, or whatever you call it, is you can't be scared of love. Were you ever, Maggie?"

"Ever what?"

"Scared of love?"

The plastic cup of lemonade went colder in my hands. "Probably. Sometimes it seems so, so, risky." Even if I had loved Bob, he wasn't risky. Bob was safe as Fort Knox. I took a long drink. Is that why I stayed so long with him? My fingers frosted even more.

"You bet your ass love is risky. There's no goddamn guarantee you won't get your heart stomped on."

"Now you're sounding like your Aunt Juanita."

"Na-ah and here's why. Even though relationships are so damn scary and uncertain as hell, the payoff is great if they work. Shit, we live in a city built on gambling and risk. If nobody wanted to take any chances, Vegas would've ended up another ghost town in the desert."

"I guess I just have to decide whether to take the chance."

"You won't be sorry."

Frank joined us. "Was Roberta giving you her 'love is risky' talk, Maggie?"

"Yes, and it's great."

"I never knew my cousin was a philosopher as well as a masseuse."

"My talents are many. It's a wonder some guy hasn't scooped me up," Roberta said.

"Yeah, it's a wonder," Frank said. "So you seeing anybody, cuz?"

She smiled. "Now that you mention it…"

They clinked beer bottles.

"Roberta, whenever you do give that love-is-a-risk speech, it sounds like a country western song. *Love is worth the risk, so put your money down and gamble away.*" Frank twang sang it.

"Talk about a country song." Ernie now joined us, holding an imaginary guitar and singing badly, *"Love is worth the risk as long as my heart don't get stomped on."*

"Give it a rest, Willie and Waylon." Roberta moved her chin toward Aurelia, who sat in a corner. "Auntie looks tired, Frank."

"Then it's time for the cake."

Aurelia blew out the eight candles with breath to spare. She shook her head. "Eighty-eight years. *Ochenta y ocho.* I like it better in Spanish. Doesn't sound so old." Her smile was lovely.

Frank also smiled. "This will be a good year."

"I've had many good years and what more can you ask?"

Time for the gifts.

"Too much," Aurelia said as she opened each one. Books, a new rosary, and a sweater. Frank's gift was left until the last.

"*Qué bonita.*" Aurelia held up the shawl in her small hands and everyone clapped.

"If you don't like it, I can return it."

"I love my shawl."

"Really?"

"When have I ever lied to you, my son?"

"Never."

Aurelia placed the shawl over her shoulders and Frank kissed her cheek. "Happy birthday, Mama."

With more kisses and hugs, the party ended and cleanup began. Aurelia sat down, the shawl around her shoulders.

I started to help, but Frank touched my shoulder.

"We got this, Maggie. Please keep my mom company."

"Gladly."

I sat beside her. "That shawl looks so beautiful on you."

"I love the afghan. Very thoughtful."

"My pleasure."

"Son, I can't believe you picked this out all by yourself," she called to Frank.

"Maggie helped me." Frank threw used paper plates into the trash.

"I was only there for support. Frank was the one who found it."

"Ahh." Aurelia smiled.

"Two women gave me the *ojo* while we were at the store, but Maggie called them out on it."

"After I started work at the hospital, I remember a doctor gave me the *ojo*. He asked me to clean the floor in a patient's room. I told him I was a nurse and if he wanted a clean floor, he could find a bucket down the hall." Despite her age, her voice still had potency.

"Get into trouble?" I said.

"Yes, but to hell with the doctor. And to hell with the people who can't see my son as a good man."

"Yeah, to hell with them."

Aurelia hugged herself and the new shawl. "This has been a nice evening."

"Yes, it has."

"But it's time for me to sleep. Old people love to sleep."

"Let's go, Mama." Frank helped her to her feet.

"It's been so great to meet you, Aurelia. You're as special as Frank said."

She took my hand with both of hers. "And you are, too. After all, you're the gal who made the cactus plants bloom." Her laugh was profound and delightful, like the first laugh ever invented.

"Beg your pardon?"

"Nothing, just a family joke." Frank narrowed his eyes at his mother.

"He didn't tell you?"

"Tell me what?"

"One morning, when the cactus plants were in full flower at the bowling alley and at our home, I knew he must have met someone special. Blooming cactus mean love is not far behind, you know. So later when he comes home, he says he met a nice woman who wanted to learn how to bowl. It doesn't take a genius to put two and two together."

Frank put his head down with embarrassment. "Well, Mama, I think we should leave now."

Aurelia took my hand and whispered. "*You* made the flowers grow." Then, she kissed my cheek.

Chapter Fourteen

Walking into Cactus Lanes was impetuous. Taking a pottery class wasn't.

I lied to Kyla about taking a class to hide my bowling, so there was nothing else to do but sign up for one at the community college. That way I'd feel less terrible about my deceptions.

It was a miracle I even got in, a good omen if I'd believed in that sort of thing. The community college required I select a major so I entered "art" in the appropriate spot on the form. This was the first thing I could think of because there was no degree in bowling in the catalogue.

"We have a lot of non-traditional students," the young admission clerk had told me.

"Non-traditional?"

"Older people. Like you. The other day I read a report saying almost forty percent of students at four-year colleges were over twenty-five years old."

"I'm way over twenty-five so I'm very non-traditional."

The clerk flicked her long lashes at me and took my check.

In the pottery class, I *was* definitely the oldest. The class started at nine and I took a seat at the very back. The new pen I bought rolled off the table and onto the floor with a *clink*. A few of the younger students glanced back at me as if I were one of their moms who'd insisted on coming to school with them.

The other students didn't talk much to each other before the class started. Some of them played games on their tablets, but most gazed at or texted away on their cell phones. This was another reason I hated those little cases. They took the human out of humanity. No one talked anymore. Even at Bob's wake people texted, probably with the message:

At a funeral. LOL.

☒

Oh God, was I becoming an old fart waging ire at modern technology?

As I sat there, however, the seats turned a whole lot harder than they were. I experienced a bout of regret at not finishing college to become an elementary teacher. During the time I attended, I loved the environment on campus, as if I'd gained smartness merely hanging around the student union building. Then I met Bob, got married, and dropped out, always intending to return one day. After Mike and Kyla started school, I browsed class schedules to finish my degree. Bob's reaction: "We have enough money. Besides, your job is taking care of your family."

He was the Tiger Woods of Passive Aggressive.

But he held no gun to my head or forced me to stay home. The truth was I'd gotten stuck in my life like a wayward pin in the pinsetting machine. Grinding and spinning in one position.

When Mike moved out and Kyla got married and left, I thought myself too old, even though in my fifties. I was excited and proud when Mike earned a bachelor's degree in journalism at UCLA. Kyla had started college at UNLV with a focus on marketing, but she dropped out when she married Jerome and never wanted to go back. I asked why.

"I love being an at-home wife and mom," she had said.

"But you should really have something of your own, a career. Something outside of your husband and family."

"Why? A husband and family are my idea of heaven."

I should have warned her not to make the same mistake I had made but I kept silent. At any rate I had no influence on Kyla who wanted everything her way. Years ago, I recognized the terrible fact that although I deeply loved my daughter, at times I did not like her—not when she displayed arrogance or intolerance. But I knew it was because I hadn't fought hard enough, and Kyla swallowed Bob's limited idea of life.

Perfect, perfect, perfect, he had chanted to our impressionable little girl. And my own voice wasn't loud enough to stop it.

Had it been possible, I would have kicked my own butt.

I exhaled. My regrets could have filled this classroom and spilled over into the gymnasium in the next building. All those emotions I'd kept so submerged peaked even higher than the wave that flipped over the cruise liner in the *Poseidon Adventure*. Tears came on and I wiped them before the rest of the students looked at me as if I were a crazy person who wandered in for a pottery class and started weeping at the sight of a kiln.

I blew my nose and two students turned and gaped at me. I hoped they would take pity.

At five minutes before the start time, the instructor arrived. He fit the profile of someone who'd teach pottery, at least Hollywood's casting version of it. Long blond hair tied in the back. More blondish hair in a trendy beard. He resembled Don Johnson from *Miami Vice*, except he wore stud earrings. His slender build and blue eyes practically shouted out, "Yes, I am an artist." Which I bet he'd pronounce as "art-teest." He was both sexy and silly.

The thirty-some other students set aside their electronics and straightened to attention when Mr. Art walked to the front of the class.

"Welcome to Pottery 101. You will learn the skills to create your own pieces, as well as the history behind ceramics. Before I hand out the syllabus, I usually like to start off this exciting journey by having everyone talk a little about themselves and why they're here. It helps me to get to know you and your needs for this class."

He pointed to a young man with short-cropped hair and ripped jeans, which were probably expensive. "Let's start with you."

"I'm majoring in art, and I like the tactile impression of clay."

The instructor nodded, obviously appreciative of the answer. "And you?"

The next male student had hair longer than the instructor's

with his earlobes stretched into holes the size of quarters. In them were black circles.

"I'm into dirt, man."

The instructor and the student bowed their heads as if they were communicating by cool alone. I'd never been cool.

"I can dig it. How about you?" The instructor pointed to another student.

She had eyes lined in black, straight black hair, and bad teeth as if she was starring in an advertisement for a Goth dentist's office. "I visited Rome recently and got a chance to see Michelangelo's David. I was totally inspired by it."

"It is magnificent."

"I want to see what my hands are capable of." She wiggled thin fingers topped by black fingernail polish and heavy with silver rings.

"What about you?" The art teacher looked at me. Everyone looked at me.

I took a breath and clasped my hands on the desk. "I told my daughter I was taking a pottery class because I don't want her to find out I'm bowling, but I hate to keep lying to her, so I thought, well I better go ahead and sign up for a pottery class."

"Pardon me?" The instructor scratched the side of his chic beard.

"My daughter..."

"On second thought, let's meet the other students."

Chapter Fifteen

The food on my plate was so perfectly arranged it could have been made of plastic. "This looks like it came from an expensive restaurant, Kyla."

"Excellent," chimed in Kyla's husband, Jerome.

"What the heck is it?" said my grandson, Jonathan, studying the dinner placed before him.

If he had on glasses and a tie, he'd be the spitting image of his dad.

"Tonight, we're eating herb-crusted halibut in a balsamic reduction, kale and potatoes, and new green beans," Kyla announced as if she was Gordon Ramsay's little sister.

Jonathan touched the halibut in balsamic reduction and grimaced. "Looks gross."

"Well, it's not. Now eat it, young man, or no dessert or TV."

"Can't we have burgers and fries or chicken nuggets sometimes?" Jonathan picked up his fork.

"No. This is healthier."

He sank lower into the chair.

"Please sit up."

He obeyed and poked the fish with his fork.

My daughter had been asking me to dinner once a week since Bob's funeral. But during the last few months, I'd pushed it back to twice a month because of bowling and volunteering. "Well, you've outdone yourself, Kyla."

"I'm glad you like it, Mom. I made this for my gourmet club last month and it was very successful."

This was a typical dinner at their house.

Mushroom risotto. Pesto lasagna with cauliflower. Lamb kebabs with dried apples. Potato and scallop stew. And they were complimented by the best wines. Tasty dishes, yes, but when I got home, I headed directly for the Pepto Bismol. Like my grandson, I wished Kyla would whip up meatloaf and baked chicken every once in a while. However, the gourmet dinner fit in with the surroundings.

Tucked away in a gated community in north Vegas, their house held even more square footage than mine and was twice as extravagant. Jerome brought in outstanding money as an accountant partner at a large firm and the revenue was paraded in all the swank my daughter could purchase. And did she ever, until it'd become one of those places featured in interior design magazines. The kind inhabited by the ghosts of the people who could afford such luxuries but who died before they got to enjoy them.

My daughter thrived in such conditions. She expected the entitlements as if they were air and water, all of which made me incredibly depressed.

"I'm happy you came to dinner, Mom. I miss you and so

does Jonathan," Kyla said. "Right, Jonathan?" He wasn't paying attention. "Jonathan."

"Huh?" He pierced the fish with his fork as if examining a dead raccoon.

"You miss seeing your grandma, don't you, Jonathan?"

"We see each other plenty." Jonathan smelled the fish.

Twice a month, I took my grandson out to the movies or miniature golf when it wasn't so hot. "We'll take in a film this weekend, sound good, kid?"

"Jonathan, your grandma wants to take you to the movies," Kyla said.

"What?"

"He never listens, Jerome."

Jerome pointed a fork at his son. "Listen."

"Anytime, Grandma. I like movies." He nibbled as little of the food as possible.

"So what have you been doing with your time, Margaret?" Jerome came off relaxed in a polo shirt and khaki pants.

"I was thinking about getting a job, but discovered I have no marketable skills."

"Why do you even want to work, Mom? I'm sure dad provided well for you." Kyla took a sip of good wine.

"Yes, but I want something more in my life."

"You have us. Aren't we enough?"

Kyla laid on the guilt with a trowel that night. Whenever I came to dinner, she'd serve it up along with the gourmet dishes, working in the emotion like Michelangelo worked in oils. Best to ignore it, otherwise the stuff might cling to me like paint.

I took a bite of the halibut in balsamic reduction but it was hard going down. "I am volunteering as a senior companion."

"But ain't you a senior too, Grandma?" Jonathan said.

"Don't say ain't, son," Jerome said.

"My senior is older than me, if you can believe it, Jonathan."

"She must be a hundred years old." The boy buttered his bread.

I laughed. "Not even close."

"Outstanding, Margaret. The volunteer work certainly agrees with you. You look ten years younger," Jerome said.

"That's what the volunteer coordinator told me."

"Do you drive them to the doctor's offices and shopping?"

"Well, the woman I'm assigned to loves to watch the horse races. So we go to Caesars Palace twice a week. We sit and gamble and she drinks Bloody Marys. We've been having the best time."

Kyla hooted out a breath. "That can't be very healthy for an older woman. Those places are so touristy and gauche. Is she trailer trash?" She never hid her dislike of the Strip. "Nevada would be the most perfect place to live if it wasn't for all the gambling."

Jerome and I and even Jonathan looked from one to another. We'd all heard this before.

Annoyed, I folded my napkin and placed it on the table. "Mrs. Granger is a retired teacher, Kyla. Far beyond trash. She's got a good sense of humor and is very intelligent. I like her a lot."

"But … horse racing? Come on."

"Snobbery isn't attractive." In reality, Kyla sported it like designer shoes.

"Not snobbery. Good taste."

"Horse racing sounds fun. Can we go, Mom?" Jonathan said and I winked at him.

"No."

"Still sounds fun."

Jerome seemed to be studying the ceiling as if to avoid getting into the conversation about gambling. All of this supported my decision not to tell my daughter about bowling. I was having a great time at Cactus Lanes, and my bowling skills were improving, though slowly.

"Kyla, betting on the horses makes Mrs. Granger very happy."

"Well, I still say it's kind of low class."

My tooth fillings ached. "That my dear, dear daughter is your opinion."

Kyla changed the subject.

When we finished dinner, she brought out desserts. Also gourmet. Mint chocolate mousse sporting miniature hazelnut biscotti on the side of the dish. Jonathan dug in.

"I can eat this," he said through a mouth of mousse.

"Please don't talk with your mouth full, darling," Kyla said.

Before I started in on the dessert, I folded my hands on the fine linen tablecloth. "I'm thinking about other changes."

"Like what?" Kyla's eyes contracted.

"I *am* going to sell the house."

"Mom!"

"It *is* kind of big for her, babe," Jerome said.

Kyla stared at him as if he had confessed to shopping at Kmart.

"Jerome is exactly right," I said.

"I thought you loved our house, Mom."

"I loved the people who were in it. Now it's a building with too much lawn and too much space to clean."

"If you're lonely you can always move in here. I'd love to have you. Think of all the good times we'd have together. Golfing, shopping, playing cards. You could see Jonathan every day."

She sneaked a look at Jerome and Jonathan who both appeared unsure.

"Kyla, I'm not lonely. Besides, I'd never do that to Jerome or my grandson. They don't need a live-in in-law and Grandma."

Jerome smiled.

"What will you do if you sell?" Kyla crossed her arms.

"Move into a trailer park and go to the horse races."

"Mom!"

"Kyla, I'm kidding. Maybe."

"Mom!"

"Relax. I'd move into a much smaller house, something easy to clean, something cozy. And I'd get a dog."

"Cool." Jonathan raised his spoon.

"That would be nice." Jerome raised a spoonful of mousse to his mouth.

Kyla sent him a withering glance. He quickly ate the dessert.

"Dad loved our house. If you sell it'd be like getting rid of the last of Daddy."

My daughter quivered with misery. How could I cause her more hurt? My heart took on an extra palpitation or two. My panic attacks had decreased since I started bowling, that is except for the times I visited my daughter.

I had to nip this in the bud. "You and Jerome can always buy the place. I'll sell it to you—cheap. Although it'd mean downsizing." I included a mischievous smile.

"This is *our* home."

"And a spectacular one it is."

Kayla clasped her hands on the table as if in a business meeting. "What does Mike say?"

"Haven't told him yet. But he'll agree."

"He's always on your side, Mom." Kyla took a tiny bite of the biscotti.

"And Mike probably doesn't want the house because he thinks it's too big."

"I'm done. Can I go to my room?" Jonathan sucked chocolate off his fingers.

"Go ahead." Kyla still looked at me with worry.

"I'm done, as well. Come on, Johnny, show your grandma your new video games."

I led him upstairs.

When he was younger, he loved to hang with me. We went to the park, movies, museums, and out for ice cream. He'd sleep over at my house where we'd watch cartoons, work on massive Lego projects, and in the morning, I'd cook him a gigantic breakfast. We had a blast. He loved to talk fast, do puzzles, and play with his imaginary friends all named Gungee. Since Jerome's parents lived in San Francisco, I was the number one granny by default, a title I cherished.

As Jonathan got older, my specialness waned like last year's fashion. I'm sure he still loved me now that he was nine years old, but our relationship had changed and probably would even more as he grew up. I was just Grandma now. An older woman who gave good presents at Christmas and on his birthday. I just hoped he'd remember all the other fun times we spent together laughing and playing.

"Don't worry, I won't move in here, Jonathan." We walked up the stairs to his room.

"Our house has so many rooms I wouldn't see you a lot anyway."

I laughed. "Probably not."

Bob had been a good grandpa, when he was around, which had not been often. Either incessantly golfing, on golfing trips with his friends, or at work, he hadn't believed in the words "slowing down". I urged him to spend more time with Jonathan, but he said he had many years left to teach the boy a mean swing. Last Christmas he had bought his grandson a new set of clubs, miniature and mighty. Yet, he'd only taken Jonathan out once to try them before he had died. It pissed me off as much as saddened me that Bob had squandered the precious time with this great kid.

"How about spending the night at my house after the movie, Johnny? You can eat whatever you want. Burgers, fries, pizza. Nothing gourmet, I promise."

"You got it, Grandma."

As with the rest of the house, Jonathan's room was textbook designer with matching furniture and tasteful masculine décor including a mural of men playing football, soccer, and other manly sports.

"You really want to play a video game, Grandma?"

"I'll spare you tonight." I wagged my fingers. "These old digits can't keep up with you when it comes to *Call of Duty*."

"Love you, Grandma." Here was the hint of the boy who used to think I was the greatest thing since video games.

Jonathan would be the primary reason to move in. To watch him grow and, more importantly, help prevent him from becoming too spoiled, and chip away at the legacy of entitlement instilled by his mother. But I could never move in with them because I'd end up a massive wreck. I'd be pressured by Kyla into golf, bridge, shopping, and other activities all guaranteed to age me faster than a ride in a DeLorean heading thirty years into the future.

Heading downstairs, I checked my watch. Eight o'clock. If I hustled, I could still roll a few lines at Cactus Lanes. I wanted and needed the practice.

Mostly, I wanted to feel at home.

Downstairs, Kyla and Jerome sat in their family room with a television screen rivaling the ones at the Caesars Palace sports book. Their screen, however, showed *American Idol* instead of horses and riders zooming around a track.

"Think I'll be going. Thanks for the nice dinner and evening."

"Watch TV with us." Kyla patted the place next to her on the couch.

"Thanks, but I have lots to do tomorrow."

Kyla walked me to the door. "You always have a home here."

She said it so tenderly that I hugged her.

"You'll have plenty of time to move me in when I can't remember my name or the last time I brushed my teeth."

"Mom, please."

"It's called a joke, honey."

"If you do live with us, there'd be no more hanging around with old gamblers drinking Bloody Marys at casinos." The tenderness had vanished.

I couldn't wait to get to Cactus Lanes.

———

Peeking over the ball, I held my breath, calmed myself, and rolled. This had become my routine on the lanes. Breathe, calm, roll.

Forget your daughter's arrogance and the fact you hadn't done a better job of raising her.

Nine pins down.

Remember the times Jonathan believed you were SuperGrandma.

Missed the lone standing pin, but I was meant to be at Cactus Lanes.

And I had proof.

Within a month of starting the bowling lessons, I'd also reduced my antianxiety medication. Crashing a ball into a perfect triangle of pins had improved my mental state, much better than the white pills I'd been shoving in my mouth for years. I cut back on the medication as my average grew.

Anyway, I had no need of meds.

I had bowling. I was determined to become Maggie the Terminator.

Six pins down.

To be a terror with a round plastic projectile.

Picked up the four pins.

My final score totaled 120.

"All right," I said out loud. It was perfectly fine to talk to myself at the bowling alley. The lanes were so noisy no one heard me. One time after eating Cactus Lanes chili fries, I kept farting when I rolled my ball down the lane. You have to love a place where you could fart and get away with it.

When I'd arrived at Cactus Lanes after dinner at Kyla's, I looked for Frank, but he was gone. I couldn't expect he'd be at the alley every hour. He wasn't Bob.

Finishing my third game, I put on my street shoes.

"Looking real good, Maggie."

"Hey, Jo. Just get here?"

Jo sat down, pulling up her bowling bag. "Yeah, I want to put in some practice time. Keeps me sharp. I want our team to win city this year."

"And I want you to win."

"I'm impressed by your progress as a bowler, Maggie."

"I have Frank to thank for the lessons."

"You're talented. You can't teach that."

My eyes watered with gratitude. I rescued a tissue from my purse.

"Sorry I made you cry."

"No one's ever told me I had a talent for anything." More tears came. I wiped them and blew my nose.

"Now dry those tears. I hate seeing women cry. Men don't so why should we?"

"You're right." I dried my face. "Want company?"

"Aren't you tired? You bowled three games."

"Not at all. Unless you want to be by yourself. I'll understand."

"I'd love your company."

I put my bowling shoes back on.

Tying the laces, Jo gave me a bent smile.

"What?"

"Maggie, I don't want to offend you, but you're kind of a strange person."

I wasn't offended. At least that made me sort of interesting. "I'll take strange over boring anytime of the day."

"You're nice and sensitive and funny. But it's like you lived your life sheltered away with a cult leader and escaped to Cactus Lanes."

"You're not far off."

Chapter Sixteen

I flopped down on the seat and covered my head with my hands. I'd thrown more gutter balls than ever before, as if I've never had any lessons at all. "Frank, I get better and then I get worse. The more I try, the more I suck. I'm inconsistent as a bladder condition."

Frank took the seat beside me, and I started to perspire. Whenever he was near me, I began sweating and thanked the heavens I had layered on the deodorant that morning. With every lesson he was becoming more attractive. My bowling average had hit 125 but reposed there like a bad meal on a stomach. I wanted to be better. To exceed my expectations.

"Maggie, you have to concentrate on what you're doing, but in this case, I think you're concentrating too damn hard. As a result, your body tightens, and your limbs aren't fluid."

"Isn't that what you call lack of ability?"

"We're going to try something."

"Euthanasia?"

"Quiet." He was trying not to smile. "Close your eyes. This is serious."

"What?"

"Come on." He full on smiled now.

Those marvelous dimples appeared.

I followed his instruction but peeked to see if he was making fun of me. His eyes were closed, as well.

"Now listen and breathe. Relax your whole body."

Around me, the sound of the balls tumbling down other lanes in their rhythmic tumble. The pins snapping as they toppled over. Bowlers clapping at each other's strike or spare or swearing if they missed. I smelled the warm oil of the lanes. The strong coffee. The burgers spitting. The spicy aroma of those awe-inspiring Cactus Lanes fries. Frank's shaving cologne, which was a bit musky. His smell beat them all.

"Maggie, remember what you liked about bowling in high school."

"That was so damn long ago."

"Not in your memory. It's right there. Reach out and grasp it."

I breathed out.

"Now focus on those days when you were throwing boulders. When you were having a great time with your teammates and winning the state championship. When nothing else mattered but bowling and doing it well. Breathe and remember."

I felt foolish at first but then what the hell did I have to lose? I had tried meditation for a time when The Beatles and all the rock groups ranted about it. I sat up in my bedroom in a lotus position, breathing like the Maharishi Mahesh Yogi. But every time, I became so relaxed I fell asleep. I switched over to naps instead. Now I was meditating with the Maharishi Mahesh Frank, so profoundly all the air in my body reached the tips of my toes before I exhaled it out. Let go of everything, dammit for once in your life. Remember when you were seventeen. When you carried with you a vast potential for the years ahead. Let go. I shut my eyes tighter. I was lighter than unbuttered popcorn. The floor fell out from under my feet.

Holy crap. I was in high school. Thinner with thicker hair. Smaller jeans. More hope. Out on the lane, swinging the ball behind me as if it was an extension of my arm. My steps toward the lane straight as a line from A to Z. Sending my ball crashing into my target.

Hold on.

I threw a hook back then. A friggin' *hook*. Where'd I get a hook? The bowling team coach must have showed me. The tall balding guy who also taught social studies. Nice guy who stunk of Old Spice.

My ball had curved like a mathematical arc into infinity and then crashed into the white triangle of pins. Into the pocket. All the pins erupted. I had achieved my goal, short term though it was. Namely, knock down all those pins. The calm and single deliberation of each throw to be repeated for ten frames. I had transformed into an entity solid as the ball I held. I had years ahead of me to find the right pocket on the lanes and in my life.

I opened my eyes. "Oh, man."

"You were there."

I turned to Frank. "I could even smell the pimple cream I used."

"That's deep all right."

"You're not only a bowling instructor, but a damn Zen master and psychologist."

"Sometimes, I need to be all of the above." He sat back with a satisfied smile, hands behind his head. "Maggie, the real question is are you having any fun doing this?"

"Bad as I am, yes. A very good time. I look forward to our lessons. They've become the highlight of my week." I bunched up my fingers.

Frank smiled. "It's a highlight for me too."

"You probably just need a good laugh."

"That's not it."

I'd never heard anything so caring. *Margaret*, I had to remind myself, *you're paying him fifty dollars for the hour lessons.*

"Now recall the feeling of relaxation and bowl, Maggie."

I stood up and gave a nod of uncertainty as I walked to the approach.

"First, let's try something without the ball."

Frank came up behind me and softly put his hand around my wrist. I panicked. My stomach vaulted worse than the waves in *A Perfect Storm*. I perspired anew. Together, we swung our arms back and forth.

"Kind of like dancing isn't it." His lips were near my ear.

I muttered. "Oh, yes."

"Feel the rhythm?"

Hell, yeah.

I nodded.

"Now you try." He let go of my wrist.

Picking up the ball, I glanced to the side. Other bowlers

155

moved out of the way, some a bit unnerved I was ready to bowl. Others laughed.

"Oh, shit." I moaned.

Forget about them. You used to be skilled at something. You won the first place trophy in high school. Remember.

"And have fun, please, for God's sake, Maggie."

I threw the ball, aiming at the one-three pocket. The ball rolled where I wanted it to go. The triangle blasted apart.

"It's a miracle." I jumped up and down. In my months of lessons, I had taken down spares, but hadn't yet racked up a strike.

Frank's eyebrows rose not in surprise but in satisfaction.

I was so buoyant I could have floated home. Bowlers on the other lanes applauded. I bowed to them.

"My first strike in forty some years, Frank."

"Then you were way overdue."

As my hand rose for a high five, I took a step toward him and slipped once again. Maybe from oil on the bottom of my shoe. More likely from the excitement. Whatever the reason, I came down hard on my butt cheeks.

I didn't feel a thing.

———————————

When I first started my lessons, I ended with scores of thirty or less. That day, I hit the high of 135. I took another photo of my score with my phone.

"Good job." Jo gave me a hug.

My chin pointed toward Frank sitting in his glass-enclosed office changing his shoes. "He's an incredible teacher."

"Yes, he is. He taught me and I now carry a 170 average."

"Fantastic."

Jo motioned for me to follow. On the wall near the bathrooms were posted the weekly scores of all the leagues at Cactus Lanes and their team photos.

"Here we are. The Bowling Broads." Jo and four other women hammed it up for the camera. Standing tall, they all sported yellow shirts and pride.

"I like your name. It's spunky."

"City champions three years in a row, but we got beat out last year by a team from Bulldog Lanes, damn 'em."

"Yeah, damn 'em."

"Maybe one day you'll be ready to join a team."

"I'll probably be too old to lift the ball by then."

"You have the makings, Maggie. You certainly have the drive." Frank stood behind us. He turned to Jo. "How about making me a tuna sandwich? Please?"

"I live for it."

"Why I bear such impudence from my employees I'll never know."

"Because you love me like a sister."

He coughed. "Bullshit."

Laughing, I headed to the counter.

"Come have lunch, Maggie, unless you have another appointment," he said.

"I'd like that."

I also ordered a tuna sandwich, which was good. We sat at the counter. I swiveled around on my stool. "I can't tell you how much I love your neon art, Frank. It's dazzling and poignant. Fun and touching."

His eyes widened from the compliment. "You make me sound like the Picasso of neon."

"You are. How the heck did a former bowling pro get into such art?"

"I worked for a sign company during the summers when I was in high school and began playing around with the neon. It's very relaxing, except when I cut my hands. It's a way to express myself other than by knocking down a rack of pins."

"Ever sell any of your pieces?"

"Once in a while, but I'm not doing this for money. Mainly, I love bending the light."

"Bending the light. God, you're also a poet. I can barely recite a limerick."

"What'd I tell you? A renaissance man," Jo commented as she passed by with two burgers for other customers.

Frank waved off Jo who stuck out a tongue at her employer.

"Well, you're truly an artist, Frank."

"I like to create. What are your hobbies?"

"I tried knitting once. What a disaster. Everything turned out crooked and warped."

"You work?"

"Not since I got married."

I gripped the sides of the stool. What in the hell had I been doing during the years before Bob died? "I visit my children and grandson. I garden, clean house, swim, go on long walks, go to the movies. And I love the classic movies on TV." In other words, I'd been lounging about in limbo, a shady place inhabited by women who lose their husbands either to death or golf.

I took a drink of iced tea wishing it was whiskey. Then, I sat up. "I have become a senior companion to a very nice woman who loves to bet on racehorses. At least I have that on my sheet."

"Great. And gardening's kind of a hobby."

"Then I'll count it. I was also in a book club. But I quit because the women read boring books. And I used to be in a garden club but that also turned out to be boring."

"Those count too."

"I still love to read."

"Me too. Tom Clancy."

"I haven't read anything by him, but I like almost everything else, except romance."

"No romance, huh?"

"From what I've read, they're all formula stories. Boy loves girl. Boy loses girl. Boy gets girl back." My voice held acidity, so I grabbed my iced tea to drink and stop my big mouth.

"I guess I won't be reading any romances now that I know how they all end."

"Sorry."

"See you've done a lot with your life."

"I should have done much more." I almost whispered it.

"Somedays for me, it's just work, bowling, home. Repeat. Not a bad life, but something's…"

"Missing," I finished.

We both smiled nervously at each other.

"I've never even told that to my kids, Frank."

"I haven't told my mom, either, and she lives with me."

We had exchanged an understanding. What was he? Some kind of over-the-counter truth drug? A type of sodium pentothal emitted through his penetrating eyes. In all probability, I'd just kept quiet too long and I was ready to talk. All those years with Bob, I had lived like a queen in a palace reigning over the kingdom of emptiness. What a damn fool.

"It's not too late, Maggie. Besides, now you have another hobby to count." He stretched open his arms as if to encompass Cactus Lanes. "All this."

"I broke out of purgatory when I walked through those double doors, Frank, and I'm so very happy I did."

"I'm glad you did too."

I almost tumbled off my stool with his admission, but he steadied me with a hand on my arm, softly. With care.

"Maggie, I promise I'll help you to become a good bowler. Who knows, perhaps even a remarkable one." His voice lowered and his hand moved to mine.

"I believe you, Frank. But I need more help. So how about two lessons each week?"

Chapter Seventeen

"What's up, *mujer*?"

Consuela stepped out of the patio doors. I'd forgotten it was her day to clean. She came out to where I sat beside the pool, her hands on ample hips, her stare more powerful than the bat signal.

"You were smiling. Margaret."

"Was I?"

"You forgot it was cleaning day."

"To hell with that. Hang out with me and I'll help you clean later."

Consuela smiled and sat in the lounger next to me. Removing her tennis shoes, she rubbed her toes keeping her gaze on me. "Never saw you so happy."

I felt my lips. I had on a huge smile.

"So why are you grinning?"

"Hold that thought." From the kitchen I located the bottle of wine Kyla had given me. It had to be good because my daughter would accept no less. I poured us two glasses.

"You're starting to worry me now, *mujer*."

I liked when she called me *mujer*. Woman.

"No need to worry, Con."

She sipped the wine. "This is good stuff."

"Kyla gave it to me."

"Then it certainly costs more than the ones they sell at Smiths. So why are we drinking this expensive stuff in the afternoon?"

"You know I trust you."

"I know you do."

During the summers, I'd invite Consuela's grandkids to swim in the pool. One time, Bob came home between work and golf and saw a group of Latino kids splashing about. I held a breath worrying about a response from a man who was not exactly a bastion of liberalism or forward-thinking. Fortunately, he liked Consuela, but in what my friend had termed a semi-professional "employer-employee" manner. Thankfully, he smiled, announced "Enjoy," and changed to go out and play golf.

Consuela had invited me over to her house when she made tamales at Christmas. I loved her home, which was way smaller and much more enjoyable and laid-back than mine.

I never mentioned the pool parties to Kyla. Consuela and her family were my guests. I didn't want my daughter to mess with them.

"You obviously have something to tell me, Margaret."

"Maybe."

"Come on, come on." Consuela waved her hands.

I launched into the story about how I started bowling

lessons down at Cactus Lanes. How I'd grown to love the game. About Jo. About Frank.

"Hot damn." Consuela downed her wine. "How long has this been going on?"

"Five months."

"Whoa."

"I'm sorry I didn't tell you all this earlier. I wondered myself if I was going to stay with it."

"Everyone's entitled to secrets. You're gaining confidence, which is a very good thing. So tell me more about this Frank."

"Why him?"

"Because your eyes lit up like Bally's when you mentioned his name."

Consuela loved to gamble there.

I put my hand on my forehead, which could have been feverish. "I like him. He's a very nice man."

Now Consuela's eyes sparked. "So have you gone out on a date?"

"No. God, no. How can you ask me that? It's been just over a year since Bob died."

Consuela slipped on her wise woman face. All knowing, all seeing when it came to relationships, and she was an expert. Her husband was a stocky guy with the thickest black hair and a soul patch to match. He ran the service department at a Ford dealership and was mad for the woman. Kissing her. Holding her hand. Hugging her. They fought. They talked. They laughed together. Whenever I watched them, I held on to the profoundest shade of envious green.

Consuela placed the glass down on the ground. "*Mujer*, you've been widowed a hell of a lot longer than a year."

The truth had been compacted as the dirt piled on top of Bob's grave. "You're right. I only started wearing black when his body got cold." I shook my head.

"I'm sorry." She placed her hand on my arm.

I hadn't confided in Consuela about the state of my marriage. No need to. When she came in the kitchen to clean, there I was stirring a cup of coffee as if it was the last brew left on Earth. She'd seen me in the same position many, many times. Alone.

"This Frank sounds like the type of man who wouldn't abandon you for some stupid game with little sticks and even smaller balls."

I laughed. "You have a way with words."

"You going to pursue this relationship?"

"I'm not going to hunt him down with a net if that's what you mean."

"Why not? I'll go see if there's one in the garage."

Laughing, I studied my good glass of wine. "I'm not sure if he even likes me, I mean as a woman. He probably sees me as a bowling student and buddy. No one has looked at me as a woman for a long time, not even me."

"You're a woman, my friend. You've got the boobies to prove it."

I pushed up my chest. "You're saying all this so I'll help you clean the bathrooms."

"What are you talking about? You always help me clean."

I jerked forward. "And please, Con, keep this our secret."

"You know I will, *mujer*. But Kyla and I are such BFFs I don't know how I'll be able to keep it quiet." Sarcasm spilled over in her voice.

"I wish she knew you like I do." Picking up my glass, I gulped the rest of the wine.

Consuela examined her hands, which were beautiful amber. "I'm sorry about putting Kyla down."

"Con, I can't seem to smash her wall of superiority. I never could."

"You might try a sledgehammer."

"Not hefty enough. I could put this all on Bob but she's a grown woman."

"Look at it this way, Margaret, what Kyla learned, she can unlearn."

"Think so?"

"Anything is possible."

"Yes, it is. And look at what she's missing." I poured another glass of wine for Consuela and myself. "The friendship of a good *mujer*."

Consuela accepted the salute but checked out her watch. "Ay, the time."

"Come on, then. Let's clean."

Chapter Eighteen

I held out the ball. In my head I chanted. *I am a pro, I am a champ, I am rocking thunder*. I inhaled and tried not to think about Frank watching me or to not think about Frank at all to avoid sweating.

Breathe, Maggie.

"Anything wrong?" Frank said.

"I'm contemplating my shot." From my starting position, I took four steps down the approach and threw. Seven pins dropped.

"Your form is improving. During the last two lessons, you've hit pins every time."

"A vast improvement from taking down the ones in the other lane or none at all."

"Yeah, it is." He added a laugh.

I loved his laugh, how it burst with kick and soul.

"I've been studying the professionals on TV." I also mentioned my research into the game, especially about its roots in Egypt and how it was played by Henry VIII.

"Hell, I've been bowling all my life and never knew that." He bowed. "So by all means, bowl." His British accent was terrible.

My second ball picked up the remaining pins. In bowling lingo, it's a conversion. A carry. To me, a phenomenon.

Frank nodded at my achievement. But I could do better. I had to do something better.

Picking up the ball for the next frame, I slowed my breath. The room stilled as if this was a chess alley instead of a bowling one. No sound of people talking, pins falling on other lanes. No whirring of the pinsetter machine.

Remember. Remember. Shooting missiles in high school. The trophy in my hands after state. The bowling ballet in Frank's arms.

Swinging back the ball, I let it go. I experienced every step. The ball headed to its mark. All the pins fell over. I whooped in victory.

"Well done, Maggie."

Jo ran down. "I saw your strike from the counter. That's my girl."

"Thanks, Jo."

"Well, get up on the lane and repeat those moves," Frank said.

For seven more frames I threw strikes and spares. Glancing back, I noticed the mouths of Frank and Jo as they gaped in amazement. I wasn't hurt by their astonishment. Those strikes amazed me too.

Was this me?

For each successive frame, the very air halted as I sent the ball on. Even though the pins were made of wood, I wanted them cringing with fear at my throws. I never believed in ghosts, ESP, nor telekinesis. I never even watched an episode of *Supernatural*, but I swore I could see myself from the pins point of view. Granted, they weren't seeing Earl Anthony, the PBA's number one bowler of all time, or Dick Weber, standing on the approach. They beheld Margaret Helen Brandt Adams targeting a round lethal weapon and they quaked with panic.

Crash.

The pins produced the most exhilarating sound when they flattened. An explosive dream come true. With a strike, an X filled the frame box like an equation for victory.

I ended with a score of 180. Taking out my phone, I shot another photo of the telescore to certify I wasn't hallucinating. I fought the urge to take over the microphone at the front desk and announce my total score over the loudspeaker to everyone in Cactus Lanes.

"Your ball was right in the pocket," Frank said.

"May I shoot another game? I'm in the zone. It could be the Twilight Zone, but I want to convince myself this is happening."

"Why not? Go for it." On the computer screen, he ordered up another game.

I blasted round warheads. During the next game, I scored more strikes than the last game. Who was this woman? I needed to know. Maybe I'd stepped into a parallel universe where I was a professional bowler. Like the *Star Trek* episode where Kirk, McCoy, Scotty, and Uhura transported into a parallel universe where they were pirates. Spock wore a great goatee in that episode.

I flung another strike, my own photon torpedo.

On the tenth frame, I readied for what I hoped would be a colossal finish. The ball took down pins, but an awful split remained. A pin stood on each end of the lane. The seven-ten split. A damn bedpost, which was its official bowling term.

"So ugly." The leftover pins halted my streak of strikes and spares.

"The deadly seven-ten," Frank said with exaggerated solemnity.

"That's got to be impossible to pick up."

"Not impossible. It can be done. And if you do, you even get a patch from the local Women's Bowling Association."

"You ever pick up one of those?" I narrowed my eyes roguishly.

"Not for a while."

"Well, then."

"Doesn't mean you can't do it."

"Then tell me, Mr. Instructor, how do I take down those two?"

"Since you're right-handed, aim at the pin on the right. But not head-on. More to the right side of the pin so it'll skid across the lane and knock over the other one."

"You've got to be kidding."

"Never about splits."

After drying the split sweat from my hands, I threw at the impossible. My ball sped right in between the two pins. Everyone watching put their arms up in the air and yelled, "GOAL!"

I remembered that tease from high school bowling. I didn't care though because I ended with a 190 game. I took another photo. I intended to frame this one and have it buried with me.

"Frank, you're a great teacher. You're Anne Sullivan, Jaime Escalante, and Aristotle all in one. You took a woman who threw Jell-O and turned her into someone who threw comets. That, my friend, is a tremendous feat."

"I can't take all the credit."

"Yes, you can."

As I put on my street shoes, my face ached from beaming. When was the last time I felt such a pleasant ache? Probably ten years ago when I went to a Moody Blues concert. I had to go by myself because neither Bob or Kyla was interested. Consuela wasn't a rock fan, but I still liked her anyway, and Mike was out of town. The Moody Blues and that last game had inspired my sincere utter, down-to-my-toes-and-up-to-my-hair-follicles joy.

At the front counter, Frank sprayed antiseptic into rows of house shoes.

I paid for the lesson. "I can't wait for the next one."

He placed down the spray can. "Maggie, you've graduated from lessons. You're just going to have to keep practicing now."

He could have been talking about a breakup, a divorce. "I *want* more lessons, Frank."

"It'd be like stealing your money."

I placed my hands on the counter. "I want to learn how to throw a hook."

"A hook?"

"I want to be a better bowler and in all the videos and on television, the best bowlers all have hooks. I had one in high school, for Christ's sake."

"Then I'd love to show you."

Jo passed by and nudged me in the left side of my ribs and then walked on.

"What was that about?" Frank's eyebrows raised.

"Jo said I have to stop using house balls and you're too polite to try to sell me anything."

"It's astonishing how well you *are* doing with a house ball, but just think of what you'd accomplish with your own equipment."

"Then set me up, please."

"Follow me to the pro shop." He wiped his hands with sanitizer.

Located across from Frank's office, the pro shop displayed shelves of balls, shoes, and bags. I'd never been in there. Behind the sales counter on a work bench sat a wicked-looking drill press at least three-feet tall. The drill bit was the size of a thumb, which made sense since it was used to drill finger-sized holes. Above the workstation was a neon light sculpture in the shape of a pair of hands in repose. More of Frank's work.

"Looks like you can burrow to the middle of the earth with that drill, Frank."

"I'll have to try it one day."

"You drill the holes? I mean, yourself?"

"Yes, ma'am."

"You do a little bit of everything around here don't you?"

"The pleasures and responsibilities of ownership. I also sweep and fry up burgers when Jo lets me."

I examined the selection displayed on one wall. "Bowling balls measure eight point six inches in diameter. I read it online."

"I know."

"Geez, of course, you know. I'm just showing off my study of bowling."

"Good, because I'm going to give you a quiz later."

My attention set on a new red ball. "This one is pretty. Looks like a cinnamon candy. And I love that shade of red."

Frank nodded. "Yes, it's pretty but here's a suggestion." He showed me a rack of black balls. "You've been rolling a thirteen-pounder. Ah." He picked up one. A shiny black model.

"This is a good one for most lane conditions, short oil, long oil, dry heads."

He placed the ball down and took up a dark blue one. "This one's good on oily conditions or in the back end of the alley."

"Frank, you're talking more bowling speak and I haven't learned all the jargon yet. But I trust you to select the best one for me."

He decided on the first ball. "I'd say this one and we'll try fourteen pounds. You'll have no trouble working up to that weight."

"I'll give it a shot. So, what'd we do now?"

"I have to measure you. This way." He headed to the workbench. "Put your right hand in mine."

Slowly, Frank spread my fingers apart. One by one and as if he handled fragile ceramic, he measured my thumb, pointer, and ring fingers by placing them in a plastic wheel with lots of finger sizes. He wrote down each measurement on a pad. I was beginning to like this process. It was pretty damn intimate.

I looked up from watching him and saw Frank's head move in a "get lost" motion, but not to me. I turned. Ernie stood outside the glass of the pro shop giving Frank a thumbs-up and puckering his lips in a kiss.

Ernie saw me, started whistling, and walked away.

"Ern's such a kidder." Frank's cheeks went red.

"I think he's great."

"Sure he's great. But he can be annoying." He continued his work. "Believe it or not there's an art to measuring hands and fingers for bowling balls."

"I believe it, Frank."

"Now I'll need to check the pitch of your thumb."

"Pitch?"

"The angle of your thumb. Without a good pitch, your shot might be off, and you'll end up with a sore thumb. I need you to grab your wrist and let me see what finger your thumb points to."

He noted the information. I hadn't experienced anything so erotic in years.

"Since you want to learn a hook, I'll place inserts in for fingertip bowling."

I probably looked confused, which wasn't anything new.

"The insert were those plastic things in the holes."

"Ah." I gave my head an irritated shake. "I need to do more bowling research."

"Maggie, none of my other students has ever brushed up on bowling facts like you." He cleared his throat as if the flattery surprised him.

"It's an old habit. Anything I'm interested in I study everything I can about it." Like you, Frank. "But you're right about taking the dimensions of my hand. It is an art."

"A lot of people think bowling is a matter of throwing a ball down a wooden lane. But everything is important when it comes to the ball. The span between your thumb and fingers, the angle the holes were drilled. They all affect your release or the ball revolutions." He stopped with the measurement. "Everything has a purpose. Like where you drill the finger holes in relation to the pin."

"Pin?"

"Here it is." He showed me a yellow dot on the ball.

"I've never learned about that."

"Every ball has one. It marks the top of the weight inside the ball. The ball spins around the pin." He wore a kind of blissful look.

He could have been reciting bowling nirvana.

"Pin and pitch. How very Buddha-like. I sometimes wonder where *my* pin might be, my center. Not on my bowling ball, but in my life. And where my pitch will take me." I glanced up and blushed because my thoughts poured out of my mouth.

Frank bowed his head with appreciation. "I've never heard it put that way. It's beautiful."

The pro shop seemed to have shrunk about us like a cocoon.

I smiled. "Now how about new bowling shoes and a bag for my brand-new ball?"

Chapter Nineteen

Thud, whir, clatter.

Thud, whir, clatter.

With my new ball, I hit strike after strike with mostly spares filling in between. Rarely did any pins remain after my second ball. When I completed each frame, I glanced back at Frank and Jo who showed a mix of awe and disbelief. I waved at them like a kid who'd passed her first driving test.

To be truthful, they weren't half as surprised as I was by my newly developed skill on the lanes. With great instruction from Frank, I'd become Maggie the Strikemaker.

Maggie the Pin Destructor.

MAGGIE THE TERMINATOR. *Hasta la vista* pins.

Bam.

Another strike. The pin triangle burst apart in its surrender.

The day I got my new ball, bag, and shoes, I was infinitely more excited than the time Bob had given me a pair of diamond earrings for our twentieth anniversary. The new bowling ball shone grander than any gem. Heavy with the possibility of bringing havoc to those ten pieces of stoic wood. My new bowling shoes were light gray with pink highlights, and my bowling bag dark blue. Such treasures.

For the past three weeks, Frank had showed me fingertip bowling so I could master a hook. Instead of placing all my fingers in the holes, I inserted the thumb and the other two fingers up to my knuckle. How the hell the ball even stayed on my hand was a mystery. Then came the lessons on the release. My preliminary attempts at a hook resembled awful angles more than elegant arcs.

Still, I managed to pick up the technique like a virus. My ball curved when and where I wanted it, taking the pins down and out. The ball spun like the wheel of a tiny sports car. Since that instruction, I'd regularly been hurling strikes and spares, including that day.

For my last game of the lesson, I scored a two hundred. My best ever.

Frank touched my back. "Maggie, your hook is so good you're probably making the pins weep whenever you step on the approach."

The man's compliments caused weakness in my arthritic knees.

"You've graduated from my teaching. Now all you have to do is practice and play."

The thought of no more lessons depressed me. Maybe, I could learn to bowl with my left hand and be ambidextrous on the lanes. But what a molecule-thin excuse. I decided to return regularly to Cactus Lanes to bowl for fun and *that* was no excuse.

"Woman, you must have been a pro bowler in a past life."
Jo bestowed a huge hug.

"That means a lot."

"More importantly," Frank said. "Are you having fun, Maggie?"

"Oh, yeah."

I packed my ball and shoes in my bag, which had a roller so I could move it like a piece of luggage. I took my time, not wanting to go home.

Frank manned the lunch counter.

"Thanks for everything, Frank."

"My pleasure. Just keep practicing."

"You bet. I'm planning to bowl twice a week to do so." Of course, I'd practice when Frank was there. After months of lessons, I knew his schedule by heart.

"I think it'd benefit your game if you watched the league play. You'd get to see different styles and who knows, you might even want to join one later. Leagues have already started but you could be a sub." He served a plate of nacho chips to a customer.

"When's the next league night?"

"Friday. They start at six thirty."

"You bowl in a league?"

"I happen to bowl on Friday." He smiled

I attempted to be more demure. "Then it's a date. I mean, not a date, but … I'll come watch." I blew out my breath to compose myself. "One more thing, Frank. I'd like to buy one of your neon sculptures."

"Maggie, you don't have to. You've paid me plenty of money for the lessons."

"I want one."

"You're just being nice."

"This is not a bonus for your splendid bowling instruction. Your work is very beautiful."

He smiled. "Which one?"

"Follow me." I led him to the one I wanted. "How much? I'm a wealthy widow so by all means, overcharge me."

He scratched his chin. "I've never been good at pricing my art."

I stood in front of the neon piece I had coveted since bowling at Cactus Lanes. "I'll give you eight hundred dollars."

"That's too much, Maggie. Too damn much."

"I won't give you less because my dear Mr. Frank Martínez, you've given me so much. In fact, I should pay more."

"Eight hundred is great."

"Then sold."

Chapter Twenty

At night, the Cactus Lanes sign was even prettier. The letters flashed on in a brilliant red.

C-A-C-T-U-S L-A-N-E-S.

At the bottom of the sign, the cactus plant in neon appeared particularly brilliant. Had it always been that beautiful or was I seeing it for the first time as a real bowler?

Cars and trucks packed the parking lot for the bowling leagues. Since my lessons took place in the morning, I'd never seen so many people there. Before entering, I checked myself out in the front glass. *Not bad at all*, I heard Bob say. *Shut up, old man*, I told him.

The place was hectic with men and women wearing the matching shirts of their respective teams. I took in the smell. The deliciousness of the famous chili fries and burgers frying up. There was also a wisp of cigarettes from the bar at the back where smoking was allowed. Rock music played on the jukebox in one corner while video games pinged and rang. Teenagers equally laughed and cursed as they shot pool.

The exhilaration inside amounted to a friendly contagion and it caused me to add an extra jaunt to my step. Frank talked with a bunch of men all wearing a dark blue polo shirt with the team's name: the Bowling Aces. On the back was the name of the team sponsor: SAL'S PLUMBING. His eyes sparked when he spotted me as if I was Amelia Earhart returning from the dead. How incredibly accurate. I had returned from the dead. I suspected I held on to the same expression, the same glint.

"Never been here at night. Very exciting, Frank."

"I wanted you to see the best in the city. I wanted to show you what you can strive for." He waved one arm. "Welcome to the leagues."

"The leagues," I repeated with veneration. Although I'd been taking lessons for several months, I was too intimidated to watch how good the league players were compared to how bad I was. But scoring a two hundred chipped away at the intimidation.

I scanned the place from lane to lane. Men and women stepped into their own bowling shoes—not house ones. Many of them strapped on black wrist braces as if gladiators entering the Colosseum. They removed multiple balls out of large bags on rollers. They all seemed to know each other, smiling, waving, or chatting like old friends, although soon they'd be competing.

"Study their form and approach. I'll be over on lanes sixteen and seventeen if you need anything."

I took a seat at one of the tables overlooking the lanes.

"Nice to see you, Maggie." Jo wore her yellow team shirt. Her name was embroidered on the front under the team name in fine lettering.

"If it isn't a Bowling Broad."

"And damn proud of it. My whole family bowls. My husband and sons are all on teams. Hell, I even got a grandson in the junior league."

"My family has no legacy except money."

"I wouldn't reject that, honey."

Several male bowlers took two or three balls out of large bags.

"Why do those men have so many balls?"

"Better than none at all," Jo answered deadpan.

"Hell, I walked right into that one."

"Different balls for different conditions. Dry or oily lanes. Frank'll explain it." Jo laughed.

"He tried but I'm still confused."

"Got to go. Have fun looking around."

The men's leagues bowled on lanes at one end of the alley and the women were on the other section. The front-counter night-time employee, a middle-aged guy with an infectious grin, announced the play was about to start and the machines started up with a pleasing click and hum. Strolling up and down, I studied the players. The bowlers exuded seriousness when they rolled. Then their attitude changed into friendship with high fives and knuckle bumps. However, missed pins and splits elicited shaking heads and cuss words.

At several tables, bowlers played a card game in between their shots. They placed quarters in a bowl, while others took quarters out with a grin. Jo was going to have to explain this ritual to me.

Some bowlers weren't as good as others, not taking down the ten pins in one or two balls. But the good ones…

The good ones.

They bowled with drive and style. Their demolished pins sounded as if they might shatter into splinters. How easy they made it look. Smoother than a Shari's strawberry pie.

Frank was such a bowler. He exhibited so much poise as if willing the ball to move on its own to knock down the pins. I envied his focus and endeavor. Even his teammates all stopped to watch him.

Bam. A strike.

"Holy shit." I breathed out.

"Everybody is so good," I told Jo between her turns.

"A lot of them are, yes. Averaging more than one ninety or better per game."

"Wow."

"I could do a lot better if I got more practice in."

"I've seen you, Jo. You're great."

From where he bowled, Frank waved at us. I waved back, probably a little too enthusiastically. I yanked down my arm.

"You like him."

I choked at her statement of fact.

Jo patted my back. "Struck a nerve, huh?"

"My husband died just over a year ago."

"Know how often you say that?"

"A lot?"

"Like you're using the deceased as a reason not to live. Well, *you* ain't dead. Oh, oh. I'm up." Jo hurried away to bowl with her team. The name of their sponsor, VEGAS AUTO REPAIR, was emblazoned on the back of her shirt.

Jo and her teammates cheered each other with almost a sisterly love. Two of the members appeared to be about Jo's age, and the others a tad younger. All of varying build and hair color. After finishing her second shot, which was a spare, Jo huddled with her partners. They all turned in sync and stared at me. I twisted around to see if they were checking out someone behind me, but no. They were clocking me. Inspecting me. All of them smiled, except for a strongly built woman with blonde curly hair who appeared capable of chewing through the ten pin. Skepticism shaded her eyes like a cataract. Not knowing what else to do and not wanting to insult them, I smiled like a goof. They returned to bowling.

What the hell was that?

At about nine thirty, the leagues began to wrap. Frank joined me.

"Enjoy the play?"

"Very much. You're an amazing bowler, Frank."

I was surprised when he blushed because anyone who had ever watched him must have told him the same thing.

The clamor as the players talked about their games and replaced equipment in bags fell off in a quiet space between Frank and me. This was not my imagination. In that space was a question I had to ask. I glanced over at Jo, who mouthed "What are you waiting for?"

"Frank, do you want to go have coffee? We can talk about … bowling."

"I'd love to."

"Great."

"Let me put my equipment away in my office."

"I mean if you're tired, we can have coffee at the snack bar."

"Have you tried the coffee here?" He put his hands to his throat in a mock yuck.

He headed off. I gazed at Jo with an expression of "What do I do now?" She tossed me an encouraging nod.

"It's coffee, Margaret, not sex," I whispered to myself. "God, I can't believe I said, 'sex'. God, I can't believe I'm thinking about sex."

Suddenly, Frank stood beside me. "You say something?"

"Nothing."

"Ready?"

"I'll drive."

"I like a woman in charge."

I wished I was one of them.

"You a native of Nevada, Maggie?"

"Yup. I should get a patch or something."

"You should."

"How about you, Frank?"

"My family ran a small grocery store in Henderson."

"Hey, I grew up there. Where was your store?"

"On Sixteenth Street."

"I'm sorry to say I never shopped there."

"It was one of those stores selling a little bit of everything. Food, pots and pans, detergent. I used to sweep up and stock the shelves."

The memories must have been happy. They were reflected on his face.

"I remember stores like that. Lots of characters with candy behind glass. Sausages hanging from the ceiling."

"My dad's place had tons of character, not to mention fruit in bins and a small deli."

"I miss those. Now it's like shopping at corporate grocers. Wide aisles. Clean floors. Stepford Wife clerks. No heart."

"They scare me too."

"How come you left the grocery business, Frank?"

"One word."

"Bowling?"

"I loved it better than selling groceries."

"Totally understandable."

The only place I could think of to buy coffee was a Denny's a few blocks away because there was always a Denny's a few blocks from any point in the universe. Not the most romantic place, I thought as I drove into the parking lot. God, Margaret, it's not a date, I assured myself. A meeting between teacher and student, or two bowling friends. Still, I glanced at myself in the rearview mirror before I got out of my car.

He ordered a large black coffee, none of those soy latte, non-fat beverages. I loved the simplicity. I ordered the same, although I'd been known to purchase a full-on, calorie-choked mocha every once in a while, especially when in a reckless mood. I should have asked for decaf because I was going to be up all night with the caffeine, but I didn't want to be a wimp.

"Let's get a piece of pie." He eyed the dessert menu.

"I won't say 'no'. But I may only take a few bites of mine otherwise I might as well just rub the fat directly on my ass." God, I actually said ass.

"Maggie, why'd you really come in for bowling lessons?"

"At this stage in my young life you mean?"

His nod was gentle. "I wasn't going to put it that way."

"I would. Bowling looked like something fun to do." I took a quick sip of the coffee, but it was still hot. I charred my tongue.

"Coffee hot?"

"Yesshh."

"Were you craving the excitement? The cheap beer specials?"

"Maybe it was the famous Cactus Lanes chili fries."

"Those too. But I'm serious, Maggie."

I covered the top of my coffee cup with my hand. "You have the worse habit of bringing out the truth in me. You should've been a cop."

Intertwining his fingers, he placed his hands on the table. "So tell me or do I have to pull out the lie detector?"

"Not necessary." His eyes were enough. Two beautiful brown doses of sodium pentothal. "After my husband died, I was looking for a little direction. Maybe a little of my old self. I seemed to have lost her somewhere along the line."

"I don't understand."

"For years I was Mrs. Margaret Adams. I was 'Mom' and 'Grandma', but I'd lost track of Margaret, I mean Maggie. So I searched for who was I supposed to be."

"In a bowling alley?"

"As good a place as any and better than most. One night I dragged out one of my old yearbooks and saw a photo of me and the bowling team. Then I remembered your place. I was coming home from the cemetery after having buried my husband when I saw your cactus neon. I loved it."

"And so you returned to bowling."

"It took long enough. The first time I bowled I was

seventeen. As part of our gym class in high school, we bowled for two weeks. Turns out I had a knack so the teacher told me to go out for the team. I did because there weren't many things I was good at."

"I don't believe you."

"Believe it, Frank. I was an average student and follower. But I was voted captain of the bowling team and we won the state championship." I smiled and held out my hands as if still grasping the prize. "The trophy was heaven."

"So why'd you give it up?"

He could handle this. "My friends at the time weren't bowlers and not very supportive. I never went back."

"They thought bowling for inferior class people who lived in trailers and couldn't afford to ski." He crossed his arms. Not angry but tolerant.

"Not in so many words, but yes."

"Well, I guess there aren't too many doctors, corporate executives, and Supreme Court justices who bowl."

"Justin Bieber does, and so does Kevin Hart, at least according to the Internet."

"You don't say."

"And Dwight Howard once carried a 185 average."

"I'll be damned. But no court justices, oh well."

"No, but they should. And if they do decide to roll, they should hire you as their teacher, Frank. You're excellent. And with the kids you show great patience."

"I love it, though I do get a gut ache when the kids manhandle the equipment. They'll loft the balls on the lane and mess around with the computer telescore. I usually have to reset it three times during each lesson."

"I love how they skid about on their socks."

"It's like wrangling very short college kids."

"Do you have children?" I inwardly cringed at my impertinence, but the question seemed natural.

"No." He smiled but it was dampened with sorrow.

I wanted to pinch myself for causing him sadness. "Sorry for asking. It wasn't my business."

"No need to be sorry. What about you?"

"A daughter and a son, and one grandchild. I helped create and raise them. But they're their own people now and my contribution seems more one of passing."

"Then you were blessed to be loved so much."

I wrapped my arms around myself. His response was so much warmer than I expected. "Never thought of it that way. I thought I was the one doing all the loving." My cheeks heated. "All this talk about love."

He insisted on buying the coffee and pie, which I considered a date move.

It was midnight by the time I drove him back to Cactus Lanes.

"I had a good time," I said as we sat in my car.

"As did I."

"Let's do this again."

"Heck, yeah."

He clutched his hands on his lap.

"Everything okay?"

He looked up at me, his eyes glistening even in the relative darkness. "I had a son, Javier. He was my joy for four months. My wife and I mourned him and her inability to have more. She used to say, 'We only have our love now,' but part of my heart was buried with him." Then he glanced up at the blinking lights of Cactus Lanes. "Now, when I teach the kids, sometimes I imagine I'm teaching Javier the game. Like one of them might make it to the professional level like their *abuelito*. Or they'd end up bragging to other kids, 'Our grandpa was in the PBA.'" He wiped his eyes.

I was full-on crying. I handed him tissues from a box I kept in the car and we dabbed away tears.

"I haven't talked about it in years."

"Then I'm honored and I'm so sorry."

"Me too."

He got out of the car and waved as he headed to his truck.

I watched him drive away. He was more real than any man I'd ever met.

For the next two weeks, I came in every other day to practice and my average rose to a staggering 210.

God bless bowling.

Chapter Twenty-One

Mike buckled the seat belt in his car. "What'd you feel like eating tonight?"

"Sushi." I rubbed my hands together in anticipation.

"Raw fish it is."

"Your dad hated sushi so we'd never go."

"Remember what he used to say?"

"What?"

"You're overcharged for raw fish and a little rice on a thin green paper."

I choked a little on my own spit. "God, you sounded exactly like him right then."

"Weird, isn't it?"

"Your dad was kind of a meat and potatoes guy."

"And that's probably what killed him."

"Mike."

"Sorry. Dad would have laughed."

Looking at each other, we said at the same time, "No, he wouldn't."

We ended up at an atmospheric restaurant a few blocks from the Strip. The kind with real orchids and subtle Japanese décor. This was our ritual when my son came to visit. Dinner and gambling. It started on Mike's twenty-first birthday. Bob said he had to work, and like her father, Kyla didn't gamble even when she turned the right age. They both had called it a waste of money.

"But what a fun way to waste money," Mike told them, and he and I went to dinner and gambling until four in the morning.

Sometimes, Mike and I hit a show at one of the casinos to see a vintage rock band playing their hits, or a band imitating a vintage band playing their hits. I'd seen the Cirque Du Soleil Beatles show twice and he was wonderful enough to go with me both times.

"Mom, you would've made an awesome groupie," Mike had told me after the second showing.

"The nicest compliment I ever had, son."

Mike loved rock as well. When he was small, he particularly loved the song, "One After 909" by The Beatles. In his little socks and briefs, he'd sing into a pretend microphone, "Come on baby, don't be cold as ice."

One of my best memories of momhood.

No rock music that night, just sushi dinner and good talk, mostly about his work.

"You were always a good writer, Mike. As a kid, you made up stories and told them to *me* before bedtime. I loved the one about Cinderella from the prince's point of view. You should turn it into a kid's book."

"I like the story too, but I'm so busy at work. Still, it's not a bad idea." He took out his phone and typed a note to himself.

"Seeing anyone?"

A warped smile. "Not yet, but a new freelance photographer signed on. Interesting girl."

"How?"

"Intelligent, very witty, and lovely but in an off-beat way. You know the more you get to know someone and like them, the better they look?"

"The story of my life, son."

"Mom, you always run yourself down. I hate it."

Best to keep the conversation off me and my activities. "We were talking about the interesting photographer."

"I'll let you know what develops. Get it? Develops?" He laughed with earnestness even if it wasn't his best joke.

"Eat your spicy tuna roll, son."

When delivering more sushi, an attractive server also delivered her best smile for Mike. He didn't notice.

The summer before Bob had died, Mike's five-year relationship with another magazine writer named Corrine ended. He never brought Corrine to our house in Vegas, though I'd invited him to do so. Whenever I visited him in San Bernardino, I thought her very bright as well as beautiful, but closed as a trunk belonging to someone who'd lost the key. Eventually, Corrine left the city for another job, and Mike stayed behind with a heartache. After hearing the news, I drove to be with my son. We ate Chinese food and watched old movies that had nothing to do with romance. Bob was too busy to make the trip, which irritated me most of the way to California.

"How you doing, Mom?" Mike gave a pretend forceful stare. "Though I have to say, you look great. New hairdo and clothes. I like it."

I longed to tell him about bowling, even about Frank. My son wouldn't judge me as I knew Kyla would with a pronouncement faster than Judge Judy's. Of this I was certain. But by confiding only in Mike I'd be playing favorites. So I'd keep my secret like a poker hand, close to my chest. I'd tell him what I could. About the senior volunteer job and the art class.

"Your senior volunteer gig is great, Mom, but is Kyla forcing you to take that pottery class?"

"Not really." Well almost.

"Do you even like it?"

No. "It's something to do. Something creative."

"I hope you aren't going to let Kyla talk you into golfing. You hate it as much as I do."

"I won't, son."

Mike glanced at the lavish casino lights out of the window. "Dad never forgave me, you know."

I touched his hand, and he turned his head, his eyes still wounded.

I loved that we could talk like this. Mike and Bob couldn't, not by a long shot. Hell, they barely shared the same room. As a boy, Mike had also heard Bob's be-perfect-perfect-perfect speech, which he disregarded instantly. The real problem between them stemmed from golf, which caused me to despise the sport even more.

By the time Mike was nine, Bob had him take lessons from a pro and they golfed together at least twice a week. Turned out, our son happened to be a prodigy with a set of clubs. A downright Mozart of the mean swing. By fifteen, Mike had claimed most every youth title at the country club and at the private school he attended. By seventeen, he started beating out everyone, including his father. Captain of the high school team, he was offered a scholarship to several colleges.

Mike turned them down flatter than a newly-mowed green. He announced to the whole family one evening after dinner he was through with golf. He had played just to please his father but couldn't endure the hypocrisy any longer.

"It's slow and elitist. I'd rather write," he said.

This was no surprise to me. Notebooks filled with stories, journaling, poems, and observations on this world were piled up in his room. He allowed me to read some of his writing and it was great, and I wasn't saying that because I was his mother. He was a talented storyteller.

Mike knew what he wanted and showed the courage to follow through with it. How I envied and took pride in him.

However, Mike's declaration struck his father worse than a steel beam to the groin. Anger followed the disbelief while we all sat in the living room after dinner.

"You a homo or something?" Bob shouted.

Bob never shouted unless it was at the TV when a golfer missed an important shot in a tournament.

"Bob!" I yelled and I never yelled. "It's his business. And if he wants to quit playing golf that's his business too."

Mike kept his natural coolness. "I like girls, but even if I were gay it shouldn't matter at all. I'm through with the game, Dad."

"You could be a pro."

"I'd rather not."

"Golf can give you so much, son."

"You've given it too much already, Dad."

Bob stood up, his mouth quivering. Outside of the movies —including *Lifetime* ones—I'd never seen anyone storm out of a room before. But he couldn't stand the truth, though he never would've admitted that. I understood the situation very well because the reality of my marriage floundered at the bottom of a bottomless pit.

Taking a cue from her father, Kyla started shouting at her brother. "You're stupid, Mike. After all the time Dad gave you, to teach and support you. You're an ungrateful son."

She marched out of the room, also.

I sat near Mike, placing my arm over his shoulders. His hands trembled.

"So what'd you think about tennis?" I asked innocently.

Mike laughed until he gagged.

But the golf incident, as I had now filed it away, distanced our son from his father and his sister. Even growing up, Mike and Kyla were more adversaries than siblings, choosing allies in the struggle. Kyla selected her father and Mike, me. After Mike's confession, their relationship degraded even more.

I couldn't point a finger. My connection with my two older brothers hadn't been much better. Joseph had moved his family to Sacramento and Sidney followed to be near him. They had visited at holidays until our mother died and then the contact whittled down to Christmas cards via the US Mail.

The coolness in my own family was not much better during the holidays or Mike's visits home from college or San Bernardino once he found a job at a magazine. And when people asked Bob about Mike, Bob replied he was doing fine and nothing more. This enraged me and I boasted how Mike was a darn good writer.

Goddamn golf.

My son stirred around his drink, the Vegas lights illuminating his head like an aura.

"Mom, even though we had troubles, I miss him. I keep wishing he'd told me, 'Mike, I'm proud of you for doing what's best for you, golf or no golf.'" He took another drink of his scotch. "I should have talked to him more. Made up the differences between us."

"I believe he loved you very much."

"He did a good job of keeping that to himself."

"You know what he was like." I licked my lips. "Showing emotion wasn't in his vocabulary."

"I know. We both know. You more than anyone."

I blessed him for his understanding. "Focus on the good times with him. That will help you cope, Mike."

"Forget the not-so-good ones."

"Exactly."

"You doing the same, Mom?

"That a trick question?"

"Man, this is one depressing conversation." Mike finished his drink. The cute server asked if he wanted a refill. He caught her smile this time and returned it. Then he took my hand and squeezed. "So where do you want to lose your money first?"

Chapter Twenty-Two

Though it was one hundred degrees outside, my anticipation kept me cool. I waited for Jo in front of Corky's Diner, which was located four blocks from Cactus Lanes. The cafe appeared to be older than most in a city full of new construction. Jo had asked me to meet her for lunch, but she also specified to wait out front for her. I wondered why but followed her direction. Standing under an awning, however, wasn't much relief from the drumming heat. Still, taking in the fantastic smells from the diner helped pass the time. I enjoyed the scent of the diner's special—meatloaf.

Jo came up the sidewalk and waved. She was a good walker, like she knew where she was going at all times. I'd never seen her outside of Cactus Lanes in the daytime. Her hair was much redder in the sun. In place of the usual outfit of a T-shirt and jeans, she wore nice capris and a sweet blouse.

"Sorry, I'm late. I had to drop my son off at this job. His car broke down."

"No problem. But let's go inside. It's hot."

I was happy she'd invited me. To have a friend. Someone I liked. This was earth-shattering to me. Counting Consuela and Frank, she made three.

I was so pathetic.

The diner had a small waiting area where the strong smell of coffee practically knocked me back. I could breathe in the caffeine so I wouldn't even have to order a cup. Heady with character, the diner came right out of the 1950s. Black and white checked linoleum covered the floor. Diners sat at chrome tables. Booth seats covered in red leather showed wrinkles from all the behinds that sat on them. Cooks flipped burgers in the open kitchen area, causing me to wonder whether grease from the 1950s also clung to the walls. The young servers took orders and delivered food wearing skates.

"I'm so happy we could have lunch together, Jo." We stood in the small lobby area.

"I'm happy that you're happy. I wanted to talk with you about our team." She motioned to the hostess that we weren't ready for a table yet. "We happen to have an opening. One of our teammates had to leave the Bowling Broads. Her husband retired and made her move to Phoenix. Damn him."

"An opening? Me?"

"I want you to join. Your scores have been through the friggin' roof."

My stomach imitated a wayward baton. "Jo, it's been more than four decades since I bowled on a team."

"So?"

"What if I mess up? What if I muff an important tournament?" My head was about to implode with the "what ifs."

"Must I drag you inside to meet the girls?"

"Oh God, they're here?"

"If you're going to bowl with us, you need to meet them. Kinda goes with the territory. They'll love you. If not, they'll love your average."

My underarms were awash with nervous perspiration. I hadn't been scared of meeting people since the first dinner with Bob's wealthy parents. And that meeting was comparable to walking up the gangplank to the Titanic. My fear was justified then. His parents turned out to be as friendly as the iceberg that sank the ship.

I couldn't move. "What if we aren't compatible?"

"It'll be fine. But you're going to have to pass inspection with the girls."

"Why do I feel like I'm going on a blind date?"

"Because you are."

Jo led me to a large round booth at the back. Sitting at it were the women I'd seen at Cactus Lanes during the league play.

"Well, here she is." Jo slapped my back.

She introduced me to the team.

A Black woman, Bonnie Ralston was slender and perky. Even her short brown hair and comely brown-green eyes were perky. Bonnie waved.

Full-bodied, Suze López appeared to have shy ways compared to Bonnie and Jo, but her eyes flushed with friendliness. Brownish-red curls surrounded a round face.

Then, there was Violet Smith.

Lean with the arms of a female wrestler, she had an expansive bosom and small waist. Despite the threatening physique, she was quite lovely. Blue eyes, blonde hair reaching to shoulders. Still, she cracked her knuckles as if preparing to pin me in a ring in less than thirty seconds.

For a better look at me, Violet put on the glasses hanging from a chain around her neck. "Well, sit down," she said with such authority I immediately obeyed.

Jo swept her hands in my direction. "Maggie's bowling like a champ. She'll fit right in."

"So you want to take Karen's place?" Violet took off the glasses.

"There's no way I can replace her, but I may be able to contribute something to the team." My toes seared with pressure, like a murder suspect being grilled over a slow flame. I fought the heat.

"Karen *is* going to be hard to replace," Suze said. "I do miss her." Her eyes moistened.

"A 187 average. Five times women's city champ and editor of the state women's bowling association newsletter," Bonnie added.

"Karen was also named Bowler of the Decade by the state women's bowling association." Jo grinned.

I thought Jo was on my side.

"And what a hook. She could be five lanes down, throw it, and still get a strike," Suze said dreamily.

"Size eleven bowling shoes to fill." Violet nodded.

How could I even compete with a local bowling legend? I wondered what they would think if I ran out of the side door. I could tell them my house had caught fire.

Violet put her glasses back on and gave me another once-over. "You look like a bridge kind of gal to me. Cocktails and cribbage, whatever the hell cribbage is."

"Not nice, Violet." Bonnie sent me one of her contagious smiles.

"I want to know who she is and whether we can trust her. That's fair, isn't it?" Violet placed her hands down on the table as if extending a challenge.

"Does seem like a good question," Suze answered quietly, head down.

I placed my hands on the table. Either I was going to do this or not. Either I was going to sit alone in my affluent tomb of a home with not much to do or I was going to get involved.

Where was the pin and pitch to your life, Margaret?

I addressed Violet directly. "You *can* trust me."

One of her eyebrows lifted with doubt.

"And I like the people I've met at this table, at least so far." I smiled.

A verbal gauntlet.

"Oooooh," pronounced Jo, Bonnie, and Suze.

Violet grinned and she was even prettier. "You've got guts."

"You too. You know what else I have?"

"What?"

"A 205 average." I raised my eyebrows.

Violet whistled and smiled.

I blew out a breath. "So, am I in?"

The other women put their heads together and whispered. I stood up like a prisoner in a docket ready for the decision from the court.

"You bet your asphalt you're in." Bonnie held out her hand.

Funny how easily women share things over lunch. Eating salads and sandwiches. Disclosing your life. Listening to the particulars of someone else's. Taking bites, sipping iced teas, and giving of themselves. I loved each minute. I had very few friends because most people I knew didn't want to give of themselves or let you into their lives. They were stingy. But during the past hour, the women in the booth proved generous. I wondered how much I could share of my life. The lonely well-off woman who didn't cry when her husband died. Best for now to be a good listener and share what I could.

The team members were in varying degrees of relationships. Jo and Suze, both in their mid-fifties, had been married for more than twenty-five years. Bonnie, who turned fifty-eight, lost her husband ten years before and lived with her divorced daughter, and Violet had been divorced for six years. She was the youngest of us at forty-four.

"I ain't looking for love." Violet stirred sugar into her tea.

"What if it came looking for you?" I leaned on one elbow. I liked her pluck.

"Maybe, I'll have to answer the door. I mean, depending if he's a good man."

They asked about my relationship, and I replied I'd lost my husband more than a year ago. Their condolences were genuine, and I wondered where these women had been all my life. The answer was simple, however. Down at Cactus Lanes.

Each of them had grown children and a few had grandchildren. We all pulled out cell phones to show photos of our kids and grandkids to each other and remarked on the cuteness of the others'. Suze stayed at home and was heavy into volunteering for her church. Bonnie worked in a bank, and Violet was a case worker with Nevada welfare services. I suspect the job must have accounted for her hard casing but holding a grand heart within.

"Bowling is my outlet." Violet's voice was rough. "Sometimes I imagine the pins are my pain-in-the-ass co-workers and the crooked people trying to defraud the welfare system."

"Yeow," Jo said.

"It's all very therapeutic."

"Whatever you say."

But the talk soon switched over to bowling. They'd been on the same team for six years, but all of them had bowled for much longer, even starting in high school as I had.

"After my husband died, I decided to get back into bowling. And I haven't felt this alive in years." Like Frank, these women had the power of a truth serum.

"Dammit, that's 'cause bowling is fun." Jo clapped her hands together. "People don't comprehend how much there is to bowling. Sure, there's skill involved but also determination, strength, intelligence."

"Three out of four in your case," Violet said, causing the others to laugh.

I'm not sure if I should but it was funny.

"Violet, you're hilarious," Jo countered sarcastically.

"Thank you very much," Violet replied in her best Elvis impression, making everyone laugh that time, including me.

"Bowling teaches us so much about life," Jo tried to continue.

Violet shook her head. "Here we go."

"Everything reminds Jo of bowling." Suze nudged me with her elbow.

"I have this speech memorized," Bonnie added.

"Well, I'd like to hear it." I wasn't lying.

The other three groaned.

"Quiet, all of you, while I talk to Maggie here. Now as I was saying, bowling teaches you skill and concentration. How to work as a team but still excel as an individual. And bowling is also like love." She grinned with wickedness. "Some days you get strikes and some days you get washouts."

"But if you're lucky, you get a turkey." I grinned very wide.

Jo, Violet, Suze and Bonnie exchanged looks of admiration. It certainly paid off to study bingo lingo.

"See, what did I tell you?" Jo said.

Bonnie reached over and hugged me. "You're one of us now." I hugged back. I could get used to this.

"Welcome to the Bowling Broads, Maggie," announced Suze.

"Thanks. I've always wanted to be a broad."

———

Running into my bedroom, I slowly opened a bag and removed a bowling shirt with the name "Maggie" written in elegant lettering. I touched the name delicately as if it had been sewn with stringy gold.

Whipping off my shirt, I put on the new one and checked out myself in a full-length mirror. I picked up an imaginary ball and narrated myself like an ESPN announcer covering a national bowling tournament.

"Maggie Adams, a newcomer to the game after a long hiatus, gets ready to bowl."

I lifted my fantasy ball and started my approach.

"Adams has demonstrated an uncanny ability to control the ball, right, Chuck?"

I lowered my voice for the role of Chuck the Color Analyst. "Yes, indeed. But she gives a tremendous amount of credit to her amazing teacher Frank Martínez. He reminds her of an older Ricardo Montalbán with a little Edward James Olmos thrown in the mix."

Back in the announcer mode, now she hushed her voice, "Let's see how she releases this throw and whether she's worthy of the title, Bowling Broad."

I sent the phantom ball down the lane with impeccable form.

"Good spin. Good spin," said the announcer.

"And what a hook," added Chuck. "You could catch a marlin with her hook."

I peered into the mirror, watching the imaginary ball spin down the lanes.

"Strike!" I jumped up.

Sunny with pride, I bowed to my audience.

Chapter Twenty-Three

M y stylist Hillary stepped back from me. "Special occasion tonight?"

"Very special. You might call it my coming out party. Kind of the prom date I never had."

"No prom? You're kidding."

"No interest until now. At any rate, I want to look fabulous."

"You got it." She winked.

I ended up giving her a fifty-dollar tip.

Later in the evening I was about to enter Cactus Lanes wearing my new team shirt but stopped. Who was that woman reflected in the glass doors? The one with the nifty shirt and bowling bag. In my purse was a new membership card to the local and state women's bowling league associations. As far as I was concerned it might as well have been a pass to heaven.

Was this the same person without a clue after her husband died? The mom stuck in the mother of all ruts? The person who'd messed up her life until that point?

The woman with all the money in the world and nothing to show for it?

No, it wasn't, dammit. And not because of a new haircut and color. No doubt hackneyed, here was a damn spanking brand-new me and I liked her.

Please, let me be worthy of her, I prayed.

As usual the league players prepared for the evening. The vitality in Cactus Lanes was tangible. A wall of chat and competition. A grin broke out as if I'd been dipped in a vat of happiness. I added another prayer.

God, don't let me screw up.

Straightening my back, I headed to lanes four and five where my new team members were set to play. When Jo spotted me, she gave a loud yippee.

"What?"

"We were taking bets you wouldn't show."

I smiled. "Why are people always betting I won't show up?"

"Dammit." Violet opened her purse.

Jo, Suze, and Bonnie held out their hand and Violet forked over five dollars to each of them.

"That's what you get for not having faith in human nature." Bonnie folded her bill in half.

"Ah, shut it, Bonnie."

"Violet really does love us and her family but no one else." Suze tied her pink bowling shoes.

I unpacked my gear. "If it's worth anything, Violet, I would've bet ten dollars on my no-show. I haven't competed in anything since high school so I'm nervous as hell."

"If that's the case, maybe I should only pay you guys two fifty." Violet's hand went out.

Jo clenched the dollars and stuck them into her purse. "A bet is a bet."

"I didn't want to let you down so I came. Now that I'm here, I really don't want to let you down."

"Good enough for me." Suze hugged me.

Violet put on her glasses. "You got your hair done, Maggie."

My cheeks flushed. "I wanted to look my best tonight."

"We don't care how you look. Just how you roll."

"I'll come in rollers next time."

"Ha!" Bonnie pointed at Violet. "Forget her, Maggie, or she'll make you crazy. She pulled the same routine when I joined."

"And me," added Suze quietly.

"You guys are exaggerating." Violet placed her ball in the ball return.

"No, we're not."

"She comes off as scary only if you let her." Jo plucked one of the balls out of her bag.

Violet huffed. "It's a good thing I like all of you or I'd bowl elsewhere."

"No one else would have you." Jo's smile was impish.

"You're right. No one would."

We all smiled.

Our opponents for the night began to arrive at the lanes. Our teams appeared to be matched in ages, but when I smiled at them, they returned a stiff nod.

"They look tough," I whispered to Jo.

"They are," she whispered back.

"They're kinda serious."

"I know. They haven't caught on that this game is also fun."

I placed my ball on the ball return and turned to my team. The corners of my mouth drooped at the floor. "What if I don't roll any strikes tonight?"

"We'll have to kill you." Suze gave a friendly wink.

"Remember it's just a game," Bonnie said.

"No, it's not," Jo and Violet proclaimed together.

Jo typed the player names into the computerized scorekeeper. The other women on my team then paid her cash or with a check.

"How much do I owe?" I reached for my purse.

"Thirty dollars. Most of it pays for the three games of bowling. The rest goes to the association and for prize money at the end of the season." Jo placed the money in an envelope.

"We've cashed in most years," Bonnie added with pure pleasure.

"Is that legal?" No doubt it probably was since Vegas was nothing but gambling.

"It's not betting. It's putting money aside to reward good bowling," Suze said.

"And so it should."

Off to the side, Violet studied her thumb.

"Can I help you, Violet?"

"I have a cut and it might throw off my bowling."

"I know what to do." I smiled with new bowling knowledge. "LiquidSkin. I read about it in my research." I made sure to pack it along with a bag full of accessories such as cornstarch for sweaty hands, Tylenol, and Zantac for heartburn. I took my antianxiety med before I left and had to stop myself from taking a double dose.

"Thanks anyway, Maggie, but Super Glue works better." Violet took a small tube from her bag, applied it to the cut, and blew dry the stuff. She held out her healed thumb. "Good as new."

I inspected her hand. It *was* good as new.

"Here." Suze handed me a yellow towel. They all had a matching one. "To wipe the excess oil off your ball."

"Or to wipe oil *on* your ball if the lanes were dry," Bonnie said.

"I don't understand."

"Forget about that for now, Maggie. Bowl."

"Well, thanks for the towel. If I suck, I'll cry into it."

The game started. I was set to bowl last for the team because as I learned at the diner, I had the highest average of all of them, so I was their anchor. The role frightened and exhilarated me. My duty consisted of boosting the team score if necessary, or so the others explained. But it was a burden too if I muffed the game. I was no longer in a *Lifetime* movie, but one of those World War II films where I was a pilot and it was up to me to drop the bombs in order to save my whole squadron. Then I fumbled the mission and the rest of my squadron ended up shooting down my plane.

Maybe not such a good scenario to think about at the moment.

"We're turning on the lanes for practice," announced the man who worked at Cactus Lanes during the league night since Frank, Ernie, and Jo were all on teams.

"You get two practice rolls," Jo told me.

At my turn, my hands turned clammy with uncertainty about whether I could deliver a high score. My ball dropped with a thud. My new teammates, the bowlers we were playing, and any others nearby swiveled to look at me. Keeping my head lowered, I picked up my ball. I finally rolled and knocked down five pins. On the next one I missed them all.

"Dammit."

I had to face the others. "I screwed up. I'll try my best not to for the rest of the game."

"No worries. I did the same thing, but *I* dropped the ball on my toe," Bonnie said.

"I remember that. I was ready to throw you off the team, but you were so pitiful we had to keep you," Violet said.

"Was I really pitiful?"

"Yup," Suze said.

Jo adjusted the brace she wore on her bowling wrist. "Maggie, roll strikes and we'll forgive all."

"Oh, God."

When practice ended, play started, and we rotated turns on the two lanes. My teammates earned mainly strikes and spares. Then it was my turn for real. Stepping onto the approach, my shoulder blades prickled as if their eyeballs and those of the opposing team were pasted on there. Please don't let me drop the ball or crush my toe, I prayed some more. This was an evening of prayer.

I rolled. *Crack.* A seven-ten split.

"Oh, shit."

I dared to look back at the others when I retrieved my ball for the second roll. My belly weakened from the hesitation shadowing their eyes. They're going to kick me off after the first game and summon a substitute probably already waiting in the parking lot.

Then I saw Frank waving at me. "You can do it," he mouthed. Because the lanes were noisy, I couldn't hear him, but I'm sure that's what he said. He then sent me one of his wonderful supportive smiles, fueled with so much support it could have sent a rocket to Saturn.

I threw my second ball, aiming for the ten pin in the hope it might skid over and bump the other one into submission. Holding my breath, I watched my ball hook but not enough. The ten pin fell over.

"Good try," Suze said.

I breathed with gratitude at her. "Sorry, guys."

"You're nervous, I'll give you that one," Violet added.

The next time I rolled a strike. Then another strike, another strike and then a spare. Each time, my new teammates clapped or held out hands for a high five or knuckle bump. I ended the first game with a 190. The Bowling Broads took the first game.

"I knew you could do it." Jo placed her arm around my shoulder.

"For a bridge kind of gal, you're good." Violet glanced at the telescore.

"I had every confidence in her." Suze nodded wisely.

"Thanks for taking a chance on me."

"Enough patting ourselves on the back," Bonnie said. "We got another two games to win."

In between the games, I searched for Frank.

"Congratulations, you're an official bowler."

"And I've got the logo to prove it." I modeled my bowling shirt.

"If you still want the neon, I can deliver it tomorrow afternoon."

"I'd like that."

We set a time.

"Back to bowling." I spun around with excitement and plowed into a hefty male bowler.

"Sorry," I uttered with embarrassment.

My teammates had their own style of bowling, each reflecting their personalities. Jo was straight-forward in her execution, her hook narrow and lethal. Bonnie walked fast down the approach. Suze took deliberate steps on the approach and added a little hop to the last one before she threw the ball. Violet was pure power.

While the men on the leagues weren't as talkative, the women bowlers laughed and chatted between the games. Nevertheless, with ball in hand, the females were as serious about scoring as the men. And like their male counterparts, profanities often accompanied a roll failing to clear the rack, which left a split, or missed completely.

I couldn't remember when I'd had such a good time with other women. In the end, it only mattered that I did.

The Bowling Broads won all three of our games, which was a bonus.

Chapter Twenty-Four

I watched the clock on my nightstand. For the fifth time in an hour, I checked my hair in the mirror. I put on lipstick, although I panicked when I couldn't find my new one.

Earlier in the day I'd gone to the mall and stopped at a makeup counter at Macy's. I headed in for a new lipstick, but the young woman recommended a professional makeover.

"Ever had one?"

Her skin was flawless. I was tempted to touch it to make sure it was real and not flesh-colored ceramic.

"The last makeover I had was on my wedding day and look how that turned out."

"Okay." She smiled through her obvious puzzlement. "Then I'd say it's about time to try another one. It'll be fun. It's kind of slow today and I need practice."

Certainly, she wanted to sell me more products, but I agreed. Trying new things was becoming a habit with me and I liked it.

Usually, I wore eyeliner, a hint of mascara, and lipstick. But when I stayed home, I wore nothing but Chapstick. Bowling changed everything. I'd come to care about what I looked like when I walked out the door.

Thankfully, I still had my eyebrows. Lots of women my age at the country club had lost theirs somewhere. I ran a finger over mine. Not Groucho Marx thick but acceptable.

The young woman at the makeup counter first examined me before taking her time to find the right foundation. I squirmed a little in the chair hoping I wouldn't end up resembling Bette Davis in *What Ever Happened to Baby Jane*.

After cleaning my skin, she went to work, although it was a little weird for a stranger to apply foundation, line my eyes, and apply mascara. In other words touch my face. She was at it for a good twenty minutes and I was sure I'd be ready to sing, "I've Written a letter to Daddy," when she had finished.

Then she stepped back, and her flawless skin gave a flawless smile. "Go on, check yourself out in the mirror. You look fabulous. I did a great job, if I do say so myself." The young woman then leaned in and added quietly, "And I'm not trying to make a sale. I like to help people look their best."

I looked.

"Oh, man. What'd you know? I have cheekbones and eyes."

She'd emphasized my good points such as they were.

"You bet. Your eyes really stand out."

"You are a genius."

My skin tone was even. The makeup wasn't caked on. No sign of Baby Jane Hudson anywhere. I was kind of attractive, if you didn't look too hard or too long.

I ended up purchasing more than three-hundred dollars'

worth of products. My best investment since the Keurig Coffee Maker.

Back at home, I glanced at the clock for the thirteenth time.

"Where's my lipstick?" I finally located the new one in the bottom of my purse where all items not wanting to be found ended up, such as keys and change.

A vehicle pulled up outside and for a second, I worried it might be Kyla. I peeked through the curtains, but the sound came from a car passing on the street. Terrible as I felt for doing so, I released a grateful fizz of a breath it wasn't my daughter. Anyway, Kyla was going to be busy with her family this afternoon. This I knew because I had called an hour before and asked her what she was doing to absolutely guarantee my daughter *wasn't* coming over.

"Do you need anything?" Kyla said when I had called.

"No, just calling to say, 'Hello.'" I'd gotten used to lying though the shame still pricked me like mosquito bites.

"How's pottery class?"

"Interesting." No fibbing about that. The class was not boring, but it was frustrating. When it came to molding the clay, I had Vienna Sausage fingers. "Everything's good so I'll talk to you later. Love ya." I wanted off the phone in case Frank drove up.

"Well, okay." Bewilderment spilled in her voice.

After ending the call, I applied more lipstick and rechecked my hair.

"Margaret, you're going to wear down your lips to nothing with so much lipstick."

"I'll stop," I answered but checked my clothing. I had on a pair of jeans and a new shirt. I hadn't bought this much clothing for myself since I was in my twenties. The jeans were loose, which meant I'd lost weight. All due to the fact I was more active than I'd been in the last hundred years. However, my days of sporting a supermodel body were not only over, they were extinct. Not that I ever had one of those bodies in the first place. I was what my mother called solid. Petite was a stranger in our family. We were a clan with bones hardy as a Neanderthal carrying a mastodon leg home for dinner. Wide shoulders and muscular arms.

The clock ticked and taunted me.

Trying to read a new book, I scanned the same paragraph over and over.

The sound of another vehicle outside the house.

I threw down the book.

Jumping up and running to the balcony, I spotted his blue truck parking in front. Frank was right on time. I still rushed down the stairs. Half-way there I stopped and slowed, not wanting to break my neck, which would have spoiled my day. A little out of breath, I inhaled a few gulps of air, not to mention smoothing my hair, before opening the door.

Frank stood on the step, holding the sculpture wrapped in a blanket.

"Oh heck, I thought you were the pizza man." My hands on my hips. How I wished I could be cool.

"I bear art instead of pepperoni."

"I like 'em both. Come on in."

Standing in the foyer, he whistled. A long whistle. "This is one beautiful house. And huge. Ever get lost?" He smiled.

"Frequently."

His voice echoed a bit and I turned self-conscious as if I

217

were a way older Scarlett O'Hara in an overdressed Tara. "You could fit a family of ten in this mausoleum."

"Hey, if you have the money, then spend it."

"I'm glad I'm spending it on your art."

Frank set the neon piece down on a table. "Were you going out to dinner?"

"No. Why do you ask?"

"Because you look very nice. I mean you usually look nice, but today, especially so." He blushed a bit.

"Thanks for noticing." My toes burned from the recognition. I reminded myself to go back and buy hundreds of dollars more of makeup.

"Now where do you want this?"

I pointed upstairs. "My bedroom. This way. Need help?"

"It's not heavy. Neon tubing, remember?"

"And light."

"Of course."

To make way for the sculpture, I had removed a print of one of Vincent Van Gogh's Iris paintings. He had painted a series of them when he was in the Saint-Paul de Mausole asylum in France or so I'd read on Wikipedia. For years, I'd wake each morning, sit in bed, and stare at the painting as a reminder not to go insane in this lovely lonely monstrous house.

I indicated the spot on the wall where I wanted the neon. Right across from my bed. "Need any tools?"

"Brought my own."

I hadn't noticed, but he wore a carpenter's belt.

Frank installed a few screws into the wall to hold the piece of artwork.

Sitting on the bed, I watched him and his muscles at work. Like scoping out a male stripper at Chippendales. Well, an emeritus one anyway. "Always been a handyman?"

"It's a mandate if you own a business. Something always needs fixing, so you better learn how to do it."

Regrettably, the installation was quick.

He plugged in the piece.

We both stepped back. The sculpture glowed. A bowling ball knocking over a pin with lightning erupting from the contact.

"It's wonderful, Frank."

He acknowledged the compliment and removed the carpenter's belt. "From all the blossoms in your yard, I thought you might have wanted one of the sculptures of the cactus flowers."

I shook my head. "No, this is the one. I want to see it every morning." I turned and he smiled at me. "What?"

"You looked beautiful when you said that."

My cheeks flushed and I handed him a check for eight hundred dollars. "Best one I've ever wrote."

"Listen, let me take *you* to dinner. I'll spend some of the money you gave me."

"All right."

"I know a place off the Strip, awesome Italian food and an outdoor patio. You like Italian?"

"Who in their right mind doesn't?"

My senses hummed on max overload from the lights and odors. The taste and the company. The good wine and delicious sauce. Frank and I sat on the patio, which overlooked a small lake where a group of swans glided by. We could have been in Venice, Italy, or Venice, California, for that matter. Lights from the massive casinos created a LED horizon topped by a faint beam shooting into the sky from the top of the Luxor pyramid.

The scene was so romantic. I had imagined—and yes, wished for—such a time with Frank, but now that it was here, I wasn't sure how to act. Of course, I almost blew it.

"Did you know three years before women got the vote in 1919, the Women's International Bowling Congress started in St. Louis?" It was the first thing out of my mouth. The moment I said it, I wanted to jump into the lake with the swans.

I took a bite of breadstick so I wouldn't spout any more bowling trivia he must have known anyway.

"You nervous or something, Maggie?"

My foot shook under the table. "Yeah, even though this is not a date."

"I'm nervous, too, even though it's not a date."

"You are?"

He nodded.

"Thank, God."

With such admissions, talk came easy, as if we had removed our shoes and expectations. We chatted about bowling and families. He about his mother. Me about my children. We drank more wine, which made conversation even more laid-back.

"You gamble much, Maggie?"

"When my son Mike visits, he and I will go out to dinner or a show at one of the casinos and then we'll play for a few hours."

"No table games?"

"I'd love to try Blackjack but I'm too daunted by the people who know what they're actually doing. I'd get so excited I'd probably say, 'Hit me, hit me' even if I didn't need a card."

He waved a breadstick in the air. "I do love Blackjack, but like you, I gamble only once in a while."

"Good. I was afraid you were going to say you're a recovering gambling addict."

"And I was afraid you couldn't count to twenty-one."

I laughed so hard I choked on a breadstick.

He got up and patted my back. "I'm sorry."

"You can't help it if you're funny."

"It's a curse."

I caught my breath. "I thought you might have to do the Heimlich maneuver on me."

"That might have been fun."

I laughed again.

"From the neon sculpture you chose, you appear to be in love." The candlelight skipped in his eyes as he talked.

The breadstick stuck in my throat again. "Pardon?"

"I mean in love with bowling."

"There's a lot to love, Frank. The game has come to mean so much to me. It's injected my life with friends and strikes." My cheeks singed from the confession. "Man, saying that out loud sounds corny as all hell."

"I know exactly how you feel."

"So tell me about the world of professional bowling."

"Lots of pressure and very intense."

"I have to admit this, Frank. I looked you up online. You're mentioned on more than two thousand pages."

"So many, huh? Never counted them."

From his expression, he hadn't judged me for cyberstalking him. "Who taught *you* how to bowl?"

"My dad. He carried a 185 average. He was a good man and a good father. He died twelve years ago this January. I was happy he'd seen me become a professional bowler. He was very proud."

"How does a bowler turn pro, by the way?"

"One Saturday, I was watching a tournament on TV. My wife told me I was as good as those guys. I decided she was right. I qualified and became a professional. My wife was so proud. She told everyone, even people on the streets."

The memory softened his face.

"Miss the money? The excitement? ESPN?"

"At times it took all the fun out of bowling."

"But that's not why you quit." Not a question. Jo had told me the reason.

"No." Grief dimmed his eyes. A large shiny tear glided down his left cheek. I'd never seen a man cry. I almost jumped across the table to hug him. More than twenty years she had been gone but his sorrow endured. I barely cried for Bob.

With a napkin, he dotted his eyes. "Didn't mean to bring down the evening."

I shook my head that he had not.

"It's all life." He wadded the napkin in his hands. "I started on the tour when I was twenty-nine and for a good part of the next twelve years, I was away from her. I should have spent more time with my wife instead of playing for money and PBA glory." He stared out at the lake as if ashamed to look at me. "I should have been there. I should have had more days and hours with her."

"She loved you, so she understood." I put my hand over his. "Listen, I'm the damn queen of regret. It gets you nowhere but running in place."

He looked at my hand on his and we stopped talking. I could ask him anything and decided to do so.

"How did Anna die?"

His hand slipped out from under mine. "Breast cancer. After she passed, I went back to work as an electrician but didn't bowl. I stopped for seven months, but I couldn't stay away. Any pleasure—aside from Anna and my family—came from playing that game. I wanted happiness so I bought Cactus Lanes."

"It's a great place. Homey. Fun."

"Yes, it is, which makes me very proud. What happened to your husband, Maggie?"

"A heart attack while golfing. He was a workaholic and a golf fanatic, not necessarily in that order. He lived and breathed the game. You love bowling, Frank, but you're not consumed by it."

"Bowling is what I love, but it's not all I love."

I took another drink of wine. A long one. I was tumbling for this man. I took a larger gulp.

"I don't know how to thank you for your patience over these last months, Frank, and for the incredible lessons."

"Maggie, you paid me."

"Oh, yeah. I forgot."

We walked to the parking lot and got into his truck.

Frank placed his hands on the wheel and looked over at me. "You know the best thing about Vegas? It's an all-night town. Lots of places open twenty-four hours a day. Coffee houses, grocery stores, pharmacies, Taco Bell."

"So why are we still here?"

———

We parked behind the Flamingo and walked along the Strip. The lights and noise turned background to our talking and laughing. The next day I probably wouldn't remember what the hell we had even talked about. I simply knew it would become a valuable element to my existence like oxygen in my lungs. At two in the morning, we finally drove to a place he liked and split the best green chili burrito I'd ever tasted.

As he drove me home, the fledgling dawn slinked over the vista in gray-yellow. When we arrived, he walked me to the front steps.

"You'll be all right?" Frank's eyes shot up at the dark house, which appeared even more daunting in the faint light.

"I'm used to an empty house."

"Well."

"Well."

With such delicacy as if not to hurt me, he drew me close and kissed me. A strike detonated in my body. Ten pins downed by thunder. When we pulled apart, I touched my lips. "Hot damn."

He started laughing.

"I wasn't even sure my lips still worked."

"Then we should double-check." He kissed me again.

After another kiss and another, he said good night. I drifted upstairs to my bedroom. Not bothering to turn on the light or even kick off my shoes, I clicked on my new sculpture. Lying back on the bed, I admired the neon. The calm light illuminated the whole room and then some.

Chapter Twenty-Five

R uth tossed down her tickets. "Dammit. Serves me right for betting on a horse with the same name as my chiropractor."

"You're too much, Ruth. Who do you like in the next race?"

But racing was the last thing on my mind as we sat at the Caesars Palace sports book. Ever observant, she eyed me like a doctor.

"Sweetie, you're a little green around the gills as my old dad used to say." She giggled. "He was a fisherman and had fish sayings for everything. Like 'Life is like a tuna. Either it's fresh or dead in a can.'" Her smile was crooked. "I know, a dumb saying. Come to think on it, they were all dumb."

She sipped on her Bloody Mary. That day I joined Ruth in one, although I'd need two cups of coffee before driving us home from the casino.

"Man trouble, isn't it?"

I gulped my drink. "Am I that transparent?"

"Like Saran Wrap." Ruth had a twittering laugh. She

burped from the Bloody Marys and pardoned herself. "You don't get to be my age and not recognize the signs. And you got the signs stamped all over you."

"I do?"

"I may be old, but I haven't forgotten a thing."

"I always thought I did a good job of hiding my feelings."

"Nah, you still look miserable."

"Thanks, Ruth."

She motioned with her fingers. "Let's have the steamy details."

"I've kissed a man and I care about him a lot."

"And that's making you miserable? You *are* messed up."

"Right on as usual, Ruth, but what shall I do about this? Incidentally, he hasn't called me back and it's been three days. Maybe I was a bad kisser. I haven't used my lips or mouth like that for years. Or maybe he just likes to kiss and run."

Ruth blew a nice raspberry. "Bullshit."

I waved my hands about. "I blame all those old romance movies I watch on TV." The *Lifetime* ones included. "They show you it's all so damn easy to fall in love, but the movies end and the credits roll before they tell you what happens after that first kiss."

"I like those movies too, even though they're mostly crap."

"But what if he wants to, you know…" I glanced around first and then moved my hips up and down.

"Go to bed with you?"

"Yes," I whispered, quickly making sure no one heard me.

She chortled. "Stay calm. Who wants to listen to two old ladies talking about intercourse?"

"Not funny, Ruth."

"Yes, it is. Maggie, you're making up lame excuses for not getting into bed with him." The older woman held my hand and took on a whiny voice. "Oh, I can't have sex because I broke a nail. Oh, I can't have sex because it's a full moon. I can't have sex because I'm too old."

I was *so* happy no one sat near us. "Maybe he doesn't want to sleep with me. That might have been platonic kisses. Pity kisses for a lonely widow."

"Did they feel platonic?"

"No, my toes almost caught fire."

She shook her head at me. "Never saw a woman so insecure. Let me ask you a personal question."

"This has been very personal so far. And Ruth, you've missed a race."

"Hell with it. Do you want to go to bed with him?"

Oh God, I did.

I slowly nodded, but my chest began to tighten up with heart palpitations. I started to sweat. I was panicking, all right.

Ruth had articulated what I'd been thinking. Namely, sleeping with Frank. Who was I kidding? That had been on my mind, granted hidden underneath, from the first time I saw him at Cactus Lanes. When we admired the cactus flowers out front. Ever since, the image set off quivers, shakes, and tremors through my body. I needed more than a cold shower. I needed to jump into the Bellagio fountains.

"Ruth, I haven't had sex in years and years. I mean lots of years." I whispered the confession.

She whistled. "Hold on. I thought you said your husband died a year ago."

"Like I said, I haven't had sex in years and years."

Bob's maneuverings in bed resembled a car tune-up. I guessed he was thinking about foreplay at the country club instead of on me. What happened between us was always more sensible than sensual, trade rather than tenderness, as if he was closing a deal. If there had been passion, I sure didn't remember. With such taciturn connections, sex wasn't on my mind much until Bob came knocking at my bedroom door with a little smile, the one signifying he wanted under the covers. A year after he had stopped coming at all, I put on sunglasses and ordered one of those masturbation wands online, which were cleverly called personal massagers—though the name fooled no one. When it arrived in its nondescript packaging, I conjured up fantasies of the Ragnar guy in the *Vikings* TV series to get in the mood. But I felt silly and finally tossed the thing.

After being with Bob I'd had enough plastic.

Personal wand or not, I wanted to feel something.

I downed the rest of my Bloody Mary. "Ruth, maybe it was my fault Bob lost interest."

"Because you didn't love him?"

My feelings were coming out of Ruth's mouth.

"So now you're facing the prospect of going to bed with someone you really want to go to bed with and this is a bad thing?" She used her teacher's voice.

"What if I climax the moment he touches me? What if my body collapses like a crushed aluminum can? Or worse yet, what if sexual enjoyment has passed me by like the time I wore a size ten? Ruth, my insides might have already dried up like a raisin."

The older woman placed down her drink. "Do you want to be with him?"

"Yes, dammit." I said that too loud. "He's wonderful. One of the most wonderful men I've ever known." A hammer hit my head. "Ruth, I'm falling in love with this man."

Hell, it was true.

"No need to get mushy."

"Am I too old?"

"Maggie, you act like you're a hundred years old." She squeezed my hand and gave me a hard stare.

"What it is?"

"You're scared, aren't you? Damn, girl, you're terrified."

The heart palpitations amplified so much they could run a small factory.

"You got to get over your fear, honey." Ruth held up her hand to stop any more of my objections. "And don't worry about when you finally get him in the sack. It's like bike riding, Maggie. Going uphill is hard, but the ride down is fun." She finished the last of her drink.

The older woman blinked her eyes fast as if to keep back tears.

"Ruth?"

"I had man trouble once. He was the love of my life, something I never even told my dead husband. This other man was poor and couldn't afford to marry me. But I loved him something powerful."

"What happened?"

"He joined up with John Dillinger's gang."

"Wow."

"Probably a lie. I loved him, but he was the biggest liar ever born." She took my hand. "Maggie, you know when you pull a thread on your panties and keep pulling and pulling until the next thing you know the elastic is all gone, and your underwear is down below your ankles?"

"Sorry, Ruth, I don't understand."

"Honey, sometimes you got to pull the damn thread."

I leaned over and kissed the woman's cool cheek.

"No need to get sentimental. Now, who do you like in the next race?" Ruth studied the form.

———

After dropping Ruth off, I headed to Cactus Lanes. Along the way, I outlined my lips with my finger. Ever since we'd kissed, I felt him on my lips like a layer of new skin.

Frank's truck was still there. It was after seven and he was probably going to be heading home soon. Gripping the steering wheel, I tried not to be negative. I tried not to read too much into those kisses. But Ruth was right. I had to confront what I felt. I could live with disappointment. I had for more than thirty years.

Frank came out of the building, and I got out of my car. He saw me and smiled. I walked up to him and hugged him. A gesture so natural. But I pulled back. "Sorry."

"Not at all."

"Frank…"

"You're probably wondering why I haven't called."

"I did wonder." Boy, how I wondered.

"I've been confused is all."

"Whatever you say, Frank, I'll accept it. But I hope we can be good friends."

"Maggie, I loved Anna very, very much. And for a long time, I felt if I got involved with another woman, I might be betraying her memory, and our life together. I worried she might disappear altogether. And that meant a part of me might disappear along with her."

No way did I feel that about Bob. I was going to hell.

"I told this to my mom and she said, 'Francisco, you've kept her memory like a small altar in your heart. But there's no betrayal because she's gone and you're still here. Live, my boy, live.'"

He took my hand. "I agree with her. 'Live, Francisco, live'."

I placed my hand over his. "I didn't know what to think when you didn't call and my speculations were wild. But Frank, it's been an eon since I felt kissed, really kissed. I felt cherished, dammit." I stepped closer. "I wouldn't mind a repeat."

"Me, neither."

Chapter Twenty-Six

The ball careened down the lane. My hook arched before contact. The pins blasted away.

My teammates hooted in joy. I'd come alive and it only took forty-some-odd years to do so.

While I improved with each game of bowling, such wasn't the case in the pottery class. My hands weren't so magic there. The clay was not putty in my hands, but a living thing fighting me back. One of my first attempts at pottery, which wasn't so good in the first place, I gave to Kyla to demonstrate that, yes, I was taking a pottery class. My ceramic bowl appeared to have been mashed by a truck, but I'd painted it a color to match her dining room. At dinners at her house, she still tried to talk me into bridge classes and going golfing with her, but I said I was too busy. Lying to my daughter no longer bothered me ... and that *did* bother me.

My best pottery project did not impress my instructor or fellow students, but I loved it. I had formed a bowling ball sitting in between two bowling pins. I painted the ball a bright blue with yellow lightning strikes on the side. The pins were blazing white with a band of red. The piece failed to be accepted into the student art show and received a C plus from Mr. Art, my instructor. Who cared about the grade? I placed the finished work on my bedroom chest of drawers. It was a Rodin to me.

I couldn't create a ceramic to save my life, but I could bowl, darn it, and proved it later at leagues.

When it wasn't my turn on the lane, I took two quarters out of a plastic dish full of coins from a table above the action. Since I landed a strike and Violet and Suze had open frames, I earned a quarter. If I ended up with an empty frame and they pulled down a strike, I lost a quarter. At home, quarters filled a jar.

"I win again." I exaggerated glee.

"You gonna buy another house with all the money you're winning off us?" Violet said.

"Maybe an apartment in Paris." I fluttered my eyelashes.

Violet laughed. This amounted to a small but awesome victory since she had taken the longest to warm to me. For weeks after I joined the team, I'd catch her observing me with overt suspicion and a dash of aggression.

"You're bowling great tonight." Suze held out her hand for a high-five.

"She's inspired by Frank, baby." Bonnie formed a kiss.

"He's in Henderson on business," Jo said.

"And you're still bowling well, Maggie?" Violet said. "You're probably thinking about him."

"Enough. I'm up."

I *was* thinking about him. We'd gone on dates and necked

234

like kids, but nothing more. I didn't want to jinx it by wanting more. I enjoyed what I had.

The team won all three games. After stowing away my equipment, we studied the team's standings posted on the wall.

"Yes, friends, we the Bowling Broads are number one," Bonnie said.

"And look who's got the highest average and series again this week?" Suze nudged me in the ribs.

"You talking about me?" I smiled innocently.

"Smartass," Violet said.

"We've got first place tied up for the first part of the season," Jo said.

"Off to Corky's to celebrate," I said.

"Naturally," Jo added.

"It's tradition," Suze said.

"And there's no screwing with tradition." Violet crossed her arms.

"Damn right," I said.

After league play, we headed to the diner where I first met them. We ordered up burgers and shared French fries if any of us weren't dieting, otherwise we ate salads. At Corky's, we usually took over a corner booth where we could be loud. This is what I loved about the women. They were loud about living. They could be shouting from a rooftop, "YES, I'M HERE, DAMMIT AND HAVING A GOOD TIME." I wanted to join them on the rooftop.

We usually recapped the night's games. I desperately wanted to invite them to my house, but I was embarrassed by the opulence and believed they might think less of me for it. As if I was slumming it by bowling with them or something. Besides, if I wasn't comfortable there, how could they? The sooner I sold the place the better. Later in the week, I had an appointment with a real estate agent. Once it sold, I'd buy a small house and invite them all over to watch movies or for barbecues.

"I'm proud to say you're fitting in quite nicely, Maggie." Jo placed her hand on my shoulder.

"That means a lot to me."

"Except for one thing, and then you'll be one of us."

"What's that?"

Jo held out her right hand. "Touch my palm."

"Mine, too." Violet set out her hand.

They all held out their bowling hands.

Were they playing a shared joke on me? Similar to the one my oldest brother used to play where he'd encourage me to yank his finger. When I did, he'd release the loudest, grossest, and smelliest fart.

I touched their hands. "What am I supposed to feel?"

"My bowling callus." Jo pointed to a thickness at the base of her thumb.

"We all have one." Suze waved her hand.

I felt their hands one more time. "I get it. Kind of like a rite of passage, huh?"

"Forget you own all the equipment, or you play on a league, Maggie. The callus shows you are a serious bowler," Violet said.

I felt a slight thickening at the base of my right thumb but nothing as pronounced as theirs. "I think I'm starting to get one."

Violet gave the nod of a shaman. "Someday, my girl, someday."

Chapter Twenty-Seven

F rank waited on the passenger side. "You going to get out of the truck now?"

I couldn't move. To stall, I checked myself out in the review mirror to apply more lipstick.

"How long has it been since you've been to a man's house?"

"I was twenty-five. You do the math."

"My mother will chaperone us. So, keep your hands to yourself, at least until later." He smiled wickedly.

Although I'd already met Aurelia, I was held in place by fear. Fear she wouldn't think I was good enough for her son. I was also scared she might be right.

"Get out of the truck, Maggie." He opened the door.

I smoothed my dress. A pink summer number with small roses, a white shawl, and sandals. "Do I look like a slut?" I wasn't joking.

Frank laughed and held out his hand.

"You hesitated before you answered, Frank."

"Come on, slut."

His house was more at home in New Mexico than Vegas. Covered in adobe-colored plaster with plenty of Southwestern amenities, including a small courtyard. The wooden door was painted a turquoise blue and proclaimed its own welcome. Large ceramic pots held cactus plants on a small porch.

"Your cactus plants are blooming. They're magnificent."

"I know." Frank's smile was just as amazing.

The house smelled spicy and warm. Colorful rugs with Native American patterns lay on the floor and similar bright designs decorated the pillows on a comfortable-looking couch. I immediately felt at home.

More of Frank's art neon hung on the cream-colored walls. This time with southwestern figures in golden light. Anasazi dancers in yellowish-brown. Lizards in bright green. Smiling faces on suns with wavering beams. Thunderbirds ready to fly.

"Your home is lovely." In contrast, mine was an ice palace.

"Mama, we're here," Frank called.

I backed up toward the door, but he caught my hand.

"Mama."

No answer.

"She doesn't hear so well. Maybe she already fell asleep."

"Maybe she doesn't want to have dinner with me," I whispered.

"No, she's excited. Mama!"

"You don't have to yell. I hear you ... well, most times." Aurelia came into the room.

I wasn't sure what to expect, but her greeting was pure hospitality. I could have melted away by its warmth.

"So good to see you." She held out her hand.

"And you too, Aurelia. Thank you for having me."

"You're the first woman Frank's brought home since his wife passed."

Frank bit his lip with mortification.

"Feel special?" Aurelia smiled at me with small teeth.

"You betcha."

Frank shooed us into the dining room. "Let's eat."

The comfortable dining room smelled of sage and lavender candles. More of Frank's neon lit up the brick-colored walls.

"Dinner was fantastic."

"Thank you, Margarita." Aurelia dipped her head. "But I didn't cook, Frank did."

"It was nothing," he said.

"*Nada*, hell. He was in the kitchen all day." Aurelia touched his hand.

"And Mama, her name is Margaret. But we call her Maggie." Frank poured us all another glass of wine.

"Wait a minute. I like Margarita. Sounds very alluring." I lifted my glass to Aurelia. "Like I'm a woman with secrets."

"Do you have any?" the older woman asked.

The question was akin to a plywood board hitting my gut. I did have secrets. Frank also looked at me. "If I do, they aren't interesting."

"Frank tells me you're a tremendous bowler, Margarita."

"I still have a lot to learn. Frank's a great teacher."

"She's being modest, Mama. She's great. Lots of natural talent."

I blushed and smiled at the same time.

"You people and bowling," Aurelia said.

"We love it," Frank answered.

"When Francisco first mentioned to me he was going to buy a bowling alley I thought he had gone crazy."

"She wanted me to be an accountant," Frank said.

"Accountants are boring," I said.

"And they don't bowl."

"Do you like bowling, Aurelia?"

Frank and his mother laughed. They had the same laugh.

"Frank took me once. You do realize all the game consists of is knocking over a bunch of rolling pins with a ball?"

"That's bowling pins, Mama."

She waved off the correction. "So, where's the fun?"

"I'm glad not everyone feels this way, or I'd be out of business."

Frank arrived with more dishes, and I loaded them into the dishwasher.

"How's your mom?"

"She fell asleep watching a *NYPD Blue* rerun. She loves that program."

"It's a good show."

"More likely she just enjoys looking at Jimmy Smits."

"I totally understand. He's a honey." I cleaned the counter. "I like your mom a lot, Frank. She's very special."

"Yes, she is."

"You're lucky to have her. I lost my mom nine years ago and my dad when I was twenty."

His eyes glanced toward the living room. "I'm grateful every day. But she's at the age that when I come home and she doesn't answer, my heartbeat doubles. My cousin Rachel stays with her when I'm at work. But every time they call me to the phone I worry."

"I understand. Life is more delicate and precious now than when we started out. That's why I also thank God for each day when I wake up and can still take a breath."

"Amen. Mama likes you, Maggie."

"She does?"

"Let me put it this way. You'd know it if she didn't. She's honest as hell."

"She's so kindhearted and welcoming that it made me think about my late husband's mother. Isn't that strange?"

"Was she kindhearted and welcoming too?"

"She hated my guts."

He blasted a laugh.

"Yeah, go ahead and laugh but up until the day she died she kept telling Bob it wasn't too late to divorce me."

Frank placed the leftovers in the fridge. "Let's go out to the patio. It's cooled down."

On our way out we tiptoed so as to not wake his mom who rested in a large chair in the living room. *NYPD Blue* played on the TV. On the bookcase by the door was a large photo of a lovely woman in a bright summer dress. Dark full hair and eyes. Gentleness dwelt on her face. Her long black hair brushed over one shoulder. Her toes playing in the grass. Laughing.

That must have been his late wife. For a second, I wondered if her spirit might warn me off her territory, but the beauty in the photo appeared as if she could never hold on to any malice.

Outside his garden was a tribute to native plants. Cactus, yucca, and Joshua trees.

"This is beautiful, Frank."

"Saves on water bills."

We sat on lounge chairs.

"Frank, the photo in the living room. Your wife?"

"Anna."

"She was stunning."

"She was. She was also terrible at telling jokes, but she loved to laugh." He snapped his fingers. "Ay, but she had a temper hotter than jalapeños on those occasions I managed to make her angry. Anna wasn't much of a reader but loved old movies and got me to love them too. We went dancing on Saturday nights and she was the one who planted the cactus garden."

"No wonder you loved her."

"Anna also loved children, which is why she became a pediatric nurse. A tragic irony came when our son died and she couldn't have any more. But maybe the gift the living receive when a loved one passes is that we remember the good times and not the bad. Any troubles and fights are not worth remembering."

"I believe that. You're so very fortunate to have so many good memories of her." Me, on the other hand, could count them, well … on one hand.

He studied the sky. "Years ago, I'd forgotten the sound of

her voice. Now she's a beautiful memory, fragile as a feather blowing about in a storm."

While he talked about her, I wasn't jealous. I admired one person lovingly remembering another.

He turned to me. "What do you miss about your husband?" His voice was quiet.

"His barbecue ribs."

Now it was my turn to stare at the sky, but I couldn't let this moment fly between us. "Frank, my marriage was not good."

"I got that impression." He placed his hand on my arm. "You don't have to say anything more."

"Yes, I do. I fell out of love with my husband one hundred years before he died."

"Did he hurt you?"

"Not physically. He just wasn't there." I gripped the sides of the chair. "My husband was a decent man and we had nothing in common but a last name. We woke up each day with our eyes closed."

"What about a divorce?"

"I thought about it, but made no move to act. It was pure inertia. No, it was more than that. I was…"

"What?"

"Nothing. Forgive me."

"For what?"

"For sounding whiny. Bob was just Bob."

"You're a good woman."

I patted his hand. "And you're way too generous with your praise."

"No, I'm not."

"What are you two talking about?" Aurelia came out on the porch. Around her shoulders she wore the shawl Frank had bought for her birthday.

"Memories and regrets." That shot out of my mouth.

"Ah, such is life. I have to admit, I was eavesdropping."

"Want to join us?"

"No, too late. My bedtime." She turned back to the living room.

Frank and I stood up and joined her.

"If I might add to your conversation, I'd like to say that without someone to love, there's another kind of loneliness." She placed her hand over her heart. "One in here. I know because I've felt it ever since your papa died."

"I know you have," Frank said.

"He'll always be part of me. He's in my bone marrow now." She pointed at her son. "But life is not meant to be spent in the past. Sometimes we have to say goodbye to say hello." She looked right at me and smiled.

"Mom, I have no idea what you're talking about," Frank said.

"You're right. I'm rambling like an old person."

"You've never rambled in your life. But it is late."

"I know, son."

She told us good night and hugged me.

"Margarita, time to say 'hello'," she whispered.

I embraced her and she went to her room.

Frank excused himself to check on her.

"I want you to see my studio, Maggie," he said when he returned.

"I'd be honored."

245

A flagstone walk lit up by solar lights led the way to a building in the backyard.

"It used to be a garage, but I fixed it up." Frank unlocked the door.

The room was dark until he flicked a switch and then it came alive with light from his neon sculptures in various forms. Southwest figures of cactus, coyotes, old churches, moons. Willowy forms in soft light. A long work bench dominated the middle of the room. On top sat a stack of large paper and a jar of pencils. Shelves of tubing, large and small lined the back wall.

He turned on a stereo. The Rolling Stones.

"I approve of your music, Frank."

"There's no other. I do love Mexican tunes, but I was raised on rock 'n' roll. The Beatles are in my Latin blood."

God, I loved this man.

Slowly, I inspected each sculpture. "How the heck do you make them?"

"First, I sketch out my idea on paper. I used to make the sculptures out of glass tubes. They put out the brightest light, but they're too much trouble. I had to heat the tubes, bend them, vacuum out the dust, *ay*, what a hassle. I burned myself and broke lots of glass. And thank the Lord in heaven I was an electrician or I'd have electrocuted myself ten times over."

On another wall were works in thinner tubes of light. "Lately, I've been getting more into neon tubing. It's more flexible."

I enjoyed his enthusiasm. My own accomplishments were wretched in comparison, aside from giving birth to my children. "I'm taking a pottery class, but my stuff looks like a sock puppet on drugs. Now your art, it's truly inspired. I'm very humbled."

He glanced around at his work. "It's all *la luz*."

"*La* what?"

"*La luz*. It means the light. It's what drew me to the neon art. *La luz* makes the world brilliant and hopeful."

"That it does."

"But *la luz* isn't confined to neon."

"What'd you mean?"

"My wife, Anna, God rest her soul, had the same kind of light. I saw it when we first met. She used to illuminate rooms."

"*La luz*. It's magical."

He gave a nod.

"Frank, why haven't you remarried? You're funny, generous, attractive, and lots of other adjectives. And you're a very nice guy. Half the women in the leagues have a crush on you, to use the old vernacular."

"You don't say?" He grinned and ran a hand through his hair.

"Be serious and tell me. Please."

He went around his studio, his fingers touching lightly his neon art. "I haven't remarried because I've never met anyone with that same kind of light inside of her."

"Not even close?"

He stepped up to me. "Until now."

"Frank, I—" Tears glided down my cheeks.

He dotted my face with a handkerchief. "At the birthday party, remember what my mom said about the cactus blooming?"

"I remember."

His smile was as vivid as his artwork. "The cactus flowers bloomed the day I met you, Margarita."

He took both of my hands and held them, so softly I could feel the ridges of his fingerprints.

"Oh, God," he said.

"What?"

"You have a bowling callus."

I yanked him to me, kissed him hard, and fumbled at his pants.

"Frank, can you please turn off the lights?" I said between our kissing, which was great.

I didn't want him to see my poundage. He knew what I looked like, but not what I looked like without any clothes. He might change his mind and send me home in an Uber.

"No."

"Then close your eyes."

"No, thanks."

"Oh, what the hell." I slipped out of my summer dress. So what if he saw my Chihuahua pouch? I wanted this man.

We weren't young lovers tearing off each other's clothes, grabbing at each other. The naturalness of us together was profound. We made love on the futon in his art studio, lit by his amazing neon artwork. Way bohemian in my eyes.

When we kissed, I did feel beautiful, extra pounds and all.

I stopped worrying whether I might be out of practice. I concentrated on Frank. One touch of his hand and everything came rushing back. I became as electrified as his neon art and wanted to please him more than anything in the world. I couldn't recall the last time I'd desired such a thing, but it was definitely several presidents ago, as was the last time I climaxed. And son of a gun if I didn't.

"Was I yelling?" I asked after we fell back exhausted.

"I think so."

"Oh, hell."

"It's a good thing my mom can sleep through a thunderstorm."

I laughed and kissed him again.

When we first kissed, I felt Frank on my lips. After we made love, I felt him everywhere on my body. In my belly, on my breasts and between my legs. Under my nails. On my tongue.

Afterwards, all I could think about was my gratitude to the Egyptians for inventing the game that brought us together.

Chapter Twenty-Eight

I was a spy. I wore sunglasses although it was dark.

Outside of Bowlarama, Violet rounded us all up for a briefing. "We've got to check out the competition if we go to the city championships."

"Not if—when," Jo added.

Suze giggled.

"What?" Violet tapped her foot.

"Kinda exciting."

"Well, control yourself. We have a mission."

We entered the competing bowling alley. Five other older women all wearing sunglasses.

"Be nonchalant," Jo urged us.

"How? We all look like secret agents from a senior center," I said.

"And it's so damn dark in here I can't see anything with these glasses." Suze held her hand in front of her face, wiggling her fingers.

"Well, keep them on." Jo adjusted hers and bumped into a chair.

"They're going to recognize us." Bonnie took off her glasses and cleaned them on her T-shirt.

"No, they won't. There are too many people in here," Jo said.

"I still can't see." Suze took her glasses off.

"Whatever. Take them off and then spread out." Violet shrugged with annoyance.

The bowling alley was smaller than Cactus Lanes by ten lanes. The place was also darker and drearier without Frank's delightful neon artwork on its walls.

"This *is* crazy," Suze whispered to us.

"Way crazy," I volunteered.

"Yeah." Bonnie's usual smile was now an anxious one.

Violet's countenance continued to be stern, like Mr. Waverly in *The Man from U.N.C.L.E.* "Chickens."

"Cluck," Jo added.

"Then let's get it done and get the hell out of here." I pushed my sunglasses up.

The bowling alley was as busy as Cactus Lanes on league night. Packed and energetic. Teams focused on their play. While a bit nervous at being caught, I did receive a zzzt of electricity from the clandestine quest.

"Look, it's them." Violet pointed her chin at a team of women shooting practice balls in the middle of the alley.

Written on their bright red shirts was their name, THE LOIS LANES, with a small logo of the intrepid reporter from the comic books. On the back of their shirts was the name of their sponsor: JAKE'S BREWPUB. The five of them were cute and slender and looked to be in their late twenties and early thirties. They ordered up a pitcher of beer.

We picked a table in back where we could still see them, but we wouldn't be too obvious. At least for five women—some wearing sunglasses—staring at other bowlers.

"The toughest team you'll ever meet," Suze said quietly.

"Look for their weaknesses," Jo said. "That's what my husband suggested."

The Lois Lanes all strutted between frames and were loud. From their camaraderie, they appeared to be friends. Joking with each other and supporting one another when they took down all the pins. But such love wasn't a weakness because they bowled out of their heads. Most of the teammates threw strikes or spares. An open frame was rare.

"Oh shit." I couldn't help but say that.

"You're so right," Suze said.

"They *are* damn good bowlers." Bonnie's normal optimism snaked into dread.

While Bonnie, Suze, and I continued to observe the Lois Lanes, Jo and Violet checked out the league standings tacked on a bulletin board at the back of the alley.

We left after the Lois Lanes' second game, which they won by twenty pins. We met back at Corky's Diner to review our reconnaissance.

"Their bowlers averaged about 170 to 190," Jo said.

Bonnie grinned with hope. "That's about our speed."

"But they're also twenty to thirty years younger than me." I drank my iced tea and wished it came from Long Island.

Violet placed her hands flat on the table. She did so whenever she wanted to make a point. "We've probably bowled longer than any of those girls. Our experience has got to count for something. Right, Bonnie? You're the one always looking on the bright side."

"Wait. I'm thinking," she replied.

"Suze, you look scared," Jo said.

Suze crunched her teeth like they were Corn Nuts. "I wanted to win this year." Her voice was louder than usual, which struck us in awe. "Yes, I'm worried, but we have Miss Two Hundred and Five on our side."

I placed my hand on her shoulder. "I also want to win. Badly." The potential victory had come to symbolize my new life down at Cactus Lanes. I wanted that trophy and not only for the sake of the Bowling Broads. "I suggest we bowl more than once a week at league. We should set a time for another practice."

"Maggie's right," Violet said.

"Whoa. It's strange you agree with anybody," Jo said.

"Well, she is right."

We picked Sunday afternoon for a practice round.

"Here's to winning the city championship." Jo raised her glass of lemonade.

"We shall kick some serious ass. Namely Lois Lanes'," Violet said.

"As always, well spoken, Vi," Bonnie said

We all held up our glasses in salute. But I winced in pain. "Oh, my shoulders. Bowling is tough on them, but it's a small price."

"Try a cold pack," Jo offered.

"No, a hot water bottle," Bonnie said.

"Two Tylenol," Suze said.

"The best thing is a vodka tonic." Violet gave a smile. She was quite attractive when she smiled.

The table quieted and the women looked to each other and then at me. They all grinned.

"You only sore from bowling? Maybe you strained yourself some other way." Jo's voice lilted.

"What are you talking about?" I *knew* what Jo was hinting at and it was a downright wonder my teammates hadn't brought up the topic before now. I was positive they knew why I was smiling.

The night in his studio. Our first time.

As much as I was tempted to sprint around and share the news with everyone in the diner like a herald of senior sex, what we did was ours alone. I inadvertently sighed.

"Well," Jo said.

"Maggie, come on." Violet leaned on one hand.

"We want details, girl," Bonnie said.

"All those spicy Latin details," Suze said. "Perm our hair with the details."

"Lots o' details," Violet grinned.

"How do you even know what you think you know?"

"Because you bowl like crazy when he's in the vicinity," Jo said.

"You girls want anything to eat?" said an older server.

"Not now. We're ready to hear about a passionate affair. I hope so, anyway," Violet said.

"I'd love to hear about that, but I have other customers. I'll come back later." The server smiled and left us.

My cheeks heated. I'd never been in this position. Talking to friends about sleeping with a man. How wonderful to have friends. How wonderful to sleep with Frank.

"Welllllll."

Jo slapped her hands together. "I knew it. I knew it."

"I've always thought Frank was so handsome," Bonnie said dreamily.

"Oh yeah," Suze said.

"Like Ricardo Montalbán handsome."

"An older version," Violet added, crunching on the ice from her soda.

"Hey, we're all older," Jo said. "So?" Her eyebrows danced up and down begging me for information.

I tried to sound stern as a pastor and kept my smile at bay. "I'm not telling you one single thing. It's very private."

"At least tell us how he kisses," Bonnie said.

"Pleeeeeeeeeasssse," Suze whined.

All four leaned in.

A smile broke out. "I will say this. My lips are supremely happy."

"Well, how about the rest of you?" Violet said.

I blushed and they laughed. The waitress returned and we ordered our food.

Bonnie sat back. "Makes me think of my honeymoon."

"Or fantasies of kissing James Dean. He had the nicest lips." Wistfulness coated Suze's words.

"Charles Bronson," Violet said.

"Bronson?"

"That sounds like you," Jo added. To me, she winked. "See, I was right. You may be a widow, but you aren't dead."

"And I'm eternally grateful." I kissed Jo's cheek and turned to my teammates. "There's so much to look forward to."

"Senior citizen discounts at restaurants? Guys in their seventies who still think we're hot babes?" Bonnie grinned.

"Know what I'm looking forward to? More time with you, my friends." I touched each of their hands.

"And Frank," Jo said.

"Most definitely, Frank."

Now *this* was a *Lifetime* movie, I thought as I walked to Bob's grave.

A widow beginning a new life says goodbye to her dead husband. I'd probably even seen such a movie on the network. But from wherever I got the idea, it was a good one.

There was another, more psychological and emotional word for it.

Closure.

Since he'd died, I'd visited his grave only once, to bring flowers for Memorial Day at Kyla's insistence. With my hand on her shoulder, my daughter wept. No tears from me for Bob's memory.

But that morning I decided to go for the sake of ending this particular part of my life. So I left early before the Vegas heat turned up like the inside of a microwave. The sprinklers had probably run even earlier because my exposed sandaled toes were wet. I didn't bring flowers because Bob had never been a flowery kind of man. He tolerated my garden and asked me not to bring any blooms inside because of his allergies. Apparently, his allergies didn't include grass because he continued golfing.

His place of rest was serene, but then all cemeteries were serene. His stone was simple with his name, date of birth, and death, and the etched figure of man in the midst of a full golf swing. Kyla had picked it out.

Looking around, I sighed. Despite the green, how desolate it was out there. I decided right there to be cremated and my ashes spread about so I wouldn't end up in a similar quiet, lonely spot.

Because of the time of day, no other mourners were out. I was grateful since closure was a private affair, not to mention it would be bordering on embarrassing if anyone saw me talking to a grave.

"Hello, Bob." His spirit was elsewhere I was sure, but I could be wrong. "I wanted to come and say goodbye." A cemetery worker drove by and didn't even turn his head toward me. He was probably used to the sight of the living talking to the dead.

"I should have been honest with you, but I wasn't, and I apologize. If I had been, it might have been better for both of us. Apart, yes, but better. I do appreciate what you left me, with the house and money, though I wish it had included more of yourself. We could have been friends at least."

I waited momentarily for some spiritual sign from Bob and shook my head. Margaret, you *have* watched too many movies.

"So, why'd I come out here? Good question. I'm in love with another man. With him I'm everything I should have been with you. I guess I wanted you to hear it from me. And one more thing, after today, I won't think of you anymore."

I realized someone was watching me. An older woman stood in front of a grave behind Bob's. The woman nodded and smiled.

"Closure is a bitch," she said.

Chapter Twenty-Nine

Through no choice of my own I had returned to the Clearview Country Club, and it was exactly as I remembered.

Hades in green.

Kyla asked me to go back there, and I went. I couldn't overpower the guilt I felt about lying to my daughter. Guilt about hiding my total joy with Frank and bowling. So, I wanted to please her by going to the place she loved.

Mike was there with me, so hell was at least a little more palatable.

A few days before, I'd mentioned to Kyla that Mike was going to be visiting and she suggested we all go golfing.

"You know how he feels about the game, Kyla."

"I'll talk to him."

She had replied so sweetly I had a feeling something was up with my daughter.

To my surprise, Mike agreed. He and Kyla hadn't spent time with each other in several months, even when he came to see me. They said they texted and Facetimed each other, whatever the heck that was. Their distance as siblings was another notch in my guilt belt. When you're a mom you take credit for your children's goodness, but you'll also bear all the shame for when they behave badly.

Mike had picked me up and we were meeting Kyla at the course.

"I thought you hated golfing, son."

"I wasn't about to leave you alone out here with her." He tapped the steering wheel. "We both know she is overwhelming and narrow-minded."

My silence agreed with him.

As we drove up, Kyla was talking with other female golfers. They all wore variations of the same outfit. A short athletic skirt and polo shirt, all very high end. Meanwhile, Mike sported roughed up khaki shorts and a T-shirt with one word on it: VOTE. His sister pursed her lips at the outfit.

"Mike, I still can't believe you're golfing with us," she said.

"I can't believe it either."

"It's going to be you and your brother playing. I donated my clubs about thirty years ago to a thrift store." I was quite happy about that.

"We'll rent you a set."

"No, thanks. I'll watch. It'll be fun to hang out with you two." Even if it was at the golf course. "Afterward, we'll grab lunch."

Discretely, I widened my eyes at Mike as if to say, "See? I can handle myself."

"You and mom ride in the cart. I'll walk." Mike put on his

baseball cap. At the first hole, he slammed the ball down the fairway.

"When was the last time you played?" Kyla asked her brother, not hiding the admiration at his skills.

"When I told dad I was quitting the game." He smiled. "I had to borrow these clubs and bag from a friend of mine."

Her shot was not as successful.

"I'm worried about Mom." Kyla drove the cart slowly to the next hole as Mike walked along side.

"I'm sitting right here, Kyla. I know you worry but you don't have to. Please, stop."

"I have to tell you this, Mom. It was Kyla's idea for me to visit. She wanted to talk about you. Although I could have done without the golf, sis." Mike whacked another shot and was on the green in two.

"I feel I'm being ambushed, and I don't like it." I clenched my hands together on my lap.

"Since you're involved, you need to hear what she's saying. And what are you saying other than you're worried about Mom, Kyla?"

"Mike, she's never home. She's become secretive. She never answers her phone. She even got a makeover and new hairdo."

"Oh, no." He feigned terror. "Not a makeover."

"I'm not a child or decrepit, Kyla."

"Then what's going on with you, Mom?"

Kyla's shot was crap. Her poor play wasn't all due to her concern about me. Regrettably, she just wasn't a good golfer. Despite hundreds of dollars' worth of lessons, she hovered at mediocrity. I sensed Kyla was also angry Mike had always been a natural at the game she longed to conquer.

Her father's game.

But Kyla was right. Something was going on with me, though I wasn't about to tell her what it was.

Mike lowered his voice. "Maybe Mom's joined the CIA. A pleasant woman like her, no one would suspect she's become a specialist in death."

"You're so funny I forgot to laugh," Kyla said.

He drew in a quick breath.

"What?"

"You used to say the exact same thing when we were kids. That means you haven't matured this much, sis." Mike held thumb and forefinger close together.

Kyla slugged his arm.

"Kyla. Mike. Stop."

At the fourth hole, Mike hit another superb shot. Kyla's limped along.

"I'll tell you what's happening with me, kids. I'm happy, so why not be happy for me?"

"You weren't happy before." Kyla bit her lips. "Hold on, I didn't mean that."

I was never going to win this but had to try. "I'm moving on with life, Kyla. I volunteer. I take a pottery class. I'm getting ready to sell the house."

"See what I mean?" Kyla could have crushed the golf ball she held.

"If this is the reason you invited me to come play with you, Kyla, we could've had lunch somewhere else so I wouldn't be subjected to this sport," Mike said.

As usual on the next hole, his shot was first rate while Kyla struggled.

"I wanted you to meet me here because I need practice for the women's league championship next week, so I thought I could get in a round and spend it with my family. What a win-win."

Mike and I looked at each other. Kyla was lying. We could tell because her voice took on a sing-song lilt whenever she did.

"Well, Mike, what about Mom?"

He looked at me and smiled.

"Quit worrying about her. She looks great and she's happy. That's enough for me."

"Mom lost her husband of more than thirty years. She shouldn't be cheerful. Whenever she comes to my house for dinner, she's happy."

"For God's sake, Kyla. It's been more than a year. How the hell should she look?"

"Hey, I'm right here, guys."

"Introspective, devastated. Grief-stricken." Kyla was almost in tears.

Her chip went awry.

"Missed," he said.

"Let's see if you do any better, show-off," she challenged.

He certainly did. His ball ended up six inches from the hole.

"I don't know how you're playing so well. You don't even golf anymore."

Mike shrugged. "It's a gift."

Kyla drove the cart to the next hole. Mike walked on his sister's side. "We both know things weren't the greatest for

Mom when Dad was alive. But Mom hid it away from us." He seized his bag's handle.

"Shut up. He was a good man." Kyla ended up taking five strokes to even get close to the hole.

Mike shook his head. "You were—and still are—blind when it comes to Dad. You were his princess and he was our king. But he was also very human."

"Mike, Kyla, enough."

"Quit insulting Dad, Mike. I won't have it."

"I'm not insulting him. I'm remembering him as he was. Not the easiest guy to live with, when he was even home, which wasn't a lot. Fess up to it, Kyla. You'll have to open your eyes sooner or later."

I smiled at my son. I *was* going to tell him everything. About Frank. About bowling. But later.

"We're talking about Mom, not Dad," Kyla said.

"Please lift the flag."

Kyla did.

"Mom even looks ten years younger. What do you want her to do? Wear sack cloth and cigarette ashes?" He tapped the ball in. "She's not going to find happiness at home. She's going to have to get out and find it."

"It's my job to worry about her." Kyla missed her first putt.

"No, it's not. I'll let you know when it's time to worry," I added.

Mike took his turn. "Mom's getting a life of her own and it's about damn time." He raised his putter and pointed it at his sister. "And if you try to rob her of that, sister or not, I will wrap this fucking club around your neck." He spoke with deliberation and straightened so he stood even taller than Kyla.

My mouth parched with their hostility. "We need to quit." The split between them had widened to Grand Canyon proportions over seven holes of golf.

Kyla took three tries to sink the ball. "I hate it when you use that word."

"What? Fuck?" He grinned and she grimaced.

"Why do people love saying it?"

"Because sometimes fuck is the best word to use," I said.

"Mom!"

Mike laughed.

At the eighth hole, Kyla teed up and was about to swing. She stopped and glanced at me. "Maybe Mom's having a mental breakdown. The stress of Dad's death is too much for her."

"Please shoot," Mike and I both told her.

She swung and her ball hopped in the air and dropped a little ways from them. "Darn it."

"Want a Mulligan?" he said.

"Quit patronizing me, Mike."

"I'm asking about a Mulligan."

"I don't want one."

"Suit yourself." Mike's ball took off straight and landed two hundred yards away.

Kyla dug her spikes into the grass. Conversations with her brother had always followed this route. As if they stood on opposite sides of the universe and tried to talk to each other over a string tied to two tin cans.

"Even in high school, you disapproved of me, of my

friends, of my life. You called us spoiled and self-centered." She drove her ball.

"I haven't seen much change in you since then," Mike said snidely.

"Kyla, I am doing fine. I'm out in the world. I'm not sitting in the house all day and being depressed. I'd like for you two to quit this arguing right now."

"I'm with you, Mom." Mike chipped the ball onto the green and it rolled to about one foot of the hole.

Kyla removed the flag. "Mom has always seemed vulnerable."

"You talking about our mother? The woman who raised you and me?"

"Yes. Vulnerable."

Mike shook his head hard. Kyla took four putts to get even close. She groaned with each bad putt. She threw down her club.

Other golfers stared at us. Mike and Kyla weren't yelling but their words were clipped as the grass.

"You guys going to play or talk?" yelled a golfer behind us.

Kyla and Mike turned around. Two older men leaned on clubs. From country club dinners, I recognized them as retired neurosurgeons. Kyla picked up the club and putted in.

We reached the ninth hole.

"I'm always sad to play this hole. I close my eyes and see Dad on the ground." Kyla sniffed back tears.

Mike raised his head with a thought. "Wait a second. You play on leagues at least twice a week, Kyla."

"Well, yeah, but it's still hard."

He wiped a hand over his eyes in obvious annoyance. He shot another good hit.

"She's acting weird, Mike."

"According to your standards."

"What do you mean?"

"Follow me." He headed toward a tree off the ninth-hole tee box.

"What about our game?"

"Fuck that."

Kyla gnashed teeth and followed. She got out of the cart. "What are you talking about? What do you mean, my standards?"

"You always want people to be perfect, Kyla." He set his bag down on the grass. "Dad was the same damn way. He drummed that shit into your brain, and you accepted it as truth."

"Come on, guys." One of the two old neurosurgeons leaned on his club.

"Play through." I waved them on. They shrugged and went to the tee box.

"Kyla, you can't abide people with flaws. You hate flaws. But dammit, people aren't perfect. We're defective as hell. You, me, Dad, and Mom."

"What's wrong with wanting everything—"

"What? Perfect? Your attitude makes you as unwieldly as an iron pipe. I'm surprised you can even walk." Removing his cap, he wiped his forehead with a handkerchief.

"What a terrible thing to say."

"But it's true." His breath sizzled like a deflating tire. "Remember my ex-girlfriend?"

"Theresa?"

"Corrine."

"I forgot her name because you never talked about her very much. How could I be expected to remember her name?"

"Know why I never brought her home to meet the family? Know why I loved her but kept her away?"

I put my head down. He was going to be truthful with his sister at last.

"I wondered about that. Were you ashamed of her or something?"

"She was Black."

Kyla smiled. "So you were ashamed."

I rarely saw my son angry, but at that moment I swore smoke rose from the top of his head. Thankfully, his anger dissolved quickly. His eyes went darker, and he sighed as if the air in his body had been replaced with something else.

Disappointment at his sister. Pity for her even.

"I loved Corrine very much, but I couldn't bring her home because I worried about how you and Dad might treat her."

I should have said something, but all I could do was agree with Mike, so I shut the hell up.

"I'm not prejudiced, and neither was Dad." Kyla stamped her left foot for good measure.

"You and Dad weren't exactly the welcome wagon, either though. At least to anyone who didn't look how you think they should look. The older Dad got, the worse he became."

Kyla shoved her club back into her bag. "You're lying."

"I heard Dad talk about Black people and Hispanic people. Muslims. Jews. Gays. Democrats. Environmentalists. It made my skin crinkle and crawl. Mom's too. And you're sounding just like him."

I lowered my head so Kyla couldn't see his truth in my eyes. But she had to so I looked at her.

"And you are either rude or patronizing to Consuela," Mike said.

"I *have* mentioned many times how you treat her, Kyla," I added.

"But I like Consuela."

"You have a damn poor way of showing it. Kyla. Do you even know the definition of prejudice?" He gripped his club.

"You don't have to be any more insulting than you already are. I *know* what it means."

Mike pushed his baseball cap back. "I'm going to tell you anyway. It means having a preconceived opinion not based on any rhyme or reason. And that's you all over, baby sister."

"No, it's not."

"And that's the problem. You can't even see it. There was a time you used to be fun and ready to give anything a try. Your mind was slightly open. What happened to you?"

Her mouth twitched but she set it firm. "I grew up."

Mike took off his golf glove and picked up his bag from the ground. "I'm done with this."

"Sorry, Kyla. But I'm through with this game too," I said.

"Mom, don't believe anything he's saying."

"Honey, I love you and I'll call you later."

Mike and I started toward the clubhouse and his car.

"Wait." Kyla ran up to us.

Her eyelashes fluttered helplessly as if she wanted to say

something. How I prayed it would be an acknowledgment of her brother's words. That would be a first step.

Instead, she held her golf club tight.

"I don't understand, Mike. I've had lessons and belong to two woman's leagues. But my handicap is average. You never play and you come off like Arnold Palmer. How come?"

"Because you try too damn hard to be perfect. Come on, Mom. Let's go have sushi."

I turned to watch my daughter standing there. Her mouth trembled and she appeared ready to cry. She might have finally got the message. If she had said she was sorry I would have galloped back to her. Instead, she got in her cart and drove to the tee box to play the ninth hole where her father had died.

Chapter Thirty

Frank applauded the Bowling Broads as we wrapped up three extra practice games.

"You gals rolled well today. I think you're going to give 'em hell at the city tournament."

We all bowed.

"And I respect your dedication coming in on Sunday."

"We're going to show those Lois Lanes out the door," Bonnie said.

"Yeah, out the door," added Suze.

"And thanks for the pointers to sharpen our games, Frank," Jo said.

"We like those pointers, right, Maggie?" Violet nudged me, plying on a sly smile.

My cheeks heated with embarrassment and the rest of my body warmed thinking about Frank.

"If you're free, I'd love to take you all out for dinner," he told us as we packed our equipment.

"I was born free," Jo said.

"You bet," Violet said.

"And not Corky's Diner," he insisted.

Instead, he treated us to dinner at the Italian place where he and I had first gone and returned several times. It became our place. How great to have an *our* place. We all laughed, drank wine, and enjoyed good pasta served by people not on roller skates.

"So what do you really think our chances are this year, Frank?" Suze said.

"Let me put it this way, I foresee all your names on that trophy." He looked directly at me.

"I have that vision too." Violet's smile emanated certainty.

"I *have* seen the Lois Lanes roll, though. They are tough," he admitted.

"Yeah, we scouted them," Bonnie said.

The other teammates glared at her.

"What'd I do?"

"Nothing in the city tournament rules says you can't check out the competition," Frank said. "But whatever you do, don't deflate their tires or put glue in the holes of their bowling balls on the day of the tourney."

Violet smiled. "What a fantastic idea, Frank."

He narrowed eyes at her.

"Just kidding."

Watching Frank and these women, I marveled at the number of years I'd spent alone. What a fool. What a damn fool.

Following dinner, I invited him back to my home. Four times a week, we met there or at his house and already I wished it were more. We ended up in bed. Each time we loved each other, I wanted to seal that slice of time, place it in a pretty box, and keep it for later. How he smelled of good cologne and oil from the bowling alley. The shocking tenderness. The illumination from his neon art in my bedroom. The way his bed creaked when we moved. How we'd watch an old movie afterward, hugging each other, and eating popcorn—my favorite—or chicharrónes with hot sauce – his favorite.

I hoped to carry those images with me always, like an extra rib.

Usually, we took our time undressing each other or ourselves before making love. That Sunday night was different. As soon as I opened the door to my house and locked it behind us, I started undoing his shirt buttons, even ripping one off. He sucked in air and tugged off my shirt. We were almost naked by the time we got to my bedroom upstairs.

———

We lay back on the pillows.

"Wow, what got into you, woman?"

"Must have been the fettucine Alfredo. I should have asked to bring home the leftovers, dammit."

"That pasta must have set a fire in you." He kissed my nose. "You even ripped buttons off my shirt."

"How very *The Notebook* of me."

"I'm thinking more like *Nine and a Half Weeks*."

"You're Mickey Rourke, I'm Kim Basinger, right? Not the other way round."

He laughed. "Right. What we did was incredible, not to mention we didn't break a hip in the process."

"I'm sorry about your buttons. I'll sew them back on."

We held onto each other. I took his hand and nestled close to him. "With you beside me, Frank, this house isn't so cold and impersonal as a hotel. I don't think I'll ever be cold again."

"I'll tell you something, Maggie. In the morning, I look in the mirror now and wonder who's that man staring back at me? I swear you've given me some of your light."

I had no words for how that touched me.

He glanced around the bedroom, which was larger than his living room and dining room together.

"Your house is gigantic. When I first delivered your neon, I had to admit I was intimidated because it belongs in one of those house beautiful magazines. I asked myself, 'What interest does this woman have in me? Maybe she wants to keep me like a gigolo.'" He smiled. "I thought I'd probably have to dye my hair."

I sat up. "I married into wealth, Frank. My family wasn't poor. We had what we needed but nothing like this. When you go from not having money to having lots, it throws you off balance, at least it did me. I never knew where I belonged, and I've felt that all my life."

"Like you don't feel at home?"

He sat up also and embraced me. "My mom once told me a home is not a building, but any place with your family and the people you love." He raised my chin to kiss me. "And you're home now, Maggie."

This was five hundred times better than any damn *Lifetime* movie.

"You don't realize how special you are, Frank."

Now, he blushed and I kissed him. "*Besar*. To kiss."

"I didn't know you spoke Spanish."

"I'm learning. I downloaded an app a few weeks back and I'm a real beginner in the worst sense of the word."

"Why do you want to learn?"

I placed my head on his chest. "I love the way you and your mom talk to each other in Spanish. So intimate. I wanted some of your intimacy, too."

"Let me hear something."

I cleared my throat. "Here goes. *Como pollo. Bebo agua. ¿Dónde están mis zapatos?*" I concentrated on each word.

He laughed. My accent was flat and animated as a stone.

"Bad, huh?"

"All you've learned is 'I eat chicken. I drink water. Where are my shoes?'"

I laughed and fell back on the pillow. "God, it is tragic. Frank, you taught me bowling. Teach me some Spanish, please. You're an excellent teacher after all."

His chest rumbled as he thought. "Very well, and I won't even charge you for lessons this time."

"I'm ready, teacher."

"*El maestro.*"

"What?"

"It means teacher."

"Very appropriate."

"Let's start with *me gustas*."

I repeated it twice. "What's it mean?"

"I like you."

"How do you say, 'also?'"

"*También*."

I placed my hand in his. "*Me gustas, también*. Come on, more."

"*Me gustas mucho*."

I repeated it. "Meaning?"

"I really like you."

I placed his hand on my breast. His warmth was startling. I had a difficult time focusing on Spanish.

"*Me gustas mucho, también*."

"*Bien*."

"I took a semester of Spanish in high school but all I learned to say was 'Where is the library?' I like these lessons much better."

Frank kissed me. "Here's one more. *Te quiero*, Margarita."

"*Te quiero tambien*." I kissed him hard on the lips. "I think I know what that means."

"You better."

Chapter Thirty-One

Jo and I stood back and admired our work decorating Cactus Lanes for Halloween. Paper ghosts, witches, jack o'lanterns. We smothered the place with them, as well as Day of the Dead decorations. Paper banners with cutouts of skulls and skeleton figures in fancy suits, dresses, and hats. Orange and purple lights hung over the lunch counter and from the ceiling.

But this felt more like Christmas.

"Shows how much you can accomplish with a little crêpe paper, plastic pumpkins, and skeletons. It looks great," I said.

"Halloween's our busiest night and the most fun. After the leagues, we have midnight bowling, a costume contest, and a dance. Got a costume yet?"

"Frank and I have something planned."

"Ahhh."

"We're very good friends." I couldn't look Jo in the eye.

"Maggie, you're lying."

I hugged Jo.

"Hey, I'm not Frank." Jo held me back and stared at me. "Holy shit, you love him."

I wanted to shout it on the intercom. "My first time."

She touched my arm. "Weren't you married for like thirty some years?"

"That was marriage. This is way different."

"Then I'm happy for you and Frank."

"And it's so easy."

"It usually is. The hard part is afterward."

"I'm not going to think about the future. I'll concentrate on the time we're together."

"Good thinking then."

I hugged her for good measure.

Back at home, I changed into my costume. A fiery red flamenco dancer outfit splashed with black polka dots. I felt a little sexy wearing black stockings, although my legs were way heavier than Rita Hayworth's. Thank God, black downplayed the size of my thighs.

"*Olé.*" I clicked my fingers as I looked in the mirror and laughed.

When I returned for leagues, Cactus Lanes was festive with laughter and lightness. The world outside didn't even exist.

How fun to check out the costumes and the creativity that went into them, from traditional witches to two guys who dressed as the twin sisters from *The Shining*, complete with wigs, blue dresses, and pink ribbon around their waists. They held hands and kept telling players to "Come play with us" in creepy British accents. Not to mention lots of characters from Star Wars, Star Trek, and *The Big Lebowski* film, which I loved. Frank was also a fan of the movie, which made me even more wild about him. We laughed at the number of Dudes running around in bathrobes and plastic sandals.

Our team was going to be colorful out on the lanes. Jo dressed as a Viking warrior, wearing a horned helmet, yellow braids, and armored chest plate. The costume was all wrong according to the *History Channel*, but I wasn't going to tell her.

Bonnie came as the witch from the *Wizard of Oz*. Her green face menacing and cute at the same time. Suze, not surprising, dressed as a princess in pink. And Violet reigned as the Queen of Hearts.

Bowling in my costume proved tough. I had to remove the flowing black lace mantilla on my head because it kept sweeping in front when I tried to throw the ball. The flounces on the bottom of the dress allowed me to move but I was down a few pins from my average. I wasn't alone here. Anyone wearing long costumes struggled to throw the ball and not fall down on the lanes.

On the sixth frame of the first game, I threw and knocked down all but eight. My second ball took down the rest for a spare.

"So close to an open frame, *señorita*," Violet said.

"Whew."

We played poker in between our turns. While Jo bowled, I sat at the table near the lanes and picked up my cards. "So, I get one card for the spare, right?"

"Right," said the Wicked Witch of the West.

I picked one up from the pile.

"Now it's regular poker," Suze the princess said.

Jo returned and threw a quarter in the pot. "No spare, darn it. And this Viking armor is chafing my underarms."

I studied my hand. "You know this is the first time I've played poker."

"What kind of upbringing did you have, girl?" Violet said.

"Apparently, a poor one."

Suze returned to the table from throwing. "You're up, Maggie."

I tossed a killer strike, returned to the table, and selected two cards. Forget the poker face. I grinned. "Call."

"What?" Violet asked.

"Come on."

Violet put in a quarter. "Bet you're bluffing."

Bonnie and Jo folded. Suze smiled. "I also believe you have nothing, Maggie."

"Four of a kind." I placed down my cards.

The other women moaned.

"There's nothing I hate worse than beginner's luck," Jo said as she left to bowl.

I gave an exaggerated cackle as I swept the pot of coins toward me. "All minnnneee!"

The Queen of Hearts rolled a strike. "Her Majesty is happy."

The rest of the team all curtsied and laughed. Come to think of it, I laughed a lot throughout the night.

The Bowling Broads took all three games.

"One step closer to winning the leagues." Jo put away her equipment.

"Victory within our mitts." I reattached the rose and mantilla to my hair.

Frank joined us. Dressed as Zorro, he glanced up at the telescore. "Good going, ladies."

"Are you Batman?" Bonnie said.

Frank flourished his cape. "Zorro. A do-gooder and generally all-around good guy, except I couldn't see with my mask when I was bowling."

"More like the kissing bandit." Suze said and pursed her lips.

"You wish." Jo bumped me with a hip.

"Did your team win?" I asked Frank.

"Two out of three, but one of our guys couldn't make it tonight. He took his kids trick or treating, so we had a sub. And you should be proud, ladies. Taking the top spot in the first half of the season. My money is on you to take the city championship this year, too."

"The trophy will look very nice at Cactus Lanes," Bonnie said.

"Still got to beat those damn Lois Lanes." Violet adjusted her crown.

"You're always so negative," Suze said.

"I'm realistic."

"Not worried at all. We're all bowling well, especially Maggie," Bonnie said.

"You shouldn't give me all the credit."

"Yes, we should."

With the leagues over, the lights lowered, and rock music started up.

"Now we party," Jo said.

Most of the league players hung around and were joined by other people who had stopped by for the happy hour at the bar, and the dinner special of burger and chili fries. Frank had hired a DJ to play tunes and requested a lot of rock 'n' roll classics. Bowlers could play until two in the morning trying to knock down glow-in-the-dark pins as the lights were lowered out on the lanes.

With a flourish of his cape, Frank held out his arm to me. "How about a dance, *señorita*?"

"I'd love to."

———————

After an hour, Suze had to leave for another party with her husband. She took Bonnie and Violet with them.

"Be good, you two," Suze said.

Jo winked. "If they're lucky." She joined her husband Greg, a thin guy with a tremendously catchy smile who was also dressed like a Viking.

A space had been cleared for dancing to the right of the snack bar, and a disco ball had been hung by Ernie, who danced with his wife, Linda.

"I love your costume," I told her.

She was dressed as a female pirate. Ernie was Captain Jack Sparrow.

"Yours is cute, too."

"How about me?" Ernie said.

I nodded with approval. "Better than Johnny Depp."

"Just a little heftier," Linda said.

"Hey," Ernie protested.

Linda kissed him. "He did balk at putting on the black eyeliner."

Ernie sized up Frank. "I do believe Captain Sparrow could kick Zorro's ass."

"Dream on, bro. And besides, I'm not the one wearing eye makeup."

Linda and I laughed. Frank and I had gone out with her and Ernie last week for dinner and a movie. The men loved any film based on a Tom Clancy book, while Linda and I tolerated it. Through the evening, Ernie and Linda made verbal jabs at each other, but with so much love. They were more than the salt of the earth. They were the crust and magma too. A joy to spend time with.

After our first double date, I had asked Frank if Ernie liked me. "He seems very suspicious of me and he's very protective of you."

"Yes, he likes you. Sometimes, though, I'm not sure he even likes me," Frank had replied.

"Well, Ernie loves you like a brother. It's all over him."

In the last few months, however, Ernie's look of suspicion had disappeared, which I tallied as a win.

Frank danced me off to the side.

"You do look very dashing, Frank."

"You're gorgeous."

My cheeks felt like hot rolls coming out of the oven.

He swayed his cape. "I always thought of Zorro as the Batman of old California. All he needed was a sidekick named Robinito."

"Well, if you're the Latino Batman call me Vicki Valencia."

He laughed. "Very good."

"I have my moments."

His neon artwork emitted softened light on the couples dancing close in the darkened bowling alley. Inspiration struck me.

"Frank, you know how I love your art. Well, I'm certain other people would love it too. What do you think about holding an art show, right here? We'll publicize it and even have music and food."

"An art show?"

"It'd bring more people into Cactus Lanes and spotlight your talent."

"They're that good?"

"Absolutely."

"Let me think about it."

"Whenever you're ready. I'll even plan it." Ideas zipped about in my mind like loose ping-pong balls.

He kissed my cheek.

"Not that I'm complaining but what did I do to deserve that?"

"For having cool ideas, my *hermosa* Vicki Valencia."

"*Hermosa*?" I tried to say it as he did.

"Beautiful."

"There was a window of time in high school when I was. I had the thickest hair back then. Smaller waist. Perkier boobs. Now, I'll settle for acceptable."

"I hate it when you put yourself down. You don't understand how beautiful you are. It emanates from in here." He pointed to my heart. "*La luz.*"

"When you say it, I can almost feel that shine inside me."

"Margarita, you've blossomed like the flowers on my cactus plants."

I stopped dancing and kissed him hard on the lips. I heard music and my heart. Then I placed my head on his shoulder.

"I'm scared when the clock strikes midnight this whole

thing will fade away like a magic pumpkin and I'll turn back into the old Margaret." I said this so quietly I wasn't sure if he'd heard.

"It doesn't have to. We should move in together."

I raised my head.

"Why waste time when it's so precious?"

The minutes, hours, and days *had* become treasures to me and all because of Cactus Lanes. Because of the Bowling Broads. And chiefly because of Frank.

"Think about it." A whisper in my ear.

"I promise." I kissed him.

After a few more drinks and laughing at the party, I went to the restroom. For the tournament, Frank had had it remodeled, and it was clean and bright. Alone in the bathroom, I examined myself in the mirror. Move in with Frank. Get a new life. Become the person I always wanted to be. A new home with Frank and at Cactus Lanes. But as I washed my hands, they were trembling. I had stepped into an explosion of frigid air. Above me, happiness teetered on top of Mount Everest, and I didn't know whether I could make the climb.

The party ended at two and Frank and I were both too exhausted to sleep over at each other's house.

We kissed goodbye outside of Cactus Lanes.

"Think about what I said, Maggie."

"I will."

He drove away and I stopped to look at the cactus plants.

They weren't blooming but appeared spiky and bleak in the night.

At home, I swayed up to the bedroom as if I were drunk. I checked my cell phone. Frank had called.

"I love you, Maggie."

I held onto the phone and replayed the message twice.

The real estate guy I had met with about selling the house had also left a message. He was ready to take it to the next level, or so he said, and asked that I call him. Kyla also called, inviting me to dinner next week. She had wanted me to go with her to a Halloween party at the country club that evening, but after the ordeal with her and Mike, I couldn't return there. For the week following the argument at the golf course, Kyla hadn't called to check on me nor had she returned my calls, which was a record for my daughter. I worried she was punishing me for siding with her brother.

Removing my costume, I got ready for bed. Under the covers, I couldn't sleep. Frank's neon sculpture lit the room as did his proposal we live together. If I did move in with him, I could finally have what I wanted. To be with a man who I loved and who loved me. To have a home.

But instead of a wave of music, flowers, and perfume spicing up the air, his proposal set off shudders in my chest that radiated throughout my body. I'd read the old cliché in books about how it feels if your heart might explode. Well, that hackneyed description was absolutely goddamn true. My heart was an implosion of plastic explosive.

For almost one year, I'd been free of panic attacks and now one returned with reinforcements. All those wonderful changes over the past eleven months, the bowling, new friends, volunteering.

Frank.

I'd become strong and brave—hadn't I?

I thought about how I used to identify with Brooks Hatlen in *The Shawshank Redemption* whenever I watched the movie on TV. How he became institutionalized after so many years imprisoned. When he finally got out, he killed himself because he couldn't make it on the outside.

Now here was the chance to step away from my Shawshank.

The decision to move in with Frank was the first test of whether all that change was deep, or as surface as scum floating on bath water. But my gut dropped to the basement. Any fearlessness I held was going down the tube. I could hardly hold on to a breath over such a mondo step to substantially upheave my life.

On the bed table was the card of the real estate guy. I dropped it on the carpet and then ran to the bathroom and threw up.

Chapter Thirty-Two

When I came into the kitchen carrying a bag of groceries, Kyla sat at the table. She was the last person I expected to see that morning. But I welcomed her visit. Despite our differences, she was familiar.

"Good to see you, honey."

She didn't say anything. She appeared harder than the marble countertops. Her lips were a thin pink line, which couldn't be good.

"I didn't see your car." I tried to sound cheery but she appeared ready to drop a ten-megaton bomb.

"Jerome dropped me off. We need to talk."

After placing the bag on the counter, I kissed Kyla's cheek, but she was stiff as a corpse dipped in bronze. We hadn't spent any mother-daughter time together lately. I'd been very selfish. "Let me fix you some lunch ... or do you want to go out? We haven't done that in a while. It'll be fun. We could even get pedicures." Anything not to decide my fate. To take that test. "Maybe we can go to a movie."

"I'm not hungry and I don't want a pedicure or go to the movies." Kyla threw out the words like grenades.

Hell. Here comes the bomb.

On the table, she set out a folded newspaper. An open sports page. I picked it up.

Cactus Lanes

Wednesday City Leagues

Bowling Broads

Margaret Adams—high average 200

Margaret Adams—high series 564

"You're a bowling broad." Her teeth were cemented in disapproval.

I wanted to laugh. "You make it sound like I'm shooting heroin."

"Are you?"

"Kyla, come on."

"You lied to us. You lied about bowling."

"You're right. I wasn't honest with you—at all."

"How long?"

"For almost a year." Not a record for me, however. I've held on to other secrets way way longer.

Standing up, she paced the kitchen. "And the way I found out..."

"How?"

"Yesterday, I was shopping for a dress, and I ran into Gina Southward."

Gina was the wife of a plastic surgeon, which meant she lay beyond even Kyla's dreams of wealth, and Kyla could dream a lot. Gina had a seat on the boards of the Clearview Country Club, symphony, and the library, and never let anyone forget about any of those positions. Compared to Gina's house, Kyla's was a double-wide.

Damn Gina Southward.

"Gina said her husband read the funniest thing in the paper that morning, something about you, Mom."

My toes turned numb.

"'So your mom's a bowler. How hilarious,' she told me."

Strangely, Kyla replicated Gina's lilting voice of superiority perfectly.

"Then Gina laughed and said, 'I could understand tennis or golf, but bowling?' I told her my dad's death had hit you harder than you realized. I tried to cover up the fact I had no idea what you were up to and that it made me feel stupid."

Kyla hadn't defended me at all. I hoped she would, but I couldn't blame her after all my deceptions.

"So Gina said, 'Give your mom my regards. If she's not too busy on her bowling night.' Then she laughed at us. I was mortified."

My daughter's cheeks had become small pools of lava bubbling with heat.

"I ran to get a newspaper and found your name in black and white. Then I came here to talk. But what did I find?"

From one of the cupboards she brought out the photo of me with the rest of my teammates, along with my ceramic bowling ball and pins I'd made in pottery class. She set them on the counter.

"See, I *am* taking a pottery class. But yes, I took the class so I wouldn't have to lie to you about that the way I lied about bowling. I did lie, Kyla, a lot. And I am sorry." Those deceptions had now spectacularly caught up to me like a samurai sword-carrying Uma Thurman in the yellow tracksuit in *Kill Bill* and had sliced me in two.

"What about the tacky neon thing up in your bedroom?"

I stood up. "You had no right to go through my house. And I love my neon art."

"I have every right when you're showing a total lack of judgment in your life. You and Mike told me not to worry but look what happened to you. My suspicions were right on." Tears started down her cheeks. "And that's not the worst thing."

Hell.

"I was so distraught, I skipped the Halloween party at the club. Instead, I drove to that Cactus Lanes bowling alley. I saw you, Mom."

My body hardened, ready to sink through the dirt.

"That place, Mom. All that beer. And those weird trashy-looking people who all look like they came out of a trailer park. Why do you think they call it an alley?"

My old high school friends had said the same thing. "There's nothing trashy about them. They're generous, great people. They're my friends."

"So if you like them so much why did you lie about bowling?"

"I knew how you'd react."

"How?"

"Exactly like this. Frantic and crazed." My chest ached. I don't believe I was breathing, but I inhaled as much air as I could. "I love you, Kyla, but you're not the most understanding person in the universe. Weren't you listening at all to what Mike said?"

She didn't answer my question but cried. "Why are you spending time with those people? Why more than with me and Jonathan and Jerome?"

A shame missile targeted my chest. I sat down, my purse plopped onto the floor.

"This is my life." The words sounded so false because it wasn't. It hadn't been my life for more than thirty years.

My daughter paced in front of me. "And what about the Mexican guy? He was kissing you! He had his hands on you. I almost threw up in the parking lot! I would've gone in there and pulled you out, but I didn't want to make a scene."

"You say, 'Mexican' like it's a dirty word."

"How old is he? Has he asked you for money?" Kyla strode to the dispenser of sanitizer on the counter, gave it a few pumps and rubbed her hands.

I had to stand up to her, but the inside of my chest thumped. "We were dancing. He taught me how to bowl. He's a good man, not a gigolo. He's my friend. I can have friends, can't I?"

"Dad's been dead not even two years, and you're kissing strange men dressed like Batman."

"Just one man and he was dressed like Zorro."

"You shouldn't be in such a place, Mom. It's not safe."

"Dammit, Kyla you're exaggerating."

"And you're swearing more. Are you also learning that in the bowling alley? What's next? Hustling pool and chewing tobacco?" Kyla grabbed my arm and pushed up my sleeves.

"What the hell are you doing?"

"Looking for tattoos."

"For God's sake." I pulled down my sleeves. "And yes, I've cussed before, but you chose not to listen."

"One of my friend's mom lost her husband last year. Her mom cracked up and got a bunch of tattoos and had an affair with a chiropractor." Kyla wept harder and sat down.

"I haven't cracked up." At least not on the outside.

Kyla's body shivered, and her face crumpled into a deflated party balloon. "I'm so ashamed of you. This isn't how my mom acts. My mom went to PTA meetings and took care of us when we were sick. She is respectable and someone I'm proud of." Her words were huffed despair. "Who's living in this house? Where's the woman I've loved all my life?"

"I'm here."

"No. She's gone. She's been replaced by someone with trendy hair, who hangs out with shoddy people in a bowling alley drinking beer and planning their next tattoo. You're going to be a butt of jokes at the country club, Mom. Gina won't keep her mouth shut."

"So who cares what they say?"

"I'll probably have to quit my membership."

"You're being melodramatic."

Her head bowed and her weeping renewed, even more tragically. Then she looked up at me and brushed the tears aside. Her face so small and hurt. "Why don't you ever want to go golfing with me, Mommy?"

Kyla had done it.

She threw down the Mommy card and I felt like shit. I was the worst person in the world to cause my daughter such pain. I'd expected her to be angry, but not so hurt.

"You always want to be off by yourself. You and Mike have

regular dinner dates. You go bowling with total strangers, and you take old ladies gambling, but we don't do anything together. Why, Mommy? I love you so much."

I stood up. With a tissue, I wiped her tears. "Because, my baby daughter, you don't like gambling and I don't like golf. You don't like movies. I don't like shopping. You dislike people who are not like you and I embrace them. We seemed to have taken up residence on opposite ends of the relationship spectrum." I put my hand under her chin. "But we can still meet in the middle if you'd bend a little. There's hope for us. Please bend and understand."

Her sad face disappeared.

"Bowling. Dancing. Getting a new hairdo. You're a grandmother. What kind of a role model are you going to be to Jonathan if you pal around with cheap people at a bowling alley? How can I explain you're also carrying on with another man?" She straightened so much I swore I heard her vertebrae click into place. "How can I know you won't take your grandson to those places?"

Now she pulled another family card and my insides started to cave. Sitting back down I held on to the chair to stop from shooting off into a cold, heartless space.

I thought I'd transformed into a whole new woman ready to step out from the money and the house, and all that was predictable. Ready to travel to new places to find friends and love. But at the end of it all, I was the same reliable train who never left the station.

I failed the final damn test.

I couldn't lose my daughter. So while my heart was down at Cactus Lanes, it was also with Kyla and always would be.

The little girl who'd lined up her Barbie shoes, the young woman who loved a father who barely acknowledged her off the links. I'd put my happiness over hers. Though at times, she drove me crazy, I loved her and I still might be able to help her grow up.

And now that I was being totally honest, the prospect of losing Kyla was just one fear in a groundswell.

Once before I had let freedom go. When I could have stayed in college instead of marrying. But no, I took the easier route of marriage, with the most joy coming from my kids.

Why?

I clutched the sides of the kitchen chair. Because I was a real coward and had been for years. That's why I stayed with Bob. That's why I panicked last night about trying something really hard. Living with a man I loved. Breaking down the stone I'd existed behind for decades.

Who was I trying to kid at Cactus Lanes? My teammates, my new friends, they deserved a woman of stuff and blood. Not someone made out of cardboard.

And Frank.

He should have a woman of bravery and true light. Any *luz* he saw in me was probably just the reflection of his own generous heart and soul.

The inside of my chest thudded like a machine, and I kind of wished it was a heart attack.

"I *am* goddamn Brooks Hatlen," I whispered.

"Who?" Kyla blew her nose from crying.

"No one."

"So have you got this out of your system?"

I nodded. My head felt barely attached to my body.

Kyle hugged me. My arms were too dense to hug her back.

"I knew you'd make the right decision for all of us. It's for the best, Mom. I love you."

"I love you, too." My voice squeaked. I'd fallen off the end of the earth, weighed down by the shame of my cowardice.

"I've read how widows go through phases when they lose their husbands. See, you're just going through a phase. I'm glad Daddy wasn't alive to see this."

I stood up and wavered. I hoped I'd fall and break a hip. Every muscle ached. Every freaking joint. I turned two hundred years old instantly.

She put her hand on my shoulder. "You okay, Mom? Want a glass of water. I know this has been an emotional conversation. I'm exhausted too."

"I'm fine."

"You'll probably be a little unhappy quitting that dumb sport, but you'll get over it. We're going to have fun together. I promise. I'm so happy we talked and got everything squared away and back to normal. Right?"

Yeah, everything was back to goddamn normal.

"Can you give me a ride home? Jerome and I have a dinner tonight." She took the newspaper and threw it in the trash.

On the way to her house, my daughter talked about what else I could do to fill my hours. Golf, bridge, volunteer with the symphony. Counseling.

Driving along, I merely nodded while Kyla chatted away, but my mind and heart were shot full of Novocain. I'd given up Frank and bowling and the Bowling Broads without much of a fight because I was so damn petrified of giving myself to them completely. And that's what made my heart die.

When I returned home, the house's silence reverberated in my head like the inside of a football stadium at playoffs. I had to shove both hands against my ears. I rushed to the downstairs bathroom and vomited again. All that came out was bile and disgust.

I called Jo's house. I had to call. It was the right thing to do.

"Hello, Jo Maple's phone," answered a young boy.

TV and laughing kids made up the background noise.

I asked for Jo.

"Grandma, the phone!" the kid shouted.

Jo answered.

"It's Margaret." I deserved that name now. The name of stale oatmeal.

"Maggie, what's wrong? You sound like hell. Hold on."

Off in the background, Jo yelled, "Stop that horseplay or go outside!" She was back to me. "Sorry, my grandkids are full of salt and vinegar today. What's going on?"

"I have to quit the team." I slumped to the floor.

"What?"

From the diminishing sounds, Jo had gone into another room. "Did you say you're quitting the team?"

"Not want to, have to." The words strangled me.

"Are you sick?"

"No, but I wish I were dead."

"You're kinda talking crazy."

"I'm beyond that."

"You're scaring me."

"Don't worry, Jo. I don't have enough character to kill

myself." I began to cry. "I can't say any more. I'm so sorry. So very sorry. Please tell the girls I'm sorry, and if it's any consolation, I'm miserable."

"I'll come over and we'll talk. You can tell me anything, Maggie."

"There's nothing more to say, Jo."

The silence at the end of the line dug into my belly. I doubled over in pain and started weeping.

Jo sounded as if she talked through clenched teeth. Her worry about me had transformed to angry. "We trusted you. *I* trusted you. You're deserting the team before the city tournament. How can you do this to us? To me, and Suze and Bonnie, Violet?"

"Please forgive me because I can't forgive myself."

"This is damn low leaving us hanging." Jo paused.

I could hear her fuming through the earpiece.

"What about Frank?"

"Frank." Saying his name caused the pain in my belly to cut through the rest of my body, cutting me apart.

"You're abandoning him too?"

"Frank. Oh, God. Frank." I took a breath. "Please tell him that I love him."

"Well, you have a screwed-up way of showing it."

"He's better off without me, believe me, Jo."

"You bet your ass he is. You should be ashamed of yourself. You … you … goddamn widow!"

Jo hung up.

I had no strength to call Frank. I wasn't really worthy of him in the first place because I had no spine. It was a wonder I could walk.

I trudged up the stairs to my bedroom. To Frank's neon art and comfortable glow. But this time, the light was an accusation. Falling back on the bed, I wept so hard, my body seemed to have dried up. I was tempted to swallow all the pills I could find in the house. Walk out into traffic on Las Vegas Boulevard. But I was even too chickenshit to accomplish the long dive.

For the first time in my life, I experienced true loss.

Chapter Thirty-Three

This was the second game of golf I'd played in the last week and I was ready to lay my head in the path of a fast-moving cart.

I again accompanied Kyla and her friends from a golf team, Tina Jordan and Beth Dumont, who both could have doubled as models for Botox ads. Tina had a copious amount of curly hair and a physical body from always working out, or so she had talked about for the last six holes. Like Kyla, Tina always wore workout clothes, even when she wasn't working out.

Unlike my daughter, however, Tina was a good golfer.

"Good one, Tina," said Beth, who sported a cute golfing outfit with a short skirt showing off shapely legs.

I wore capris and the cleanest shirt in my closet. I'd lost all interest in what I wore or looked like, as well as cleaning and eating.

"The week-long golf school in Palm Springs totally helped my swing." Tina smiled demurely at her good hit.

"Your play has improved a lot," Kyla said and then turned to me. "Don't you think, Mom?"

I shrugged. I was bad company. I'd been like this ever since I quit the team seven days ago.

"Do you think I should go to golf school, Mom?"

"What?"

"Golf school."

"Why not?"

I teed off but my ball flew up and came straight down. Kyla did a little better than me. Beth blasted it like a female Happy Gilmore.

"Beth's hitting well because she's in love." Tina winked.

"I *have* been seeing Timothy Marlowe. He's a lawyer and it's getting kind of serious. We're even talking about taking a trip to Paris this winter."

"I've always wanted to go there," Kyla said and looked at me. "Right, Mom?"

"*Oui?*"

Kyla and I boarded the cart and the other two women got in theirs. We drove to my ball, which wasn't too far from my last shot. Kyla hit another rotten shot. Beth and Tina waited while we hit.

"Beth, you've got to give me the recipe for those hors d'oeuvres you made for our league get-together the other night," Tina said.

"I got them from a book called, *Entertaining to Impress*."

"They certainly did. They were fabulous."

"Simply cream puffs, crab, and a pastry filler."

After a pitiful number of shots, I ended up on the green.

Tina and Beth sunk the ball in two putts. I putted and putted and putted and putted. I didn't give a shit.

My ball finally went in the hole.

"Nice one, Mom," Kyla said.

Kyla putted and putted. "Darn it." When she sunk the ball, she grinned as though she'd won an LPGA championship.

We rode to the next hole. I let out a deep sigh while Kyla drove.

"Having fun, Mom?"

"If those two women mention another word about hors d'oeuvres I'm going to impale them with my seven iron."

"Mom!"

"I'm a little tired. I'll just hammer golf tees in my ears to drown them out."

"Mom, what if they hear you?"

"Well, I can always offer them some tees for their ears."

Kyla sunk in her seat.

We reached the next hole and watched while Beth smacked her ball a good hundred yards.

"This is so healthy for you, Mom. Clean air. Sunshine. Exercise. You were looking pale."

"It's because I have no blood left in my body." I didn't understand why my daughter couldn't see how wretched I was. There was no device to measure how much. I kept her love and here was the price.

"Mom, I don't understand your jokes."

"I know, honey. Maybe one day you will."

Kyla gave a little smile. "I'm going to try."

"You will?"

"I'll try. You talked about us being on opposite ends. I want us to be in the middle. I do. I want to—"

"Kyla, check out Tina's shot," Beth said.

Tina's ball soared past Beth's. "And Beth, I loved those shrimp croquettes. Can you give me the recipe? Douglas and I are inviting some people over and I want to serve them."

Kyla sent a weak smile my way.

When my daughter dragged me to golf, I didn't think or feel, which was a good thing. Air filled the vacuum where my courage should have been. I starred in a *Lifetime* movie no one would want to watch. Woman sentences herself to the seventh level of hell.

After telling Jo I quit the team, I had put away the photo of me and the other Bowling Broads in my closet as if it was an elicit substance to tempt me into living. A few days ago, and with shaking hands, I'd removed Frank's neon art from my bedroom and placed it in the basement, along with my ceramic bowling ball and pin and all my bowling equipment and shirts. They went into yet another plastic bin, along with all the other memories of my past. I cried for an hour on my bed, which had begun to smell like the Pacific Ocean from all my tears. When I'd pulled my Bowling Broads shirt out of the dirty clothes pile while doing laundry, I cried for another hour. This time for my contemptible conduct and weakness. I started taking my antianxiety meds again but they didn't help much. Meds don't really when you act like a goddamn jerk.

We reached the eighteenth hole. I didn't care about the score but suspected I took eleven or more shots per hole. Kyla and her friends planned to eat lunch at the country club restaurant.

"I'm going to skip eating, girls," I said as they headed to the clubhouse.

"You sure, Mom?" Kyla said.

"You do look a little tired," Tina said.

"The heat got to me."

"Take lots of vitamin C and D," advised Beth.

"With hors d'oeuvres?"

"What?"

"I'm hallucinating is all, sorry."

Kyla and her friends went inside, and I zoomed out of the parking lot though I didn't have any place to go. I'd quit the pottery course last week since I didn't have to keep up the lie. Besides, I sucked at ceramics. I'd been tempted to bowl at another alley, but such a move would have made me more of a traitor to my former team and Frank.

For what seemed the hundredth time, I cruised by Cactus Lanes in hopes of seeing Frank. He had left several messages on my cell phone, but I hadn't called him back.

When I wanted to torture myself even more, I listened to the messages. With each listen, I cried. His voice so familiar and loving. The one he used after we made love and lay in bed talking. The loss of closeness and affection sunk me down lower than a Vegas water table.

"Hey, it's Frank. I heard you're quitting the team. We should talk. Please call me."

"Hi. Call me when you get a moment."

"I know something's wrong. Please tell me."

"I miss you, Margarita. I might be able to help. Please don't give up on us or yourself."

"This isn't like you. You're such a good person. I know

something is happening. I promise to understand."

"I hope I didn't scare you by suggesting you move in with me. I just want to be with you."

And the last one. God, the last one.

"I love you."

After the last message, I lay on the bed not wanting to get up ever. I heard a vehicle drive up. My bedroom windows were open. Peeking through the curtains, I saw Frank get out of his truck. He carried a bouquet of white roses.

Then the doorbell rang and rang. He placed flowers on the front step.

"Oh, Maggie," he sighed before he got in the truck.

He drove away and I dissolved onto the floor.

The day I quit the bowling team I had called Ruth Granger to say I wasn't well enough to take her to the sports book at Caesars Palace for the next week or so. She told me I sounded terrible and to take care of myself. But after a few days I *had* to talk with her. I wanted the woman's advice. Hell, I wanted someone to listen to me and understand or condemn me. Something.

When she didn't answer, I decided to drive over.

Pulling up to Ruth's house, I ran to her small cottage and knocked. I knocked a lot. She disliked people ringing the doorbell, calling it annoying.

Ruth was hard of hearing and many times it had taken her a good ten minutes to get to the door.

"Ruth. It's Maggie."

I knocked. This time harder.

"Hello?"

An older man in shorts, a baseball cap, and Miami Dolphins T-shirt stood behind me, holding a cigarette in his brownish teeth.

"Do you know if Ruth's home? I'm her friend from the senior companion program."

"Ruth died yesterday."

"What?"

"Went very peacefully, so I heard."

"Was she sick?"

"No, sweetheart, just old age. Nice lady." He puffed on his cigarette.

I fell back against her door.

"You okay?"

"Not really."

I thanked him and dragged myself back to the car. From my purse, I got out my cell phone and again listened to Frank's messages. My wretchedness knew no bounds.

Opening the door to the house, I heard the vacuum cleaner going. Consuela pushed around the machine on the rugs in the living room. I'd forgotten it was her day to clean the house.

She stopped the machine when she saw me. "You look like you did the time you ate the fast-food taco I told you not to eat."

"I've done something horrible."

"Tell me."

With the temperatures in the high nineties, it was too hot to sit by the pool, so we sat in the living room.

"So what'd you do? Give money to Republicans?" Consuela smiled. She was a hard-core Democrat.

Before I spoke, I downed half a bottle of beer and then told Consuela about Kyla, the bowling team, and Frank. All through my narrative I counted on her understanding since no one else had extended much.

My friend listened, fixed with seriousness.

"Con, I acted terribly."

"You're right. It was downright shitty behavior. You should be ashamed."

Her voice held no consolation, none whatsoever.

"I am ashamed, believe me. But I thought you'd understand why I had to quit bowling and Frank."

"I don't understand."

"Why not?"

"I have a hard time sympathizing with a person who hurts others."

"I could use a friend right now." That came out harshly, and I could see from her face I'd hurt yet another person. "God, I raised my voice to you. Forgive me."

She shook her head back and forth. "Oh, man."

"What is it?"

"You want my blessing for your awful behavior. You must have been thinking, 'Oh, I've employed Consuela for years, so she'll be on my side no matter what I've done, no matter how bad I acted.' You want me to say it's okay because you were scared shitless."

I set down the beer bottle. "I'd never think that in a million years. I've always thought of you as a friend. I've told you things I never told anybody else."

"And I counted you as a friend too and not just some lady who pays me to clean. But I don't know if I want a friend who'd jerk people around out of her own fears."

"I was afraid of losing my family. Not being able to see my grandson."

"Did Kyla threaten you with that?"

She didn't. I shook my head.

"I don't believe I'm sticking up for Kyla, but you can't put this all on her. You're a grown woman who should stand on her own two feet." Consuela stood up. "But no. You've finally turned into one of those other rich ladies I clean for. They want to relate, but don't know how. They live in their money and nowhere else. When I work for them, I do my job and I don't talk. I pick up my check and leave." She smiled with regret. "Margaret, we have talked and laughed and shared good times over the years. I've also watched you get swept up into a life I knew you hated, and you couldn't find the balls to walk out the door."

She unplugged the vacuum and hit the button to reel in the power cord.

"I had hopes for you after your husband died, and when you started bowling and really caring for another man, I was so happy for you. But this isn't the first time I was wrong. After what you did to a man who loves you and to those other people at the bowling alley, I can't work for you no more."

I stood up. "Con—"

"If you'd been one of those other ladies, then I wouldn't have cared and kept cleaning and getting paid. But I do care about you and if you can do that to them, you can do it to anybody, just because you're too afraid to change."

She walked to the door.

"Con, please. Don't leave."

"*Mujer*, you did the leaving by standing still."

I heard the front door close. The sound echoed throughout the empty house.

At least once a day I'd driven by Cactus Lanes on the chance of seeing Frank. Even a glimpse. One day, a crew was removing the C from the sign. The next time I drove by all the letters in the sign had been taken down, including the beautiful neon cactus plant that had caught my attention in the first place. Was Frank selling the place? Was he tired of the careless people who came through the door, people like me?

I hadn't heard from him for almost a week, which made me suffer all the more. But he was more than justified never to want to talk to me again.

That day I drove there at midnight when I knew it would be empty. I parked near the dark building and got out. In the weak illumination from the streetlight, I could see all the petals had dropped off the cactus flowers and lay at the bottom of the plants. I picked up some of the fallen petals. They were dry and brown. Their brilliant colors gone. I accidentally hit one of the spikes and welcomed the pain.

I had no one to talk with. Con was gone. So was Ruth. My other friends were all at Cactus Lanes, which meant I had no friends at all.

Chapter Thirty-Four

"What are you looking for? The same thing we've been doing?" My stylist Hillary put her hands on my shoulders.

"What?"

"Your hair?"

I drooped into the chair. "A touch up is all."

"Same as before?"

"Hmmm."

"That a 'yes'?"

"I guess so."

"Okie, dokie." She started her work.

I glanced in the mirror. Grays showed in my hair, which resembled the back end of a rat's butt. I had to remind myself why I was there—Ruth Granger's memorial. I wanted to be presentable at least. But my nerve endings had shut down, and I suspected I might be like this for the rest of my life. Perhaps, not a bad thing. When you're anesthetized then you're not hurting. Come to think of it, *The Walking Dead* gained a whole new meaning for me. Then again, not a new state. I'd been a zombie for the almost three decades of marriage. Now I just had a nicer hairdo.

I smiled at my reflection in the stylist's mirror.

"Going anyplace special?" Hillary said.

"A memorial service."

"Sorry."

She appeared to be waiting for me to talk more about who had died. Stylists were the bartenders of haircuts and color after all. They heard life stories of their customers in the time it took to shampoo, cut, and curl hair.

But sharing was out of the question.

Hillary nodded with understanding and continued her work.

"There you go, Margaret. All finished."

"What?"

"You look like a model for those older lady ads."

"Too bad there's no one to look good for."

"You do it for yourself."

"Oh, her."

The cut and color were good. I gave Hillary a good tip and headed to my car.

Sludge flowed through my veins, something like the consistency of old oil. I tripped on the pavement. When I looked up, Violet waited on the sidewalk near my SUV.

"Violet. It's so good to see you." I grinned with excitement before remembering what I'd done to her and the other women on the team.

She wasn't smiling.

Mine faded from shame. "How'd you find me?"

311

"Your landscaper told me."

"Violet, I'm sorry I quit the team. This is killing me."

"I'm sure you think you have good reasons, but I'm guessing they're all still lame. I liked you, Maggie. It took me a while, but I did. I really liked you."

I started to cry. The funny thing was Violet's eyes also widened with tears, which stirred up more desolation in me.

"Why did you abandon us?"

"Violet…"

"Sure, you have lots of money, but after what you did, you ain't worth a plug nickel." Violet wiped hard at a running tear. "And you broke his heart, Maggie. If you could see him, you'd know what you did. You goddamn broke his heart."

I put my head in my hands.

"You broke all of our hearts." She turned and walked away.

Ruth Granger's memorial was held in the recreation hall. I wanted to go back home and cry some more after talking with Violet, but Ruth had been my friend and I had to be there to honor her.

A majority of the attendees were elderly, and I guessed residents of the senior complex where Ruth had lived. I wore a black pantsuit and white shirt, but the rest of the mourners dressed casually in pants, capris, and even shorts. I supposed they were probably used to regularly saying goodbye to friends and neighbors.

At the front of the hall was an enlarged photo of a smiling Ruth and another of a younger Ruth. Both versions showed the same flash of mischief and arc of character in their eyes. I wished I'd known her longer than I did, but I was enriched for having known her at all.

Sitting in the front row were Ruth's children. I recognized them from the photos in her cottage. Daughter Rachel, who was in her sixties, was petite like her mom. She wept into the shoulder of her husband, a short man with a thick, white mustache. Sitting on the other side of the daughter was Ruth's son, Nick, a trucker who visited his mom whenever he wasn't on the road. He was as burly as his mom was small. Ruth always talked with love about both of her children but had a softer spot for Nick, who had already gone through two wives and was combating alcoholism. She said she'd had him in her late thirties, which made him colicky and prone to trouble.

Nick walked to the front and cleared his throat. "I want to thank all of you for coming today for my mom." He looked at the photos. "I don't think I'm wrong in saying there'll never be anyone like her. She loved to laugh and bet on the horses and drink Bloody Marys. The strange thing is she was really good at betting. She also claimed the Bloody Marys actually prolonged her life."

Several people in the room laughed, including me. Ruth and I had had fun times at the sports bar. And Ruth usually did win, though it was generally ten to twenty dollars per game because she bet the two-dollar minimum.

"My mom taught school for many years, but she was my first teacher. She taught me to work hard and never give up." He started to freeze up with emotion and gripped his big hands together. "I wasn't always successful, but Mom never got on my case about it. She supported me and was generous as the day was long. That was Ruth. She was a great mom and a good, loyal friend. I'm going to miss her."

Nick took a handkerchief and blew his nose before continuing. "If she taught me anything, it was to take hold of life with both hands and hold on as hard and as long as possible. Wrestle it and take control of what you can. I'm still trying, and I know my mom will be watching over me and saying, 'Hold on, Nick, hold on.'" He looked up. "We will all miss her very much. But as she also used to say, we have a limited number of years in our lifetime, so don't be a fool and waste them on sadness, regret, and fear."

From beyond the grave, Ruth admonished me for doing exactly that. We could have been sitting next to each other at the Caesars Palace sports book, holding a Bloody Mary, making a bet. She'd be shaking her head at me, saying, "Honey, what the hell are you doing with *your* life?"

Sitting alone at the dining table, I stared at my takeout Chinese dinner as I sipped wine.

"Mom?"

"In the dining room."

Mike entered and gave me a hug and kiss. He sat down.

"Want some Chinese food? I haven't touched it."

"No, thanks."

"Wine? It's good."

He retrieved a glass from the cupboard and poured himself a glass, but didn't sit down. "Mom, I'm sorry I couldn't come sooner, but I wanted to talk with you face-to-face, not over the phone."

"That's okay, Mike."

"For God's sake, why did you quit the team? More importantly, why did you break up with Frank?"

"You talked with Kyla."

"Her hysterical version. You were on a bowling team and kissing a man."

"You failed to include your sister's adjectives like *trashy* bowling team and a *Mexican* man."

"Yup, those were her adjectives. I didn't tell her I already knew about Frank and bowling. That would have pissed her off even more."

"Good idea."

"I did yell at her." Mike gulped down the wine, poured another glass, and sat. "Come to think of it, I cussed her out quite a bit." He smiled. "It felt fantastic."

"Mike, she's your sister."

"She's acting like an asshole, which I *did* tell her. You certain Kyla wasn't adopted?"

"Reasonably."

He reached out and touched my hand. "How are you?"

"It's a vast understatement to say these last few days have been among the worst of my life."

Mike sat back. "It was more than a kiss, wasn't it?"

"I'm wild about him, Mike. And for those women on the team. How could I treat them so badly?" I flung my wine glass against the wall. It shattered. "You don't have to tell me you're disappointed in me because I'm disgusted with me. I have been for years." Tears slipped down, and I wiped them with

315

my sleeve. I couldn't stop crying and I wondered if I had any salt left in my body.

Mike got me another glass and filled it with wine. "I was so proud of you when you told me about Frank and your new friends at Cactus Lanes." He scooted his chair closer to mine. "I was never ashamed of you, until now."

"This day keeps getting better." I fell back into the chair.

"You crumbled like a cracker. When Dad was alive you stood up to him when he was wrong, which was usually all of the time. You stood up for me when I stopped golfing. When I went to journalism school instead of going into his business. When you tried to raise Kyla so she wouldn't end up like Dad. You were a damn tower of strength."

"Was I?"

"And I've got to ask you something. Something I wanted to for a long time." His eyes glimmered with tears. "Why did you stay with him for all those years?"

"It doesn't matter now."

"Yes, it does. When Dad died, I thought, now Mom can finally do what she wants. Then you let Kyla buffalo you into quitting bowling and the man you care about."

I shook my head slowly. "She didn't."

"What?"

"Son, I can't talk about it." More tears wet the front of my top. I couldn't tell him about my total lack of nerve to change my life and love Frank and my friends, not to mention the fear of losing Kyla if I did.

"I'll listen when you're ready." He nodded and glanced around the house as if a visitor. "It's very quiet in here."

"Yes, it is."

"Dammit, I'll just say one more thing. Quiet is for the grave and you're a long way from a hole in the ground." He placed his hands on the table like a challenge. "What were you going to do now? Cry for the rest of your life?"

"Maybe." Smiling awkwardly, I wiped my face with the back of my hand.

"Whose life are you living?"

"I'm not sure anymore."

"For your sake, I hope you find out soon." He poured both of us another glass of the good wine.

Chapter Thirty-Five

"Ever play bridge before?" asked a young hostess who looked more at home at an upscale law office. She wore fashionable clothing, precise makeup and hair, with the legal efficiency of a yellow pad.

"I've played poker, does that count?"

The woman examined me as if I was a mutant.

"No betting is allowed here."

"Good. It's a bad habit."

"Yes."

"I was making a joke."

"Oh."

Kill me now.

The Palms Bridge Club held the reputation as the most lavish private bridge organization in the city. Elegant décor rivaled any new casino with sparkling chandeliers and comfortable chairs around shiny black tables. A full bar and an espresso machine stood in the corner.

Espresso, not a coffee pot, mind you.

People began to take a seat at the three dozen tables in the subdued room. I wanted to get the hell out of there but had promised Kyla I'd give bridge a try as an acceptable pastime.

Despite all the people in the room, the bridge club was disturbingly noiseless. As if the lovely wallpaper and carpeting absorbed all the sound. The players didn't chat loudly about the weather or their grandkids. They spoke in hushed tones when they bid as if talking any louder would cost them money. A majority of people there looked like me, except for Latina women serving drinks made up by the Black bartender. I hadn't noticed such diversity before I bowled down at Cactus Lanes.

Kyla had planned to join me, but Jonathan had to go to the dentist for a chipped tooth from an errant baseball. I tried to go with them, but she insisted I carry through.

"You'll love it, Mom," she had told me. "Lots of nice people you *should* become friends with."

You mean confused and desperately depressed widows like me, I was going to answer. My muscles ached from my daughter's unplanned but still effective guilt manipulations. After talking with her, I felt as if I'd visited a massage therapist who'd done time in prison for assault.

The hostess showed me to a table in the middle of the large room. On the top were wooden card holders and a fancy writing tablet to keep track of scores, along with a pricey pen that never leaked ink on hands. Already seated was a couple who appeared to be in their seventies. The man sported a trimmed white beard, while the woman's white curls looked phony. I played with the idea of sneaking a touch to see if they were synthetic.

Like the other people in the room, the players were all well-dressed. The man sported a Rolex, and his companion wore enough gold jewelry to sink a swimming pool. I'd been assigned to play with a man wearing an expensive shirt and slacks. Portly and pink cheeked, my partner wheezed when he breathed. He winked at me.

"This is Margaret Adams. She'll be joining you today," said the hostess with sugary false sincerity.

I sat and the other players introduced themselves. I immediately forgot their names because they didn't matter to me. Nothing much did anymore.

"So, we're partners," the winking guy told me and extended his hand.

"I guess." I took his hand and when I tried to release it, he slid his fingers over my palm and winked again. I was happy he sat on the other side of the table.

"Play much?" asked the older woman.

"Not at all. But I researched the rules."

She glanced at her partner and his eyes rotated up to the glass ceiling. He didn't bother to hide the expression from me.

"This is the best club in town."

"And most exclusive," added her partner.

"Obviously. The word diversity probably couldn't even get in the front door unless it was serving drinks."

"Pardon me?" the woman asked.

"Forget it."

"Vincent will guide you through a game if you forget the rules." She said it slowly, as if I was mentally defective.

Vincent was the winker. "You're my east."

"What? Oh right." East, west, north south positions.

"Well, let's start," the older man said.

Slap. Slap. Slap. Out came the cards from the machine. I placed the thirteen cards in a sleek holder.

Since Vincent the Winker was west, he opened the bidding. "One spade." He looked up at me and smiled.

The old woman passed.

"One diamond, I suppose," I said.

The old man passed.

Tricks. No trump. Dummy cards. Follow the suits. I tallied up the time like nails being pounded into my skin. We'd been playing for a whole ten minutes.

Even with the players in full bridge mode, the room was so calm I heard the ice clink in their high balls or iced tea.

"Exciting game, isn't it?" I said, not concealing the smart-assness.

The passive expressions on the other players appeared to be glued on. If I had a gun I'd have shot myself.

"You folks want anything," asked a waitress.

"Gin and tonic with No.3 London Dry." The old woman studied her manicured hands instead of the young girl. "You do have No.3 London Dry?"

"Certainly." The server then looked at me.

"Water, *por favor*, and thanks."

The waitress smiled.

"I'll have what my wife is having," the old man said.

"Scotch, straight." Vincent winked at the waitress and then at me as he distributed the cards. "You picked up the game quickly."

"Cards are lighter than a bowling ball."

"Bowling is not a game. It's a pastime for the poor," the bearded guy said.

His wife giggled. The winker wheezed out a laugh.

I sighed deep. "That's enough. I've had it."

Like drunks or other people in dire distress or addiction, I'd reached the very bottom. The lowest point in my life. I could go down no farther. Not even to hell, which I was sure was located in the basement of that very bridge club.

I grinned. I had one way to go.

"We want you to bid is all," Vincent said.

"Listen to this place. Really, listen."

They all listened.

"Peaceful, isn't it?" The woman smiled at last.

"Silent as the grave," ole white beard said.

"Exactly, but we're not dead yet. I'm not, anyway." I bolted up. My chair hit the ground. I flipped my cards all over the table and onto the floor. Then I grabbed the other players' cards and threw them up in the air. I felt giddy as a kid who'd eaten a bag of sugar.

I felt goddamn free. Really free.

"You nuts or something?" Vincent sounded irritated, like he'd been served the wrong kind of Martini.

"I am crazy as a bag of walnuts. And I'm truly nuts for being here in the first place." I grabbed more cards from the dispenser and tossed them as far as I could. They rained down on the heads of the nearby players. For good measure I swept up the cards on another table and did the same. The cards flew like liberated birds. I thought of all the damn years I'd wasted in the Shawshank prison. I could have walked free at any time but didn't. And for that I could have chewed through the nice carpeting. Instead, I threw up more cards from a surrounding table.

"Security," I heard the hostess announce.

"Well, time to go," I told the people at the table.

Most everyone in the place stared at me now. I hurried toward the exit, and then turned around and shouted, "IT'S TOO DAMN QUIET IN HERE! GET OUT AND MAKE NOISE! IT'S NOT TOO LATE! BELIEVE ME, IT'S NOT TOO LATE! RUN FOR YOUR FREAKIN' LIVES! SEE ME? I'M RUNNING TOWARD LIFE."

Laughing, I dashed out into the open air.

Chapter Thirty-Six

I stood outside the door of Kyla's house as she drove up. I tapped the *luz* in my veins. Lava.

"Mom, I thought you were playing bridge." Kyla carried a latte.

"I cut that game short." I followed her into the house. Although this might be the last time I spoke with my daughter —not out of my choice—I was ready to do what I should have done the moment I first entered Cactus Lanes.

"Are you sick, Mom?"

"I won't be playing bridge anymore, or golfing. I'm going to ask the Bowling Broads if I can rejoin the team, and I pray they'll have me." I wasn't confident, however, but I was prepared to grovel if I had to.

Kyla set down her coffee on the marble table in the foyer. "This is all a phase. Maybe you need psychiatric help."

"I'm not the one who needs help. Come with me, Kyla." I led her to the kitchen and pointed to a chair. "Sit."

"You don't have to use that tone with me."

"Oh yes, I do, and I should have used it lots more. Kyla, for once, please do what I ask."

She sat.

"I don't need psychiatric help. I'm perfectly sane because at long last I've grown a set of balls, as Consuela says."

"Mom, you're having a nervous breakdown."

"No, I'm having an attack of courage. I've finally become Wonder Woman, Ripley in the *Alien* movies. Freakin' Katniss Everdeen. Sure they're all thinner but I feel strong enough to at least lend them an assist." I couldn't help but smile.

Kyla's face reddened. "You're on drugs, aren't you?"

"No, are you?"

"You need counseling. You're like a stranger."

"That's because I located a spine, which is why you probably don't recognize me. Hell, at times I don't recognize myself."

Kyla's eyes widened and she resembled a little girl. I sat next to her and took her hands. "You, you're the one who requires counseling to bust out of the closed box of a mind you created. Forgive me for not raising you better. I wasn't strong enough then.

"I should have tried harder to make you realize people aren't perfect. To drum it into your skull that your father was galactically wrong on this point. Is it the magnificent imperfection that makes the world great. Full of wonderful shapes and sizes and colors. By accepting that you'll become part of this fantastic world. If you don't, you'll end up an intolerant snob inhabiting your own sad planet."

My daughter pulled in her lips.

"Kyla, don't you see? Holding up that humungous

umbrella of perfection will only end up breaking your back. If you're so inflexible someday you're going to shatter under its weight. As someone who loves you, I don't want to see that happen. I want you to enjoy life. I know all this because I came close to smashing up under the massive fear I'd been lugging around."

Her eyes became teary.

"One other thing, and this is important, so, you'll want to pay attention, Kyla."

She stood up. "Not that Mexican bowling alley guy!"

I stood up too. "Don't you ever say that again!" I said fiercely.

Kyla's eyes blinked with my display of guts.

"His name is Frank Martínez, and I'm going to beg his forgiveness. And if he'll have me, I'm moving in with him. I love him." I couldn't help but grin. "In fact, I'm crazy, ga-ga, madly, and totally in love with him. He is the most generous, warm, and forgiving man I've ever met. You'd discover that too if you give him a chance."

"Never." One tear slid down my daughter's face.

"Then I'm truly sorry for you. And I'm sorry you won't be able to know this good man or the good people down at Cactus Lanes. But look at me. I used to be a scared as hell, a self-depreciating woman who's become a self-depreciating woman in love and who's *not* scared anymore. If I can change, so can you. If I can be better, then so can you."

"Mom, is this you?"

"You bet. I want to grow old with Frank. If he takes me back that is."

"Oh, no."

"Oh, yes. I'm happy. Won't you give me at least this?"

"You'll never replace Daddy." Kyla stood and appeared to be a boiling pot ready to burst. Hands in fists. Red and puffing like a dragon ready to burn down a village.

"Honey, now that I'm being honest, I can't stop. I'm sorry to say this but your father swept me away with his privilege and I let it happen. I never had the bravery to leave him and take you and Mike with me. He never hit or abused me. He just wasn't there for any of us."

"You didn't love him at all?"

"I'm afraid not. I wish I could have."

Kyla's eyes enlarged as if she'd been hit with a stun gun. She started to speak, but I held my hand up and motioned for her to sit back down. I sat down across from her. "It occurs to me now that your father must have loved the fact I let him live his life separate from mine. I made no demands to interfere with golf or his business."

"You lived a lie, Mom."

"Yes, I did. A much bigger one than going bowling."

"He loved you," she said quietly. "He'd have left too, if he didn't."

"If he did love me, I couldn't tell."

"He stayed married; I'd call that evidence."

"I think you'd call that circumstantial. Poor Bob. We trapped ourselves inside a marriage of lethargy and disinterest. Such a waste of time." I stood up. "I love you very much, Kyla, but you can be one enormous pain in the ass. I believe I can tell you this since no one ever has. That's a waste too because you have so much to give, baby."

"You wouldn't do this to me, to your family. To your

grandson."

Softly, I took my daughter's face in my hands. "All my life I've done everything for everybody else. Now it's my turn to do something for me. It probably sounds selfish as hell, but if I don't learn to like and respect myself, then no one ever will. Including you." I let Kyla go. "I want to go on spending time with you and my grandson and Jerome more than anything, but if you never want to see me anymore it is your loss and *your* shame."

Jonathan entered the kitchen, making us both jump. "Mom, I'm home. Mrs. Jenkins gave me a ride from swim practice." He gawked at his angry mother, and his grandmother who was calm and smiling. "You guys having a fight?"

"We're talking about damn bowling," Kyla said.

"Mom, you said a bad word."

I hugged Jonathan and kissed the top of his head. *Stay strong, woman.* "Goodbye for now, my little love."

"You going somewhere, Grandma?"

"That's up to your mom."

The kid looked at his mother.

"If the team will forgive me, I'm going to play in the city bowling tournament. I hope you'll come and watch, Kyla."

"I'd be ashamed to be seen there." She looked away.

I wanted to cry for her but placed my hands on Jonathan's shoulders. "You know what your grandmother is, Johnny boy?"

"What?"

"A shit hot bowler."

The kid laughed. "Shit hot."

"You bet." I kissed his cheek and left.

Chapter Thirty-Seven

I sped into the Cactus Lanes parking lot, screeched to a stop, and bolted out of my SUV. The lot was empty, except for Frank's truck. I'd thought about calling him so he could meet me there, but I was terrified he wouldn't answer the phone. Why should he?

I had to explain in person. I wanted and needed to see him.

The alley's neon lettering had been covered by a huge tarp. Frank had probably had the sign redone for the tournament.

The place closed at ten on Sunday and Frank always stayed late to do paperwork. I knew his schedule because I stayed late with him a few nights. It was great. I'd fetch him coffee and file away papers for him. One night, we shut the lights and made love on the couch in his office.

Please let him be there and alone.

Despite my new found *cojones*, I didn't have enough strength to see his mom so I didn't go to his house. Although a sweet woman, Aurelia would have been warranted to call me the Spanish word for asshole and slam the door in my face. I certainly wouldn't have faulted her. If I'd been Frank's mother, I would have done exactly that.

Since my not-so-quiet exit from the bridge club and my daughter's house, I'd driven around waiting for ten o'clock. As I did, I made up the speech I'd give Frank, and came up with a thousand ways to beg for forgiveness. I avoided waiting in the parking lot. I didn't want to be recognized by other players and given dirty looks for wounding the nicest and greatest man on the earth.

Please, God, don't let me be too late, I chanted like a prayer.

Racing up to the entrance to Cactus Lanes, I looked through the double doors. A few lights were lit inside, meaning Frank was still in there.

I started to bang on the glass doors. "Frank, please let me in. Frank."

I waved at the security camera out front, but he didn't come to the door. He probably knew I was out there.

"Frank!" I pounded on the doors.

No answer.

I spun around and leaned against them, prepared the slide down into oblivion. Instead, the door opened. They hadn't been locked. I entered the empty bowling alley.

My heart did handsprings. Frank sat at the snack bar drinking coffee. He looked up and saw me. At first, his beautiful eyes widened with surprise, but then they narrowed into suspicion and hurt. I ran to him and stopped short.

"I'm so glad I found you."

"I never thought I'd see you again." He greeted me as if I were as an insurance salesman selling whole life.

All the speeches I'd practiced dashed out of my head.

"Frank, I know you must hate me for what I did, but now I can tell you why."

"Oh." He took another sip of coffee.

At the pain and mistrust he showed—and which I had caused—my knees almost gave out. I took another step forward, holding on to the snack bar counter so I wouldn't fall over.

"In your messages, which I listened to a hundred times, you said you'd understand. While it might be hard for you, please at least listen to me. I know I don't deserve your time, but you're a good man and you'll listen."

He remained silent and I became even more alarmed he did hate me—or worse, that I had destroyed any feeling he once had for me.

"My daughter isn't a tolerant person. She's prejudiced and narrow-minded. So, I lied to her about Cactus Lanes, about my bowling, and about you, Frank. When she found out she became very upset, which is an understatement. She freaked. Mostly because I was involved with you. She said she was ashamed of me and I was no longer a good role model for my grandson. She lobbed guilt grenades. So I told myself, 'Margaret, you have to give up what you love for your family.' I couldn't take the chance on losing my daughter."

His eyes stayed on his coffee cup.

"But Frank, that wasn't the only reason."

He looked up at me.

"I stayed in a terrible marriage for decades because I was too goddamn afraid to leave and depend on myself. I stayed with a man I didn't love and barely liked on most days."

Frank placed his cup on the counter.

"When Bob died, I prayed for the old Margaret to go into the ground with him. Good Ole Margaret Adams who never ventured out of her old life no matter how often she dreamed of it. She wanted to be strong but wasn't. She wanted love but didn't fight for it. She was even too damn frightened to even step into the ring. Then I started bowling and made new friends… I met you. I was happy." I dared to take a step forward. "And surprise of all time, you loved me." I placed my hand on my chest. "Then you asked me to leave that other life behind and move in with you. But instead of running towards a new future, I did the same thing I've always done. I ran for goddamn cover."

Tears felt heavy on my cheeks, but I didn't wipe them away.

"Here's more of the God's honest truth: I love you very much. More than any man I've met. I can't think when I'm around you. I can hardly breathe. But because I was such a coward, I didn't believe I deserved you, Frank, or my friends. I didn't have the strength to be happy or to love you." I gasped in anguish, and the sound spread throughout Cactus Lanes. I took a breath and I stepped forward, so close I could have touched him.

"When you told me I had a light inside me, I believed you. I was vivid. I *felt* the brilliance inside of me, me of all people. The light made me warm and strong."

I brushed the tears and straightened with a new, heady sensation.

"And as soon as I quit you and the team and bowling, any light inside me extinguished. I became cold and dead like I'd been for so many years."

He swung around on the stool toward me. I dared to reach for his hand. His warmth caused my heart to fire up like a furnace that hadn't been used in decades.

I stood taller than I ever had. "Frank, I'm not frightened anymore. I'll never be afraid again. Let me show you I can shine. I'm not worthy of you, but you have to know this, I loved you the moment we first met in front of the cactus flowers. Ever since I saw you teaching those kids how to bowl on lane number sixteen. I beg of you to give me the chance to love you as a woman full of life and light. Let me be brave for you and me."

I bent over, out of air. "Give me a moment. I've never talked this much in my whole life."

He removed his hand from mine.

"Oh, God."

"Let's go outside." He sounded like a bouncer getting rid of a drunk in a bar.

"You're kicking me out?"

"Follow me."

My legs weakened so much I had to sit down on one of the stools. "I'm too late, aren't I?"

"This way." His tone was serious.

I stooped over so much my shoulders practically reached the floor. "No need to toss me out. I'll go away quietly. I won't stalk you. Not even online." But I was tempted to grab onto him until the police had to come to pull me off.

I followed him outside, not knowing how I put one foot in front of the other.

Frank led me to the front of the dark building. "Wait here."

Pulling at a rope, the tarp fell off the sign. He ran back inside, probably to order up a restraining order.

Lights snapped on.

I blinked from the brightness and looked up. A new neon sign blinked two words:

MARGARITA LANES.

Now the cactus plant under the letters showed a remarkable red neon flower.

I fell to my knees.

I began crying. For the last three weeks I'd cried so often out of misery, but happy tears felt infinite. I hoped so, at any rate.

Frank joined me and pulled me to my feet. He wiped away my tears with his handkerchief. I threw my arms around him and hugged him hard. "I don't deserve this, Frank, not after what I did."

"You deserve it for coming back."

"How did you know I would, even when I didn't?"

"Because of your *luz*. It never goes out. Even if you tried to extinguish it, the light is there."

I hugged him harder.

"You're beautiful, my Margarita."

"No, Frank. You're the one who's beautiful. You always have been."

We kissed. Kisses of renewal.

I held him close and whispered in his ear. "Know what I want to do?"

"What, *mi amor*?" he whispered in mine.

We inaugurated Margarita Lanes with bowling. Frank turned up the juke box and played rock 'n' roll. In between rolls, we danced and kissed. Halfway through the last game, I tugged him into his office, where we made love on the couch. We ended up falling onto the carpet, laughing.

I nestled against him. "Frank, you positive you still want me?"

"Duh."

I got up on one arm. "I'm not young anymore. I have wrinkles and flabby arms."

"So do I."

"I wake up with all sorts of aches and pains."

"Who doesn't at our age?"

"And my boobs are sagging."

"Don't worry, baby. I'll pick them up."

Chapter Thirty-Eight

My head rested on Frank's chest. The absolutely best place in the world, I had discovered. Listening to his heart. What a sound.

"I have more apologies to make, Frank."

"Not necessary, my love. I explained everything to her over the phone."

"It's important to me."

He kissed the top of my head. "You *are* brave."

He'd spent the night at my house after we made up at the bowling alley. We both yawned in the morning because we didn't get much sleep after making up a few more times in bed.

On the way over to his house, I was nervous even though his mom appeared to have no drop of spite anywhere in her small frame.

We found Aurelia sitting in the shade of the porch at their house. I shouldn't have worried at all. She opened her arms and I rushed into them and cried against her shoulder for a solid twenty minutes. Through the crying, I told her my reasons for leaving. She listened with so much consideration I wished she'd been my second mom. Taking a fresh tissue from my pocket, she dried my face.

"Forgive me for hurting Frank." I found my voice through the tears.

"I knew you'd come back."

"You did?"

"Look, Margarita."

Her chin moved up. Frank and I glanced at the cactus plants in their garden outside. They had bloomed.

"I'll be damned," I said.

"When?" Frank said.

"This morning, Francisco."

The three of us spent an enjoyable evening. Later that night, Frank and I made up again. I did like the making up part tremendously.

I gripped Frank's hand as we had lunch at the Italian restaurant we liked. I had asked him not to mention to Jo that we'd gotten back together. I wanted to talk to her, Violet, Bonnie, and Suze at the same time. "Will they take me back?"

He shook his head. "I'm not sure."

"Shit." I kissed the top of his hand. "You did and I thank heaven every day for it."

He placed his hand on mine. "I'm easy compared to them. They even terrify me."

"Then I'm screwed."

"You can always crawl."

"Prostrating myself for forgiveness is becoming easier the more I do it."

I'd have more groveling practice at Corky's Diner.

Before I entered the place the next day I drew in a breath. Frank offered to come along, but I had to do this alone. I searched every cell, every membrane, and organ for my new-found bravery. Clutching my purse, I couldn't seem to move my feet.

The Bowling Broads waited inside and they weren't expecting me of all people.

I entered and the air conditioning almost knocked me back. If they held to their routine, Jo, Bonnie, Suze, and Violet would be eating there after bowling.

I peeked behind a corner. They sat at their usual booth, talking noisily and laughing. I'd been a part of such fellowship but blew it big time. My past dishonor almost made me run away down the street. But I had to make it right. Such was my penance, but also proof I could be better. That I could be brave, a word I was beginning to love. Few times in life was a person given the chance to correct mistakes, and I wasn't going to muff this one. In *Lifetime* movies the characters always succeeded in their second chances. I prayed this would happen in reality. Still, I sweated. My knees quivered like lime Jell-O. My hands were pieces of uncooked bacon.

Taking in a breath, I walked over to their table. They all stopped talking and laughing when they spotted me and promptly turned into ice floes.

"Hi."

No one replied, not even asking me to sit down.

"What the hell are you doing here?" Jo said at last. Bonnie and Suze kept their heads down. Violet seethed.

"I came to tell you how very sorry and ashamed I am for

letting you down. I messed up big time, and it's not the first time in my life. I couldn't tell you before but I can now."

The groveling *was* getting easier. They listened but didn't say anything.

"What I did was reprehensible, but what was worse was losing Frank and you, your friendship, even for these past few weeks."

"You've apologized. We're kind of busy here." Violet looked down at her fists.

"Frank took you back?" Suze said.

"Yes, he did." I couldn't help but grin. "I've put my house up for sale, and I'm moving in with Frank and Aurelia."

"Yeah, we could tell something was up when he named his bowling alley after you," Jo said. "We aren't dumb."

"Far from it. And I do promise here and now to spend the rest of my life showing him and you that I genuinely earned the honor." I smiled, but my nerves hummed like a buzz zapper, while I waited for their verdict.

Jo looked at Violet who looked at Bonnie who looked at Suze.

"This mean you're going to stay with him?" Bonnie said.

"Unless Frank throws me out." I dared to sit down. "I know I've lost your trust and I'd do anything to earn your forgiveness."

They all folded their arms. Not a good sign. With shaky hands, I stood up. I had to make them realize how much they meant to me.

"Jo, each day I thank the Lord I walked into Cactus Lanes. That I met you and took bowling lessons with Frank. Sure, I lived in a mansion knock-off and had plenty of money, but as

Violet correctly pointed out, I wasn't worth a plug nickel. Now, with you and Frank, I have so much. I am finally rich. And who would have thought it would all start with chili fries?"

Jo's eyes teared a bit, but she quickly dried them with a napkin.

I swallowed and tried to finish what I had to say. "I love all of you, and I'll be cheering for you at the tournament against those damn Lois Lanes. I'm so lucky to have known you."

They said nothing. I had lost them and started to cry. "All righty, then." I turned.

"Maggie."

My heart stopped. I swiveled around.

"We aren't going to win without you." Jo stood.

"Not without our anchor." Suze rose also.

Bonnie joined us and we hugged each other in the middle of the diner, all except for Violet who hadn't moved. I had wanted Violet's approval most of all and dreaded that she might quit if the others took me back. But a smile finally opened on her face. She became as striking as a ball smacking the pocket.

"You could have told us, Maggie."

"Who'd want to admit they were chickenshit when it mattered most? Would you?"

"Probably not." She smiled.

"May I hug you, Violet?"

"If you must."

I did, probably too hard.

"And what the hell does reprehensible mean?" Violet said and grinned.

I started to laugh and cry.

She hugged back. "Let's go bowling."

When I stepped onto the approach to roll my first night back on the league, the ball no longer weighed fourteen pounds of rubber. It was made of promise and power.

I played like a gladiator with a round weapon. Strike. Strike. Strike. *Crash. Crash. Crash.* I was freaking Maggimus Decimus Meridius.

Glancing at the yellow dot on the ball, I relaxed even more out on the lanes. I had found my pin, my center, and not only when I bowled.

I ended up bowling my best at the Friday league. 221. Before I rolled on the next game I addressed my teammates, my friends, ball in hand.

"What?" Jo said.

"I'm so blessed for knowing such wonderful humans like you."

"We love you, too, now shut up and bowl," Violet said, and the others agreed.

Within days of moving in with Frank and Aurelia, my house was on the market. We'd all agreed their house was infinitely more comfortable, so I hired an auction company and got rid of ninety-nine percent of the furnishings in mine, except for the personal effects in my bedroom and my bed. Frank and I decided to keep it because it had a better mattress than his. The day I started living with them, Aurelia treated me with kindness and respect. She made us into a family. In the evenings, Frank and I cooked dinner. Then we watched TV or movies, played board games or cards, and went for drives, when Aurelia felt up to it. I even took Frank to the Caesars Palace Sports Book and taught him what I'd learned about horse racing from my late friend, Ruth Granger. One weekend, Mike came to meet Frank and Aurelia and we had a good time. During the evening together, I felt so much happiness I could have bottled the excess and sold it on the Strip alongside the guys who handed out cards of naked women.

Through all my joy at reconciling with Frank and my team, the downside was Kyla. I had called her several times, but she never called me back. I left messages asking to spend time with my grandson. But no reply came. Not wanting a fuss in front of the boy, I stayed away from their house until invited … but I wasn't invited. I had lost a daughter and grandson. I'd have to be strong now and accept it, though I'd keep on trying.

"Want me to talk to her? I'll tell your daughter my intentions are strictly honorable," Frank said.

At the time, we were all sitting on the couch drinking coffee and eating delicious Mexican sweet bread.

"Let *me* talk to her. I'll tell her this is no way to treat her mother," Aurelia added from her chair.

But I didn't trust my daughter not to be rude to such fine people. "I shouldn't have lied to her. She's going to have to come around. She's a grown woman and I hope she'll start acting like it."

"You did what you could. The next step is up to her," Frank said. "But I still feel the cause of your troubles."

I scooted closer and took his hand. "This isn't your fault. It's Kyla's for not opening her heart. When you close it off, you miss so much. I learned this lesson the hard way. Boy, did I ever."

During the day, I went to work with Frank at Margarita Lanes, where I suggested a list of upgrades. New cooking suite in the kitchen for Jo, an upgrade in the pro shop, and large screen TVs in the bar, for a start. I'd gotten ideas from studying some of the best bowling alleys online. Proceeds from the sale of my house would pay for the upgrades. I'd keep the stocks for emergencies and—hopefully—vacations with Frank.

"This is too much," he said when I proposed the improvements.

"Not at all. This place saved my life."

Chapter Thirty-Nine

I brushed my fingers over the name on the Bowling Broads shirt.

Maggie.

I looked up at the sign. The lights blinked on and off, one letter at a time.

Margarita Lanes

Please let me stay brave. For Frank, for my friends.

For me.

The cactus flowers had long dropped off but I remembered what they looked like. I took in a copious breath of air and life and then entered the building. A large sign hung above the door.

Welcome women's city tournament bowlers

Inside, the other female bowlers wore their own team shirts. They created a wave of competition in bright colors. Oranges, blues, whites, blacks, purples.

On a table next to the registration stood the three-foot tall trophy made taller with the figure of a bowling female.

I whispered to myself. "I want it."

Searching around, I spotted Jo, Violet, Bonnie, and Suze, and they waved and smiled.

Frank had left the house early in the morning to oversee all the activities for the weekend of championship games. He'd hired extra help to man the counter since Jo was bowling and to handle the large crowd at the snack and drinks bar. For the past week, everyone, including me, had pitched in to make Margarita Lanes look its best. She had been painted and scrubbed. I loved the work, though my back ached when we got home.

Looking a bit harried, Frank joined me and the other Bowling Broads. "Since our lanes are the hosts of this event, it's probably not good form for me to cheer for my home team. So I'm going to be very neutral through the championship."

"We understand, Frank," Jo said.

"But in here." He placed his hand over his heart. "I'm cheering my damn head off for you so give them hell, girls."

He kissed me.

"Where's our kiss?" Bonnie puckered up. So did Jo, Suze, and Violet.

I held up a hand. "Forget it, girls. Those lips are mine."

"Mom." Mike arrived.

I hugged him. "I'm so happy you're here."

"You kidding? I want to see you take home that trophy." He turned to Frank, and they hugged. "How's it going, Frank?"

"Good, Mike."

Frank and my son had met a few times now and liked each other enough to attend the NBA Summer D league games at the University of Nevada Las Vegas sport center together. They had asked me to go with them, but I wanted them to bond, and they did. This brought me infinite pleasure.

"I've got to see to a thousand things. *Buena suerte*, Margarita." Frank kissed my cheek and returned to the front desk.

With pride, I introduced Mike to the rest of the team.

"Mom's always talking about you so I feel I know you too."

"Oh, no." Bonnie feigned upset.

"Well, she loves you."

"We love her," Jo said.

"Especially her average." Violet grinned and put her arm around me.

"Kyla?" I asked, looking around as if Mike had brought his sister with him after finding her wandering around outside. I had told my friends how Kyla still hadn't contacted me after my return, and it was going on three months. But I had to concentrate on what I had to be grateful for, and there was so much.

Mike placed his hand on my back. "She's stubborn and stupid. For Kyla, it's not unusual. So how many games do you have to win?"

"We won four rounds yesterday, and today it's the semi-finals. We need to beat two more teams before we enter the finals. But if we lose a set of three games we're out."

"And these women bowlers are the best of the best," Suze said. "Top teams from all the other alleys in Vegas."

"Whoa," Mike said.

"I know, son. I'm petrified."

"We better get ready," Jo said.

"Then good luck to all of you." Mike kissed my cheek.

The Bowling Broads found our lanes, put on our shoes, and pulled out our balls from our respective bags. We were ready. I hoped so anyway.

"The Lois Lanes are rolling down on lane thirteen." Suze's voice turned creaky with the tension. "They even got new shirts for the championship."

"So did we." Bonnie looked down at hers.

"But theirs are cuter." Violet said.

I glanced at our primary competition. My nerves hummed with self-doubt. "Everyone here is so good. I'm out of place. I belong in the senior leagues. I belong in one of Frank's classes for six-year-olds."

"Maggie, you're going to do fine," Jo said.

"But they do look sharp," Suze said.

"To hell with them," Violet said.

"Yeah," Jo said.

"We've got to keep our heads in the game or else we've already lost." Violet placed on the brace she used for bowling.

"Okay, then." I held out my hands.

My teammates took mine and each other's.

"Let's kick butt," Violet pronounced.

After a welcome announcement by Frank over the intercom, the championship started. Our first opponents were the Lucky Stripes from the Bulldog Lanes in Henderson. I wasn't surprised by their names. They all smelled of cigarettes, but they could bowl and were the most severe team we'd ever competed against. When one of them made a strike or spare, their teammates merely threw a sharp nod. Open frames were met with slit eyes.

Although close, we won the first game. I racked up a 211 by the end of the last frame.

"Sandbagger," one of the opponents whispered under her breath as I passed by.

"What does that mean?" I asked Jo and Violet.

"It means somebody who bowls like shit to get a good handicap for tournaments, and then bowls out of their mind when it counts," Jo said.

"An insult?"

"Oh yeah." Violet sent spears of dirty looks to the opposing team.

"Now I'm mad." I firmed up the laces on my bowling shoes.

"'Bout time you got mad, girl. If you want to get even, out-bowl the pants off of them in the next two games."

I did bowl insanely, and we won the next two games. We gave ourselves a group hug afterward. The other team continued to stare us down as they gathered their equipment and departed.

"They're bad losers," Bonnie said.

"And they stink like smokes. I was almost tempted to go and buy a pack of Nicorette gum for all of them," I said.

"Let's go see what the Lois Lanes are doing," Violet said.

We made our way down the alley. The Lois Lanes finished up beating their opponents, The Bay City Rollers, which was made up of a group of young girls who looked as though they could have done time in juvenile hall. The Rollers cursed at their loss.

"The Lois Lanes won all three," Suze said.

"Holy hell," I said.

"Damn them," Bonnie said.

"That's not nice. But I do kind of hope they fall and break their legs," Suze said.

The next team we had to beat was Bowling Mania from an alley in south Vegas. The team consisted of a mix of older and younger women. Friendlier than our other opponents, they congratulated me when I rolled a strike. I returned a smile and high fives when they scored well.

The Bowling Broads won two out of three over the Bowling Mania team and took the round.

"We're in the finals." Jo put both fists in the air.

"Good job, girls." The Bowling Mania captain was a large woman with tremendous thighs and a remarkable smile.

I held out my hand. "You were a joy to bowl with. I know this is a serious tournament, but some women look as if they have money riding on this."

"They probably do. It's Vegas after all." She winked.

Our team had a forty-five-minute break before the next and most important final round. We ate a quick lunch. Mike joined us.

"Mom, you're incredible. You have an arm like Whitey Ford."

"Who's he?"

"One of the best baseball pitchers ever."

"Maggie does throw rocks." Bonnie then took a bite of her hamburger.

"Rocks?" Mike asked.

"Boulders," Bonnie said through a mouthful of burger.

"That'll crush the pins," Suze said.

"Ah. I get it."

"Which is why your mom is our anchor," Jo added.

"Anchor?"

"Someone to come through when we need the win. Teams usually place their best bowler there."

My cheeks heated with their compliments.

"I love how she's still modest." Suze wagged a fry in her hand.

"Shit, if I bowled like your mom, I'd have my average tattooed on my arm," Violet said.

Mike laughed.

"Although my daughter taunted me about getting tattoos, the concept of stamping 200 on my arm sounds appealing."

After eating, Frank and Mike stood near the front counter talking like friends. Win or lose, I'd already gained so much.

"The Lois Lanes won their first game, and the other team took the second. So whoever wins the next one, we end up playing." Jo took a noisy sip of her drink. "They're in the eighth frame."

Our team watched the game.

The Lois Lanes ended up winning by fifteen pins. The bowlers all turned to look at us. One that seemed to declare, "You guys are next." I almost peed myself.

By then the place had cleared of lots of bowlers whose teams had lost, but many hung around to watch the finals. Frank made the announcement.

"We have our final two teams who'll compete for the championship. From Bowlarama, the Lois Lanes."

Cheers rose from the women and their supporters.

"And from Margarita Lanes, the Bowling Broads." Frank's neutrality faded as he gave a gigantic grin.

The cheers were louder for the house team.

"This is it, folks. Three games for the trophy. They'll bowl on lanes fifteen and sixteen. Please remember, no noise until the player has released her ball. Please silence your cell phones and no flash photography. We'll have a ten-minute break and then start. Good luck, ladies."

Frank joined the Bowling Broads. "You've done our lanes proud."

Catching my hand, he pulled me to him. "Focus and remember to roll the ball in the goddamn pocket."

"I love you too, Frank."

Violet got in between us. "Enough of this romantic crap. We've got a damn trophy to win."

Frank kissed Violet.

The rival team members were intense as nitroglycerin in a test tube. Despite their edge of competitiveness toward us, I liked that they were helpful and encouraging to each other.

During the first game, the Lois Lanes rolled spares and strikes, but we managed to match them on the telescore. Each bowler from each team alternated on the two lanes. The crowd of spectators went silent when the bowlers threw their ball and then clapped when they hit a strike or spare. The crowd also let out sympathetic oohs when the bowlers missed knocking down pins and ended with an open frame. I had to ignore all those watching us bowl and focus on the shot. And I especially avoided thinking too much about the Lois Lanes' anchor. A slender leftie with spiky purple hair, Katy had five earrings in one ear and a murderous hook.

I wanted no distractions. I wanted to help my team win.

Violet particularly had a good first game and a span of just a few pins separated the two teams. On the last frame, the Lois Lanes' anchor, Katy, took down a strike, which meant she earned two more rolls. Katy hit another strike, which sent cheers among her teammates. But on the last frame, she hit five pins.

I stood up. I didn't usually pray to God for victory because He had more to do than watch over bowling games. But I did pray not to mess up.

I rolled a strike. Then hit another. One more roll. If I could rack up another strike, it would mean a win for the Bowling Broads.

I pulled back my ball and let it loose. My hook was textbook. *Bam*. In the pocket. A strike. My team won by twelve pins.

My teammates hugged me.

"I knew you could do it," Jo said.

"But Violet's play was tremendous," I said.

"Yeah, it was," Violet said.

"God, I hope we can keep this up," Suze said.

"Damn right, we can," Bonnie said.

I hoped my friend's optimism would carry over into the next two games.

Before starting the next one, I drank water and hit the restroom. In the stall, my hands shook, so I put them into a fist to stop the trembling. *You can do it*, I chanted. *Then why are you shaking*, I answered myself.

On my way back to the lane, Mike threw me a smile. "You're doing awesome, Mom. Two more and it's in the bag."

"It might as well be twelve more, son."

"Ready?" Jo asked me down on the lane.

"No."

She laughed.

"How do you guys handle all this pressure?" Mike said.

"Lots of alcohol."

"But only afterwards," Violet added.

Both our team and theirs weren't as successful on the second game, but our scores still echoed each other. On the last frame, Katy the anchor bowled three strikes in a row. I had to match the feat, or my team would lose.

I rolled one strike. Cheers from the crowd. Then another strike. More cheers. I dried my sweaty hands on the hand blower at the end of the ball return. Then I used my towel to wipe my perspiring brow. Drawing back the ball, I let it go, but my thumb slipped a bit and my hook disappeared. Eight pins blasted from their spot.

"Oooh," the crowd reacted.

The Bowling Broads lost the second game by a total of six pins.

Frank talked into the intercom. "Coming up is the last game of the championship, folks. The Bowling Broads are ahead by six pins over the Lois Lanes." A cheer burst out from the crowd. "We'll begin shortly."

"I'm so sorry about the last frame," I told my teammates.

"Not your fault." Bonnie put her hand on my arm.

"I'm the anchor. If I'd picked up a strike we would have won."

"No crying over spilled pins," Violet said.

"I'm so nervous I may break out in shingles." Suze rubbed her back.

"We're still ahead." Jo smiled with hope.

"Barely," Violet added.

"Quit being so negative." Bonnie placed a hand on Violet's shoulder.

"Okay, we're barely ahead."

"Oh, much better," Suze said.

The third game started. First up, Violet rolled a strike. The crowd applauded.

"Way to go, Violet." I offered a fist for bumping.

"I knew I could do it. Well, I was reasonably sure."

Bonnie and Suze also followed with strikes. But so did the Lois Lanes. Our strikes and spares mirrored the other. We were dead even on the telescore.

"Don't know where they leave off and we start," I whispered to Jo.

"Kinda scary."

Then it was the tenth frame. The last one.

The whole bowling alley quieted. Jo, Violet, Bonnie, and Suze all loaded their frames with strikes or spares. The Lois Lane bowlers did the same. The Lois Lanes were up by six pins in the last game, which made them even with us.

On the last frame of the game, Katy the anchor rolled her first ball. A strike.

Sweat coursed down my back and settled somewhere in my panties. Katy threw the next ball and knocked down seven pins. The two, four, and seven pins were left standing on the left side of the rack. A gasp arose from the Lois Lane fans, which appeared to be their family, husbands, and boyfriends.

But their anchor smiled as if not concerned. The sweat down my back became the Mississippi and I hoped I wasn't going to float away on a current of defeat.

With the deliberation of a surgeon carrying a fifteen-pound scalpel, Katy pulled back her ball and let it go. Though tempted to close my eyes, I had to look. Her ball took out the back seven pin but the other two stood, albeit shakily. They refused to go down. Another gasp from her team's supporters.

"Son of a bitch," Katy uttered.

Her Lois Lanes teammates all patted her back for comfort.

I stood up.

"Maggie, it's up to you," Jo said.

"Quit pressuring her, Jo," Suze said.

"I think I'm going to throw up." I grabbed my stomach.

"You got this." Bonnie winked.

"The championship is riding on it." Violet smiled.

"Shit."

I walked to the approach and dried my wet palms. I needed at least two strikes for my team to win easily. Or a strike and a spare to squeak by.

I threw the ball, which found the pocket. A strike. A cheer welled up behind me.

Daring to breathe, I turned back and my teammates grinned, albeit nervously.

"You got this, Maggie," Violet said.

Taking up my ball, I rolled. Eight pins down. But the two remaining made me want to weep.

I'd left behind the dreaded seven-ten split. Pins as far away from each other as Earth is from Saturn.

The crowd also responded with groans, as if I'd blown everything with that horrible leave. I glanced over at the Lois Lanes who congratulated each other like they'd already won the game, the championship, and the beautiful trophy.

I studied the shot.

"It's impossible," I whispered to myself.

I looked back at Frank, who stood at the service desk. He smiled and nodded encouragement. I glanced around for Mike and found him. Beside him was Kyla. He beamed and pointed goofily at his sister. Kyla looked at her brother and smiled though a bit awkwardly. I smiled back and waved. God, I had tears in my eyes.

"You going to bowl or not?" asked a Lois Lanes member who crossed her muscular arms.

"She can have as much time as she needs," Violet told her in her most Violet tough voice. "So do we have a problem?"

"Ah, no," the Lois Lane said, backing down immediately.

I wiped my eyes with my bowling towel. "I'm ready."

The shot was labeled as darn near impossible to pick up, but my life until then amounted to evidence that *anything* was feasible. Holding the ball, I listened. The whole place seemed to hold its breath with me. I stepped onto the approach. *You've found your pocket. Now follow where it leads you,* I told myself.

I raised my ball and let it loose.

Time slowed to the consistency of melted taffy. Torture taffy.

The ball seemed to roll in slow motion.

Over the arrows.

Halfway to the pins.

On it went, and the alley remained silent with agonizing anticipation. I don't think I breathed. I don't think my heart was beating.

Then time caught up to the moment.

The ball struck the right of the ten pin, which skidded across the lane and knocked down the seven pin.

Margarita Lanes exploded in applause. Even the Lois Lanes got up and clapped, although reluctantly.

The Bowling Broads hugged.

"Thank you," I told them.

"For what? You rocked an insane shot," Violet said.

"For letting me be here to even try."

I stumbled up to the viewing area to my children. I hugged Mike and then grabbed Kyla and squeezed.

"I'm so happy you're here, baby. You'll never know how happy."

"It's time for me to be honest too, Mom."

"You're here and that's all that matters."

"But I had incentive to come. Yesterday, I was playing at Clearview and heard Gina Southward badmouthing you in the clubhouse afterward."

"I don't care what people say about me, and neither should you."

"They were talking about how you went crazy at the bridge game."

"Well, I did, kind of."

"They told me how I must be ashamed of you for yelling during bridge and for bowling. At that moment I saw myself in them, how I had acted toward you, and it wasn't good. In fact, it sucked."

"What'd you do then? Join them for a cocktail?" Mike said.

She smiled. "I told them to fuck off."

Mike and I both opened our mouths in shock.

"Mom, I was stupid, petty, and selfish," Kyla said.

"I wouldn't say petty."

"An enormous pain in the ass?"

"Afraid so."

"Mike told me I lived for perfection. But I'm not perfect, Mom. I made you unhappy. I discouraged you from being happy, even if it's with another man and bowling. That makes me far from perfect."

Mike and I said nothing.

"You could disagree with me." Kyla gave a half smile.

"This is your first step to open-mindedness. Watch out for a nosebleed," Mike told her.

"Shut up."

"I was going to say I'm very proud you're my sister."

"Only today?" She slugged him and he hugged her.

Kyla's eyed the surroundings, still a bit unsure. "I've got to get home. I'll call you later, Mom."

"Want to meet, Frank?" I said.

"He's a good man, sis."

Kyla bit a lip. "Another time?"

"I understand. Caesars Palace wasn't built in a day." I watched her leave. Bless her, Kyla had taken the first steps to humanhood. Maybe I wasn't such a horrible mom where she was concerned.

"Kyla'll come around. If she doesn't, I say we trade her in for an improved model," Mike said.

"Thank you, son, for everything." I smiled and searched the crowd for Frank.

"Go, Mom." He pushed gently at my back.

I made my way past people who congratulated me. I found him near the food counter. Running to him, I embraced him and swore never to let go.

"I saw your daughter and wanted to give you space."

Exactly a Frank thing to do.

"See, I told you the seven-ten shot wasn't impossible to pick up."

"What shot?"

We kissed and the place went wild.

Chapter Forty

As I dressed, I thought about Bob. Something I hadn't done in more than a year. Not since I visited his grave for the last time.

In less than two hours, I was getting married, and was surprised my late husband had come to mind.

I wore the dress Jo had helped me pick out. Not white because I was well beyond the virginal stage. But a cream tea-length dress with chiffon skirt, and lace bodice with three-quarter sleeves.

"I feel like damn Grace Kelly in this," I had told Jo when I tried it on.

"Then you best buy it," replied Jo who was to be my matron of honor.

Earlier, I had had my hair done and paid one hundred and fifty dollars to a makeup professional in a mall. Now I was ready and looked in the full-length mirror in our bedroom.

"Hell, I look good for an old Bowling Broad."

And that's when I thought of Bob and what he might have said, what I hoped he might have said.

Congratulations, Margaret, and goodbye. You look beautiful.

Frank knocked on the door. "Ready?"

"Come in."

He stepped in the room. "*Ay, yi, yi.*"

His smile held pride and longing, which made me even more crazy for him.

"You look beautiful yourself."

He pulled at the lapel of his dark blue suit.

We both glanced at the photograph of Aurelia on our dresser. Aurelia in her nice flowery dress and the shawl Frank had bought for her birthday. She sat on her favorite chair on the porch, looking so sincere I choked up whenever I looked at the photo. Aurelia had died six months before.

On a fall evening, she had kissed us, told us good night, and never woke. Aurelia's passing reflected the woman. Classy and not wanting a fuss. I had wept at her funeral.

"Wish my mom could have been here." Frank sniffed.

I placed my hand on his chest. "She'll always be your light, your *luz*."

"Come on. I want you to see something."

I followed him out to the patio. "My God."

The cactus flowers in the garden and the large pots on the patio had bloomed. Bursts of oranges, whites, and reds.

I wanted to cry but blinked back tears not to risk ruining the $150 makeup job.

The Clark County clerk had a bald head and a bottomless smile. Frank and I stood in a small office converted into a wedding chapel, complete with a wooden arbor entwined with artificial flowers. While there were many wedding chapels in Vegas to choose from, we had decided to forego an imitation Elvis singing to us or showgirls standing beside us, settling instead for the Office of Civil Marriages on Third Street.

Standing beside Frank and me were Jo and Ernie as our witnesses. I held a bouquet of yellow roses Violet had bought me, along with a boutonnière for Frank.

Before the clerk started, I raised my hand to speak. "Please, can we make this quick, sir, before he changes his mind?" I was not entirely joking.

"Not to worry," Frank said.

The civil ceremony *was* fast. The only words I heard were, "I now pronounce you man and wife."

"Mrs. Martínez."

"Mr. Martínez."

While the wedding had been nondescript, Frank and I wanted a louder celebration with friends and family. We selected the Italian restaurant where we'd first gone out to dinner and reserved a large room and the adjoining patio.

Ten minutes into the party and I knew this would be another best day of my life, one of many to come. Jo and Suze brought their husbands. Bonnie brought one of her daughters. Violet came with a guy named Max who had the body of a

Navy SEAL and tenderly kissed my cheek with his congratulations.

I hardly recognized my fellow teammates in their charming dresses, new hairdos, and makeup, and jokingly told them so.

"We do have a life outside of bowling, you know," Violet said.

"We do?" Bonnie asked.

"Hey, let's schedule an extra practice. City championship is coming up," Suze said.

"And, this year it's going to be held at Bowlarama. Home turf of the Lois Lanes," Jo said.

"How great would it be to win the trophy two years in a row," I said.

"Hey, I'm the optimist of the group." Bonnie pointed at her chest.

Ernie and his wife Linda sat next to Frank and me at one table. Mike brought his new friend, the attractive photographer who was funny and smart.

"He's a great guy. You did very well," Mike told me when we had a moment by ourselves.

"Yeah, I did."

Consuela also arrived with her husband. After Frank and I had got back together, I had called to tell my friend I'd made everything right with him and my team, not to mention standing up to Kyla.

"I've moved in with Frank and his house is smaller," I'd also told her.

"I quit, remember?"

I could tell she was smiling.

"Well, I want to hire you back, if you'll have me. And this means you'll clean the house faster so we can go to lunch."

Consuela was so happy she came right over and took me out for a drink.

When it was time for everyone to sit down for dinner, I looked around, but no Kyla. My daughter said she might be there, which was no answer.

There had been some progress though. For the art show of Frank's neon pieces at the bowling alley four months ago, I asked Kyla to find a caterer and my daughter did so and even took on some of the planning. The night was a success with Frank donating part of the proceeds to a local charity aiding the homeless of Vegas.

Kyla and Jerome did attend the show and in thanks for her help, Frank gave Kyla a neon piece she'd been admiring. My daughter's cheeks shined with what I hoped was a new acceptance of everything. After much begging from Jonathan, Kyla and Jerome had also allowed Frank to give my grandson bowling lessons. And I wasn't bragging to say that the kid has potential, which I hope he got from me.

But they still hadn't shown up and dinner was going to be served soon.

Frank nudged me. "Baby, look who just came in."

We met them near the door.

"Kyla." I hugged her.

"I—"

"You don't have to say anything."

"Yes, I do. Mom, you're radiant."

Kyla held out her hand to Frank. "Congratulations." She introduced him to Jerome.

"I've read about you online. Very impressive," he said. "I'd love to hear about being a pro."

Frank smiled. "I'd be happy to talk to you about it. I'm so happy you're here. And in time for dinner."

"Hey, coach, congratulations on marrying my grandma." Jonathan smiled. "I think that makes me your grandkid too."

"I think so." Frank hugged him.

Our wedding guests ate all kinds of pasta, salad, and drank wine, and the breadsticks kept coming. I lost count of the toasts to Frank and me.

Ernie stood up and tapped a wine glass for attention. "When I met Maggie, I was a little doubtful of her. After all, what did a rich white lady want with my friend?"

Everyone laughed, although Frank's cheeks heated red.

"But dammit, I was wrong, which is not the first time if you ask my wife."

"That's for sure." Linda gained a laugh from the party.

Ernie put his hand out for quiet. "Let me finish. Let me finish. All I can say is that my best friend is now happy and that makes me happy." He looked at me. "And here's to Maggie, one of the bravest women I've ever met."

To hell with my expensive makeup job, I cried and gave Ernie a hug. But then, a lot of hugging and kissing went on at the restaurant.

After dinner, the guests danced to the music of a DJ we had hired. Although Kyla took my grandson home by ten, Jerome stayed and even took off his tie. Another miracle.

Mike's friend took photos and promised to send me copies. Ernie bought a box of cigars, and everyone stood outside on the patio taking puffs, including Violet and my son. By eleven,

I'd changed into my comfy shoes. Frank took my hand and led me to the small dance floor. Closing my eyes, I breathed him in, his scent hinting of wine and the shaving lotion I'd bought him for his sixty-fourth birthday.

"You know we never talked about a honeymoon, Maggie."

"Maybe someday. No need for one right now."

"Not Hawaii, or Europe?"

"Nope."

"The International Bowling Museum and Hall of Fame in Arlington, Texas?"

"So tempting, but I just want to go home with you."

"Now that is sexy."

Moving around the room, I enjoyed the conversations. Jerome and Violet found common ground in their shared love of baseball. Frank and Mike chatted basketball. Jo, Bonnie, and Suze talked, well, bowling, with an occasional drift over to politics or the TV shows they were addicted to. I had encouraged my teammates to watch the *Sons of Anarchy* episodes on Netflix, a tribute to my late friend Ruth. Frank and I had already breezed through the first three seasons and we loved it as much as she had.

A little before midnight, I went outside on the patio. No cool breeze out there. They were as elusive as a million dollar win on the slots.

The night sparkled with Vegas lights in the distance. I'd once read a newspaper article about how most of the casino signs were illuminated by incandescents, LEDs, or fluorescents, as much as neon. Their radiance shimmered in all colors, lining the night with a grounded halo. Artificial brightness, yes, but still splendorous. And for several moments, the new Maggie Martínez couldn't tell if the brilliance was in the distance or inside of her.

Acknowledgments

Thanks so much to my husband Jerry and his former team members for their bowling knowhow, to my wonderful friend Bonnie Dodge, and as always to my daughters Marguerite and Gabrielle for their never-ending love and support, and my agent Leslie Truex for believing in this project. I'm also grateful for the information from the websites of Caesars Palace, the American Bowling Congress, Professional Bowling Association, YouTube, Wikipedia, Kingpinplay.com, Planetbowl, and Helpwithbowling.com.

ONE MORE CHAPTER

The author and One More Chapter would like to thank everyone who contributed to the publication of this story...

Analytics
Abigail Fryer
Maria Osa

Audio
Fionnuala Barrett
Ciara Briggs

Contracts
Georgina Hoffman
Florence Shepherd

Design
Lucy Bennett
Fiona Greenway
Holly Macdonald
Liane Payne
Dean Russell

Digital Sales
Lydia Grainge
Emily Scorer
Georgina Ugen

Editorial
Arsalan Isa
Charlotte Ledger
Federica Leonardis
Bonnie Macleod
Jennie Rothwell
Caroline Scott-Bowden
Kimberley Young

International Sales
Bethan Moore

Marketing & Publicity
Chloe Cummings
Emma Petfield

Operations
Melissa Okusanya
Hannah Stamp

Production
Emily Chan
Denis Manson
Francesca Tuzzeo

Rights
Lana Beckwith
Rachel McCarron
Agnes Rigou
Hany Sheikh
Mohamed
Zoe Shine
Aisling Smyth

The HarperCollins Distribution Team

The HarperCollins Finance & Royalties Team

The HarperCollins Legal Team

The HarperCollins Technology Team

Trade Marketing
Ben Hurd
Eleanor Slater

UK Sales
Laura Carpenter
Isabel Coburn
Jay Cochrane
Tom Dunstan
Sabina Lewis
Erin White
Harriet Williams
Leah Woods

And every other essential link in the chain from delivery drivers to booksellers to librarians and beyond!

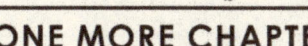

ONE MORE CHAPTER

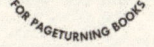

One More Chapter is an
award-winning global
division of HarperCollins.

Sign up to our newsletter to get our
latest eBook deals and stay up to date
with our weekly Book Club!
<u>Subscribe here.</u>

Meet the team at
<u>www.onemorechapter.com</u>

Follow us!
 @OneMoreChapter_
 @OneMoreChapter
 @onemorechapterhc

Do you write unputdownable fiction?
We love to hear from new voices.
Find out how to submit your novel at
<u>www.onemorechapter.com/submissions</u>